LIFE AND LOVE AT MULBERRY LANE

ROSIE CLARKE

Boldwood

First published in Great Britain in 2023 by Boldwood Books Ltd.

Cover Design by Colin Thomas

Cover Photography: Colin Thomas and Alamy

A CIP catalogue record for this book is available from the British Library.

Paperback ISBN 978-1-80415-732-9

Large Print ISBN 978-1-80415-733-6

Hardback ISBN 978-1-80415-731-2

Ebook ISBN 978-1-80415-735-0

Kindle ISBN 978-1-80415-734-3

Audio CD ISBN 978-1-80415-726-8

MP3 CD ISBN 978-1-80415-727-5

Digital audio download ISBN 978-1-80415-728-2

Boldwood Books Ltd
23 Bowerdean Street
London SW6 3TN
www.boldwoodbooks.com

AUTHOR'S REMINDER

This is book number nine in the *Mulberry* series so we thought it might help to have a little recap for readers. Some of you won't need it, others might find it helpful.

Main Characters

Peggy's family:

Peggy and Able Ronoscki and their twins, Freddie and Fay. Peggy's eldest daughter, Janet, and her brother, Pip, by her first husband, Laurie.

Peggy is now in her sixties, Able is a couple of years younger. The twins are now 19. Janet is 39 and Pip is 37; they both have children.

Maggie is Janet's daughter by her first husband and Peggy's first grandchild and is now 21. Janet and Ryan, her second husband, have a son, Jon.

Pip is married to Sheila, they have two children, Chris and Cathy. Pip works as an aeronautical designer.

Peggy has always run the Pig & Whistle pub in Mulberry Lane in the East End of London, apart from a period when she went away to the seaside and Sheila ran the pub. However, in 1958, Maggie and Fay started to take over. Peggy also has a boarding house, which is managed by Pearl. Pearl's mother, Mrs Maggs, helps at the Pig & Whistle washing up. Able has a partnership with Tom Barton in the building trade.

* * *

Maureen's family:

Maureen is in her late forties and Gordon is slightly older. Gordon's daughter, Shirley, is in her late twenties now and Maureen and Gordon's son, Gordy, is a teenager. Maureen also had a son, Robin, (not Gordon's) but he died of a childhood illness.

Gordon is suffering from a weakness of a heart muscle but is better than he was in the last book. He still manages the grocery shop that came to them through Maureen's family, but it is much bigger now, though he only goes in for an hour or two and has a youthful manager. Maureen still helps out in the pub and the restaurant kitchen sometimes. Shirley is a doctor and married to Ray.

* * *

The Barton family:

Tom and Rose Barton have two children, Molly and Jackie or these days, Jack. Tom and Able are now partners in a building business and doing well. Rose sometimes helps out in the pub kitchens. She and Maureen are Peggy's best friends and they've always done things together. They are several years younger than Peggy and Maureen and in their thirties.

All the characters are well and continuing to thrive now that life is so much better after the long years of war. This is a time when things aren't too bad for folk in Mulberry Lane, but, of course, life always has surprises round the corner...

1

It was really happening at last. Peggy looked around the Pig & Whistle's old-fashioned bar, which was about to be pulled out as part of the refurbishment she'd promised Maggie would happen if her business warranted it. The downstairs parlour, which was never used, would become the bar for the regulars of the pub and this would form part of an extended restaurant, using some of the back yard. It was a big change, but the delicious meals that her daughter and granddaughter were now serving brought in too many customers to fit into the bar as it stood.

'We'll have to do it, hon.' Able, Peggy's easy-going and much-loved husband, put his arm around her waist. 'We promised we'd come up with the money if their business expanded and it most certainly has.' He'd done his part by purchasing the building from the brewery in order to let their dreams happen.

'I can't believe it's more than two years since they started to take over,' Peggy admitted with a sigh. 'I never imagined they would stick to it the way they have, especially Fay. You know what she is like for changing her mind.'

Fay was their daughter and Freddie's twin, but Maggie was that bit older and the child of Peggy's eldest daughter Janet, who was her first husband's offspring. Laurie had been long dead now and was a part of Peggy's memories that centred here in the bar of the Pig & Whistle in Mulberry Lane, but there were so many more memories – so much love, laughter and pain. Especially during the war years when she'd taken people down to her cellar for safety as the bombs fell. The pictures flitted through Peggy's mind as she let her eyes travel the room and she saw her friends as they had been so many times, drinking, talking, sharing their lives with her, some of them still enjoying life, others gone now but not forgotten. She shook her head. Life moved on and it was foolish to cling to the past. The Pig & Whistle was a thriving business and she must celebrate that, not feel regret for what had gone before.

'Are you ready, hon?' Able's voice broke Peggy's reverie and she met his eager gaze and nodded. 'All packed? Got everything you need?'

'Yes, I made a list,' Peggy replied, a lift in her voice as she felt a flutter of excitement. 'And I know the taxi will be here in fifteen minutes.'

'Good. I'd hate for us to miss our plane.'

* * *

It was the spring of 1961, and Peggy had more or less handed over the reins, leaving the business of running the Pig & Whistle to Fay and Maggie. Now, she was about to leave for the most exciting trip in her life. Able was taking her to America and they would actually be flying first class. It was the holiday of a lifetime and had cost the earth, but Able said they could afford it and he was so happy that Peggy had given in to his persuasion. She'd thought that flying was for VIPs, like famous footballers and film stars and she was worried that it could be dangerous, but Able told her that within a very few years everyone would be doing it and only a few aeroplanes actually crashed, so she had given in. She felt a frisson of excitement as she realised it was really happening.

'Mum,' Freddie's voice interrupted her thoughts. 'You haven't forgotten I'm off to the coast this weekend?'

'No, of course not, love.' Peggy turned to look at her youngest son. Freddie had shot up these past months and looked like a confident young man. Before he started his new university course, he was going to take a casual job at the coast. He'd applied to be a lifeguard on a beach in Hastings, Sussex, and had secured the job, which made Peggy both proud and anxious, though she knew he could swim well and would receive training once he joined the team. Freddie wanted to be a sports teacher and to direct his spare time to helping those less fortunate children, who had a physical or mental impediment. He'd already joined a club in London that helped disabled kids and spent three evenings a week there. 'I've packed your cases for you and your father has put some money into your bank account,' she answered with a look of affection.

'Thanks, Mum. You always pack better than me – but that wasn't what I meant. It means I shan't be around for a while... and you and Dad are going away. The girls will be on their own – do you think they can manage? Should I put my trip off until later?'

'Maggie is very sensible,' Peggy told him. He was always so thoughtful of others. 'Maureen and Rose will still be around – and Tom. You go and have a wonderful time, Freddie. Those girls will be fine.' Maureen and Rose were Peggy's best friends and she knew they would be on hand. Tom Barton was Able's business partner – they built houses and flats as well as restoring old property now – and he had turned into a very capable man these days and was someone she could rely on.

'If you're sure.' Freddie grinned. 'Fay told me not to be an old woman and quit worrying about her.'

'Then you should,' Peggy assured him.

'Okay, if you say so.'

He nodded, walking off with his shoulders straight. He was as tall as Able now but would be broader and heavier as he grew. Freddie ate a lot but was very active; running, playing football and lifting weights had made him strong and muscular. It seemed to Peggy that girls must find her son an attractive young man and she wondered if she ought to worry whether he would be led astray in this glamorous beach job he'd taken. Freddie knew what he wanted of life – and yet he had a tender heart, which might easily be broken.

'Penny for your thoughts, hon?' Able's caressing tones made her look at him and shake her head.

'The twins are growing up so fast...' was all she could say, but a smile of understanding came to her husband's face.

'Freddie will be fine,' he replied. 'And so will Fay. She is too busy to get into much trouble – and Freddie never does.'

'I know...' Peggy laughed. 'They've both done so well in their own ways. Freddie's job this summer will help him with his sports training and a lifeguard has to be prepared for all sorts, so it is a good experience for him.'

'It is what he wants,' Able said. 'He was so good last year, giving up his time to go to France with Fay for that special cooking course. Mind you, I think they had a wonderful time out there.'

'I often wonder what they got up to that we don't know about,' Peggy said, brows lifted. 'Freddie kept Fay in line, I am certain – but I know something went on with her out there – but tneither of them tell tales about the other.'

'Whatever it was, Freddie handled it,' Able replied, a sparkle in his eyes. 'And now she is trying to make her bit of the partnership work. At the moment Maggie is paying their way; I know Fay, she won't be pleased with that for long. She'll need to be on her toes to bring in the extra business.'

Peggy nodded her agreement. Fay's part of the girls' combined business was more of a specialism and the orders were irregular – sometimes plentiful and at others slower. She baked wonderful cakes and puddings, which were a part of their private catering service. Fay and Carla, a young woman who had begun by working in the bar evenings, did most of the weddings and parties, with some help from Peggy, and both Rose Barton and Maureen Hart helped where and when needed. Fay hadn't yet found it necessary to take on permanent help, hiring in the extra waitresses for larger events.

Maggie was usually too busy in the restaurant, as she now termed the bar of the Pig & Whistle, to help with the outside catering much, and these past few months her trade had built up steadily and the pub was still popular with the locals. She'd employed a full-time waitress, as well as Mrs Maggs, who did the washing-up. Peggy just did whatever was needed, either in the bar, the kitchen or for the private catering service.

Peggy was not truly needed in the kitchen often these days; it was nice for her not to be always working, but it was hard to let go at times, especially when the memories crowded in on her and made her feel nostalgic.

'Feeling a bit like you've been hit by a whirlwind, hon?'

Peggy looked up at her husband and sighed. 'Just looking and remembering,' she said. 'I've spent a lot of my life in this bar. I was thinking of the old customers – like Alice and Mrs Tandy, Jack Barton, and a few of the others...' She spoke of three particular friends who were no longer with them but still remembered; folk she'd shared so much of her life with.

'You are bound to feel a bit sad to see the old bar go,' Able said. 'But it needs a spruce up, much more than we've done before, and

Maggie's idea to expand into the back yard is a great idea. If they open this out and add on the extension at the rear, it will nearly double the number of tables she can fit in – and we can have a new bar in what used to be the downstairs sitting room.'

'Well, we rarely use that ourselves,' Peggy agreed. 'It will be very smart – what's the word these days? Fashionable... didn't I hear Maggie say that is what we need to be? A part of the new vibrant sixties... isn't that what they're saying it will be?'

Able nodded and laughed softly. 'It's a new world they're building – I heard someone say it was the start of the swinging sixties the other day, though what on earth that really means, I have no idea. I suppose with this idea of space travel, it really will be a new world.' The Soviet Union had put a man into space for the first time in April, which still seemed incredible to him, and the United States of America had sent its first astronaut into space earlier that month.

'Well, Harold Macmillan told us we'd never had it so good.' Peggy laughed with him. 'Makes you feel old, doesn't it? All this talk of a new world and the buzz that seems to be going on all over London these days.'

'It's what is needed,' Able replied with a shrug. 'We need a brighter future for the young folk, Peggy. We have to hope that all the new ideas and the fancy talking isn't just hot air. We wouldn't want them to have the hard times back, would we?'

'Good grief, no,' she cried and gave herself a little shake. That was the last thing Peggy wanted. 'I'm glad we're off today, love. I know this is all going to be lovely when it is finished, but I don't want to watch it happen. This holiday you've organised to America is the best thing we could do.'

'We have the leisure now to do a bit of travelling and I'd like to show you where I was born.' Able shrugged. 'When I met you, during the war, I left America quite willingly to make a home here.

I haven't pined for it, so don't imagine that, hon. I just thought it would be good for us to get away and let the kids get on with it.'

'Yes, I know you're right,' Peggy agreed and then looked him in the eyes. 'Supposing we hate what they do?'

'Then we'll look for somewhere else to live. Maybe this time we will retire to the sea. Besides, Tom is in charge of the work here and I can't imagine him letting them do anything that is too horrendous, can you?'

'No, I am sure it will all be tasteful and just as we've talked about, so I am going to put it all out of my head and enjoy myself.' Once again, she felt that buzz of excitement. Never in her life had she really believed she would fly to America!

'Good.' Able tucked her into him, holding her with his one strong arm against his side as he bent his head to kiss her. He'd lost part of his left arm when wounded during the war. 'I am going to enjoy having you all to myself for once...' He turned his head as he heard a horn sound. 'I think that must be our taxi. Come on, love. It's time for us to have fun.'

2

'I just popped in to say hello – and check you are coming to lunch on Sunday?' Rose Barton said as she smiled at Maureen. 'Peggy will be in America by now – lucky her! Yet I'm not sure I'd want to fly. I think I'd rather go on a luxury liner, if we ever get the chance... but even if we could afford it, Tom is too busy.'

'Speaking of Tom's work, how are the renovations at the Pig & Whistle coming along?' Maureen asked. 'I've been wanting to take a peek all week, but I thought I might be in the way.'

The pub had been closed for several days now – the first time in many years. Even Hitler's bombs hadn't manged to shut it down, but Maggie had decided that the alterations were so structural that it wasn't possible to work round them. As it happened, Fay had booked several big events for the catering side of the business for the next week, so they were concentrating on them and the pub had a big 'closed' notice on the door, which had caused a few grumbles, even though it had been well advertised in advance.

'Tom says it is all going to plan – but you know Tom. He won't say, whatever happens.'

Maureen nodded her agreement. 'I know what you mean.

When we opened up Mrs Tandy's old shop and made it one with my father's grocery business, Tom did a wonderful job. Gordon was thinking of taking on another small shop and opening that up too, but after his heart trouble a couple of years back, he decided against it.' A little sigh escaped her because Gordon had been a little quiet of late and she worried that her husband was feeling unwell again.

'I saw him this morning,' Rose said, looking at Maureen hard. 'He seemed cheerful and well – is he?'

'Ray did what he could for him; you know what a wonderful surgeon Shirley's husband is, but Gordon may need more surgery one day,' Maureen said and her anxiety came through in her voice. 'He feels better than he did – but... he believes he is living on borrowed time. Shirley warned me that he probably won't have much more than five years or so at most – though she is hoping for a little miracle, and so am I.'

'I am so sorry,' Rose said. 'If you need anything – even in the middle of the night – you know where we are, Maureen. Please ring us at once.'

'Thank you,' Maureen smiled. 'I think he is all right for the moment – but Shirley wanted me to be prepared. Before Ray did that small operation, we thought he might not live more than a few months, so I'm lucky I've still got him.'

Rose shook her head. 'I can't imagine what you must feel, Maureen love. I suppose you just have to make the most of every day...'

'We do try. Gordon doesn't work as long hours now. He just goes in for an hour or so in the mornings – and in the afternoons we try to do things together, even if it is only a little walk or just sitting in the garden when it's nice. We've had some holidays at the sea and they were pleasant, restful.' She sighed. 'I wonder how Peggy will get on over in America.'

'You know Peggy – she is up for anything – and I think she has been feeling a bit... well, side-lined is probably the word. Maggie includes her in everything, but Peggy has always been the one in charge.'

'Yes.' Maureen nodded thoughtfully. 'I wondered if she would feel pushed out when she agreed to the girls taking over – but it was typical of her to do it. She was thinking of them, of giving them a good start in life.'

'They are doing so well. Tom wanted to book a table at their restaurant for my birthday, but he left it too late and Maggie couldn't fit us in on the day. He booked for the next day – but it just shows...'

'I know.' Maureen nodded. 'Peggy kept that pub running all through the war and that was a miracle with the way things were – but it wasn't as busy as it is now. I never expected them to do quite as well as they have.'

'Times are changing. I sometimes think of our little cake shop where we sold our home-made cakes – now Fay has it as her kitchen and headquarters. How grand does that sound?'

'Well, she was telling me she has a very posh party to cater for this weekend,' Maureen said. 'It is in the house of a music star. I think he sings rock and roll songs and ballads, but Fay says he is very popular. I'm not sure if he is American. He has ordered all sorts of exotic food. I told Fay to make sure she got paid for it in advance and she said he had already given her half as a deposit and she'll get the rest later.'

'Maggie will see they get paid – besides, we shouldn't be so suspicious, just because of things you hear and read in the papers.'

Maureen laughed. 'I suppose I was thinking of those Teddy boy types who tear up cinema seats and cause a lot of problems – usually when it is a rock and roll film...'

Rose indicated her agreement. 'It is a sign of the age, Maureen.

This is a time for young folk – isn't that what they keep telling us? We don't understand the rock and roll scene and all the stuff that goes with it.'

'Not sure I want to,' Maureen quipped but was smiling now, her worry for Gordon temporarily forgotten. 'We had jazz and the Lindy hop in the war – but we didn't tear up the dance floor or smash windows.'

'Oh, it's only a few hooligans that do that,' Rose said. 'I am quite sure this rock and roll star that Fay is catering for is fine – Jace, something or other. I understand she first met him in France when she was on that cooking course. He hadn't had a record contract then, but it happened when he was out there – someone spotted him and he went off to America in a hurry. Fay says he thinks she brought him good luck and that's why he's given her the chance to cater for his big party. Apparently, he's had a number one hit – "Loving Girls" it's called or something similar. He's celebrating and a lot of other big names will be there, as well as agents and various celebrities. If things go well, Fay could get a lot of work from it.'

'I hope she does,' Maureen said thoughtfully. 'I think she is a little disappointed that her side of the business hasn't done as well as the pub restaurant – yet anyway.'

'Well, she is catering for a different market and it takes time to build a reputation,' Rose replied. 'Maggie had a head start really. The Pig & Whistle was always known for good food.'

'Yes, that is true. Peggy's food was the kind everyone enjoys and she made it just that little bit special. So Maggie already had a business to build on and Fay had to start from scratch. She might have done better to base herself up the West End, I suppose.'

'Yes, perhaps,' Rose agreed. 'But she couldn't have afforded their prices for her kitchen and office – and she wouldn't be close to Maggie and the rest of us so would have to take on permanent staff and that she couldn't do.'

'True.' Maureen fluffed out her dark hair. 'We all have to start somewhere. When my father ran the corner shop, we sometimes counted our profits in pennies, but now it does really well.'

Rose nodded and pushed a lock of red hair from her eyes. 'Have you had your hair cut, Maureen? It looks different...'

'It's the new look they call the Italian style,' Maureen said. 'Named after that film star – Gina whatsit—'

'—Lollobrigida,' Rose said, laughing. 'She is so beautiful; everyone wants to look like she does, so we copy her hair. I loved her as Esmeralda in *The Hunchback of Notre Dame*. Did you see it when it came out in the fifties?'

'Yes, she was good in that, she is a wonderful actress,' Maureen said. 'My hairdresser suggested I try it, but I'm not sure it suits me.'

'Oh, it does – the way it just flicks round your face is very flattering,' Rose said. 'I'd have mine done, but Tom likes my hair long so I mostly just have the ends trimmed and, when I get time to go to the hairdresser, I have it put up in a French pleat.'

'It's finding the time to go regularly,' Maureen agreed. 'My hair looks nice when my hairdresser has just done it, but I'm not sure I'll be able to keep it this way when I wash it myself.' She flicked her hair again, self-consciously. 'I just used to brush it back and hold it with combs – but I've had that style for years and Shirley thought I needed a change.'

'Well, she was right and it suits you,' Rose said firmly. 'Make an appointment once a week and keep it like that.' She smiled at Maureen. 'And now I must go. I've promised to help Fay this afternoon – and I need to be back in time to fetch Jack from school, though Molly is off to her dancing lessons this evening. Paula said she would make sure she got there and back safely – her daughter goes too.'

'You are calling her Molly again?' Maureen said. 'I thought she hated the name and fancied the name Jenny instead?'

'Well, she did – and we did change it for a time, because she wouldn't answer to Molly, but now she has changed her mind and she wants to be Molly. It is a bit confusing for her teachers, but you know my daughter. She is a stubborn little madam and once she decides on something there is no changing her.'

'You wouldn't want to change her, surely?' Maureen teased.

'Tom wouldn't let me if I did!' Rose's eyes sparkled with mischief. 'She twists him around her little finger and he adores her. The little monkey knows it as well. Jack is growing up too. We used to call him Jackie, because Tom's father was Jack, but after he died... well, I suppose it didn't matter any more and Jack is better for him at school.' She smiled fondly. 'He is learning to play football and he loves it. I think Freddie got him started. Jack was very shy when he first went to school, but Freddie saw him being teased by some of the older boys and warned them off – and now he worships the ground he walks on. It is "Freddie says this" and "Freddie says that"! Jack will miss him when he goes away.'

'I don't think he'll be the only one to miss Freddie Ronoscki this summer,' Maureen observed. 'Gordy adores him too. He plays football with Freddie at the club, and Freddie is so good with him. I am really glad he decided his future was with children, teaching them to play all kinds of sports rather than becoming a football star – though that is a more glamorous life, of course.'

'Well, it was his choice,' Rose said. 'He did have a chance to join the junior squad at Manchester United but decided it wasn't for him.' She smiled. 'I wonder how he will get on this summer. You know he has taken a job as a lifeguard on a beach just until he starts university in autumn?'

'Yes. He asked his father if he could and Able told me he'd given him his blessing. I think Peggy was a bit uneasy about it at first, but Freddie is so sensible – and they give the youngsters training. It will be a good experience for him, I expect.'

'I imagine it will. Besides, he deserves some fun before he settles down to several years of study. I think it should be fun most of the time, though it is a serious job, and necessary on some of those beaches.'

'Peggy says he has always been a strong swimmer. He will be fine – and, of course, if he does have to rescue someone, I am sure he will manage.' Maureen glanced at the kitchen clock. 'Will you stay for a cup of tea, Rose? I'm going to do some baking later, but I've plenty of time this morning.'

'Thanks, but I have to get back,' Rose replied. 'I just popped in for a quick visit. We'll see you on Sunday then. I'm doing a nice roast.'

'Lovely,' Maureen smiled and nodded as she started to fill the kettle. 'We'll see you then – I look forward to it.'

* * *

After Rose had gone, Maureen got out her baking trays. She'd promised to make some cakes and pastries for Shirley, who was having friends to supper that Saturday. Shirley was always busy these days, either at the hospital or the clinic she attended two afternoons a week. She had joined her husband Ray's team, helping him with his highly skilled surgery, mostly for children, but also keeping an eye on the clinic for the people of the East End. She gave up her spare time for the clinic – something Ray wasn't too keen on, but Shirley had a mind of her own and though very much in love with her husband of nearly three years now, she was by no means dominated by him, even though he'd been one of her tutors when she was studying. He sometimes laughed with

Maureen over it, telling her that she had brought up a very determined young woman.

'Don't blame me,' she'd told him the last time he'd teased her. 'Shirley always knew what she wanted – and you knew what she was like before you married her.'

'I certainly did,' Ray had said with a laugh. 'And I wouldn't change one hair on her head.'

'I wouldn't either,' Maureen had agreed. 'She is a lovely girl – and I couldn't love her more if she was my own child.' Shirley was Gordon's daughter by his first wife but Maureen had taken her on as a young girl and won her love and affection; the two were as close as any mother and daughter, especially now that Shirley was married and often needed a hand with her cooking if she was entertaining. She simply didn't have the time to prepare fancy meals for friends, though she liked to entertain. Maureen cooked things that took time, simple cakes, pastries, also delicious casseroles that Shirley could just finish off in her own oven.

'My friends all think your chicken casserole is wonderful, Mum,' she'd told Maureen the previous week. 'I really should learn to do it for myself – but I just don't seem to have time.'

'When you have a family and are at home more, I'll teach you,' Maureen had promised. 'Until then, I am happy to do it for you, love.'

Shirley's face had clouded at the mention of a family. Maureen had hesitated for a moment and then asked if something was wrong. Shirley had frowned and then nodded.

'Ray wants to have children – and I do, too, Mum, but not quite yet. I did all those years of training and I'm a part of his team. If I give it up to have a family – what was the point?'

'The point is that you won't forget what you learned,' Maureen had responded. 'You can go back to being a doctor when your children are old enough – and you know I'll look after them for you. I can fetch them from school and give them tea here and you can collect them when you come out of theatre.'

'That sounds fine, Mum,' Shirley had replied. 'It doesn't work quite like that, though. Our hours are not nine to five – or even nine to six. We might have to work late into the evening sometimes. If an operation takes longer than expected, I couldn't just walk out because my child needed to be fetched home.'

'In that case, your son or daughter – or both – would stay here with us until you could fetch them,' Maureen had said firmly. 'Don't let a little thing like that stand in your way, Shirley. I had to give up being a nurse when I was having my first child, but I didn't have anyone who could take over for me – well, I suppose Peggy would have helped but it was different for me. I only took up nursing to get away from home and help out during the war.'

Shirley had nodded then and looked rueful. 'Ray said something similar...' She'd hesitated, then, 'I might think about it... Oh, I do want children and I know he is that bit older. It wouldn't be fair to make him wait too long and then maybe we couldn't... Besides, there's Dad to think of...' They had looked at each other because Gordon would love to see his grandchild and they didn't know how long he'd got left with them all.

'You have to decide what you want,' Maureen had smiled at her lovingly. 'I know it would please your dad to have a grandchild but only if it is what you want too.'

Shirley had laughed then. 'I am always asking you for something, Mum. Are you sure you would be prepared to take on another young family so that I could return to work? Ray said we could afford childcare but...' She'd pulled a wry face. 'I don't know...'

'They would be no trouble to us – and your dad would love having a baby around, and so would I. He wanted more children, but after my miscarriage I couldn't have another baby and we lost Robin too soon.'

'Oh, Mum,' Shirley had thrown her arms around her. 'If I have a little boy, shall I call him Robin – or would that be too painful?'

'I think it might be nice.' Maureen had blinked away her sudden tears. 'We all miss Robin, don't we?'

'Yes, Mum, we do.' Shirley had given her another squeeze. 'It looks like we'll be trying for a baby then...'

'As I said, it is up to you, love. Don't let me persuade you if it isn't what you want.' Maureen would enjoy having grandchildren to spoil but it was Shirley's choice.

'I do want children. I just thought it a waste of my training if I gave up too soon – but if I could do part-time work, even if it was as a GP again...' Shirley had nodded and smiled. 'You always make me feel better, Mum. I am so lucky to have you. Some of the children we've been treating aren't as lucky...' She'd shaken her head. 'We had a little girl brought in yesterday. She was living on the streets, taking shelter in a rat-infested hovel and was bitten several times on her leg. Because she was too frightened to go to the clinic, she neglected it and was found unconscious in the market square by one of the traders. He brought her straight in—' Shirley had caught back a sob, '—it was too late for her leg. We had to amputate to save her life, poor child...'

'Oh, that is terrible.' Maureen understood that the gangrene must have gone too far. 'If she'd only come in sooner...'

Shirley had sighed deeply then. 'At least she will be off the streets now. The welfare people have taken over and she will be fostered when she is well enough to leave hospital. I only hope she is given to good people. I think she'd had a hard time of it, Mum.'

'Poor little girl,' Maureen had looked at her thoughtfully. 'Would I be allowed to visit – take her a little present?'

'I'm not sure. We don't know if she has a family yet – but I could ask if you could be put on the official visitors' list, Mum. Would you be prepared to visit children with no family – once or twice a week?'

'Yes, I am sure I can find the time for that.' Maureen had nodded, pleased. 'You get me put on the list, Shirley, and I'll be happy to visit the children.'

'All right, I will,' Shirley had promised. 'No doubt you will have to be vetted to make sure you are a fit person, but you won't mind that?'

Maureen twinkled at her. 'I don't think I have too many wicked secrets for them to find, do you?'

Shirley had laughed. 'Oh, you probably have hundreds but none they have to know.'

3

'I am so glad you could manage to come,' Fay said when Rose entered her kitchen that afternoon. 'This red velvet cake is taking me longer to make than I thought; there are so many layers. Jace – you know the singer I'm doing this party for? – wanted it to be a big cake and I've done six layers.'

'I've never heard of that one,' Rose said and laughed. 'You do make some posh cakes, Fay. Victoria sponge or a light fruit cake is my usual treat for the family. Sometimes I buy a Black Forest gateau, but they are expensive.'

'I can teach you to make them if you like,' Fay said. 'For me that is one of the easier ones. But I enjoy cake making and I don't mind spending hours decorating them. It's just that I have so much more to prepare for tomorrow's party.'

'Where is Maggie?' Rose asked, glancing round the large and very shiny kitchen. 'I thought she was helping you?'

'Maggie made a whole batch of canapés this morning,' Fay told her with a smile. 'I know, very posh! We've put them in the freezer drawer of that fridge.' She indicated a large white cabinet in the corner. 'We'll take them out a few hours before we need them and they should be like fresh-made.'

'Will that work?' Rose looked at her doubtfully. 'I've never done that, Fay, but then, I don't have a big fridge like yours. Mine is small and the icebox only holds some cubes and a carton of ice cream for the kids.'

'Yes, it works fine,' Fay said. 'I wouldn't do it with everything, but Maggie's pastry shells freeze well and we'll fill them and finish them off tomorrow.'

Rose nodded but still looked dubious.

Fay laughed. 'Things are changing, Rose. I don't need an army of staff rushing around to prepare everything for special events when I can freeze much of it and then just let it defrost or put it in the oven to reheat. That way, things are still warm when we serve them to the guests and they really like their nibbles that way. Of course, it is different if we are serving a special dinner. Most of that has to be done on the day and it can be a rush, but Jace wanted a buffet so that his guests can just help themselves. It's fiddlier and you have to prepare a lot of stuff early...'

Rose picked up Fay's worksheet and looked though her list. 'You have six different quiches here. Are you going to prepare those today? I can do the pastry for them and most of the fillings... except I'm not sure about the goat's cheese and walnut one?'

'Yes, that's what I thought you might do,' Fay said with a smile. 'I need to finish this cake and then I'm making a batch of tiny sausage rolls, which I am also going to freeze. Don't worry about the filling you don't know; I'll do that myself.'

'I could do the sausage rolls if you like?' Rose offered, but Fay shook her head.

'I'm doing them French-style, the way Jace likes them – they are more spicy than our version and cut in little three-cornered wedges rather than a roll.'

'Fancy,' Rose said and rolled her eyes. 'You're really putting in a lot of effort for this Jace chap – I hope he is paying you well?'

'He is paying the same rate as we charge everyone,' Fay said. 'I would have done it for him for nothing, because we could get so many orders from this party – but Jace wouldn't hear of it. He wanted to make a splash and he has ordered loads of champagne and French wine.'

'You met over there when you were on your cooking course, didn't you?'

Rose had turned away and begun to prepare her bowl, board and utensils for a large batch of shortcrust pastry, which she would blind bake and then let cool, ready for the fillings. Fay was glad Rose couldn't see the faint heat in her cheeks.

* * *

No one knew much about her and Jace, except that they'd met in Paris when she was on her special cookery course, not even Freddie, who'd gone with her to France – though he'd warned her about staying out late with Jace.

'He isn't the sort for settling down,' Freddie had told her when she'd walked into her bedroom at three in the morning once and found him sitting up, waiting for her. 'I'm not interfering or trying to tell you what to do, Fay – but surely you know he is a rolling stone? He will want to move from place to place and I doubt one woman will fill his life.'

'Do you think I don't know that?' Fay had tossed back her long fair hair carelessly. 'Jace is a friend. He was working until gone one this morning. I listened to him singing in the nightclub – and he walked me home after his performance. I just like him, Freddie. Jace is fun and talented. Besides, you know I don't intend to marry until I'm older.'

'Well, I do know that,' Freddie had agreed, 'but it is easy to forget when you think you are in love.'

'I'm not in love with him,' Fay had replied, but she hadn't been certain that was true. 'Anyway, Jace and his band have been offered a record deal in America. He is flying out later today; that's why we stayed out late. I don't suppose we shall meet again.'

'Oh, I see.' Freddie had looked relieved. 'I am sorry if you think I'm being nosey, Fay, but I promised Mum I'd look out for you over here.'

'I know – and I'm glad you're here,' Fay had replied, sighing. 'I do like him a lot, but I haven't been stupid. I knew Jace was ambitious and needs to move around a lot; he wants to be rich and famous – and I think it will happen for him.'

'Well, he is handsome and he does sing well.' Her twin had laughed then. 'I should have known you had your head on straight, Fay, but I do care about you and I don't want you to break your heart over a man who isn't worth it.'

'So it would be all right if he was worth it?' Fay had quipped and then they were both laughing, in charity with each other again.

Fay had hidden her true feelings of uncertainty and hope from Freddie, even though she usually shared her thoughts with him. The friendship between Jace and Fay was in its early stages; in France he'd been too busy in the evenings singing in the nightclub to spend much time with her and she was working hard at her course in a hot kitchen most of the day. So there hadn't been many opportunities to meet privately – though they had spent one lovely day in the countryside, walking by a river. Jace had taken a bottle of wine and Fay had packed a picnic, made up of things she'd prepared the day before in class.

'You're a good cook,' he'd told her, looking thoughtful as they ate. 'I'm used to eating on the go, grabbing a sandwich or a packet of chips... I might hire you as my personal chef when I'm famous and rich.'

'You'll get fat or have indigestion,' Fay had teased as he tucked into her pastries, clearly enjoying them. 'Those things you are eating so fast you hardly taste them took hours to prepare – that pastry is flaky and the filling is a custard that needs skill to make it just right. You can't make those on the road; you need a kitchen with all the right equipment.'

'So you're saying you wouldn't enjoy being a roadie and travelling all over the world with me?' Jace had looked at her thoughtfully.

'I might enjoy it for a while,' Fay had admitted, because she was very attracted to the handsome young man she'd met by accident in the market square while shopping for ingredients for her cooking. He'd invited her to come and listen to him one evening and she'd gone to his dressing room afterwards. After that, she was his guest any night she wanted and he'd always taken her home after the performance. This was the first and only time they'd actually gone on a date.

It had been pleasant lying on the bank by the river, and when Jace had leaned over her, kissing her softly on the mouth, Fay had felt something inside – something she'd never felt before. She'd savoured the feeling as she would a slice of delicious cake, but then had sat up, hunching her knees to her chest.

'I want to be a famous cook and make lots of money – so no, I wouldn't enjoy being your roadie.'

'Pity...' Jace had said then and looked regretful. 'I'll be leaving for America at the end of the week. I've been offered a record deal and if that is a success, I'll be touring all over America, here in France, probably Germany, Spain and the UK. Maybe we'll meet again when I'm in London on tour...'

'Maybe,' Fay had replied casually. She'd stood up to hide the disappointment she'd felt at that moment. She liked Jace and wanted to get to know him, but it looked as if it would never happen. They both had ambition and it would take them in separate directions. 'When you come to London, look me up. I live at the Pig & Whistle in Mulberry Lane – that's the East End...' She'd gone to paddle at the water's edge, taking off her strappy white sandals and enjoying the coolness on her bare feet.

'I know that,' Jace had laughed then. 'I grew up not far from there – just a few streets away in a terraced house. My father was killed in the war and Ma got married again, moved away in the fifties. We moved south of the river and to a nicer area. I had singing lessons, because my stepdad was well off – a great guy actually. I liked him a lot. He and Ma died in a car accident a year ago. So I'm on my own now – and I decided to try singing as a career.' He'd shrugged. 'My stepdad didn't get round to making a will and his money went to a distant cousin. I had to get out of the house, find a home – so I bought myself a van and I live in that most of the time.'

'Oh Jace!' Fay had cried, looking at him in sympathy. 'I'm sorry you lost your parents and that you were left without a home.'

He'd shrugged her sympathy off. 'Don't feel sorry for me. It's an adventure, Fay. If I'd had Dad's money, I doubt I'd be here now. I would probably have tried to carry on his business, as he wanted me to – but now I'm a singer and I travel to gigs with the band wherever I can get them. I'm happy and I enjoy it.'

Fay had known then that she couldn't let herself fall for Jace. She wanted a settled life near to people she knew and loved, a place to call home. Jace wanted a life filled with adventure. It would be foolish to like him too much and anything more than friendship was out of the question – and yet, after he'd left her that last night, when they'd walked slowly back to the small hotel she and Freddie were staying in, Fay had felt suddenly empty.

It was ridiculous and stupid, but she'd missed him so much this past year or so, looking eagerly for the occasional postcard sent from one of his tours. Now he was back in London, living in a beautiful house he'd rented out near Hampstead Heath and already on the way to becoming very rich. It had been a huge shock for Fay when he had walked into her office a few days earlier and asked her if she could cater for a party for around fifty guests.

* * *

'How many did you say were coming to this party?' Rose asked, interrupting her thoughts.

'What – oh, about fifty,' Fay said, coming out of her daydream. 'That's why I've been cooking and freezing stuff all week. Maggie only just managed to get her pastries in that drawer this morning.' She stood back to admire the cake she'd just finished decorating. 'This goes in the fridge for now. What do you think of it?'

Rose came to stand by her and gaze on the huge cake, which was shaped like a guitar and decorated with swirls of whipped cream, strings of caramelised sugar and keys of chocolate crisps.

'Wow, that is fantastic,' Rose said. 'No wonder it took ages to prepare. I hope this Jace appreciates all the work you've put in, Fay.'

'The cake is a surprise for him,' Fay smiled. 'He told me what savouries he would like, salads and the chicken and ham, prawns. All that stuff we'll be doing fresh tomorrow, but he left the choice of cake to me. I'm not charging him for this; it's my gift, to thank him for choosing us to cater for his party.'

'You must be mad,' Rose said, shaking her head as she went back to preparing her quiches. 'I am right that you want three of each of these? So that makes eighteen altogether?'

'Yes, that is right,' Fay agreed. 'Jace said he wanted plenty of food – he'd rather have some left over than not enough. He says he can always give anything decent left over to a mission he knows of that feeds people who need it – people on the streets...'

Rose nodded. 'We thought after the war, when they rebuilt, with all the high-rise blocks, and the slums were gone, destroyed in the Blitz, that it wouldn't happen any more. We thought there would be homes for those unfortunates who had no homes, that it would be a better world with no poverty...'

'It happens,' Fay said, frowning. 'People suffer a change in life, something happens and they can suddenly find themselves on the streets with no home.' Rose looked at her, but Fay shook her head, not wanting to reveal what Jace had told her about his life. 'Anyway, Jace says the food won't be wasted.'

'This must be your best commission so far?' Rose looked curious.

'Yes, it probably is,' Fay agreed. 'I've done a lot of dinner parties and a few small weddings, but they were easier, because they were mostly sit-down, cold meals: a salmon starter, ham, chicken or tongue with salad, perhaps potatoes served hot, and a few fancy deserts, and then the cake. Most of the dinner parties were for ten people or less, but the weddings were nearer one hundred, but simpler.' She smiled. 'Mum helped me with those. She is so good at organising. If she'd been here today, she would have enjoyed helping with this, too.'

'Have you heard from her yet?'

'She rang from the hotel when they arrived, just to say they were all right, but it was a bad line so we only had a couple of minutes to talk before it started crackling. She said she would write soon. Dad sounded happy.'

'Wouldn't you have liked to go with them?'

'No. It is their special holiday,' Fay said simply. 'They've done so much for me, Maggie too – look at this wonderful kitchen. The Pig

& Whistle will be so smart when it is done. We'll be busier than ever.'

'Yes, I suppose you will,' Rose agreed. 'If this part of your business takes off too, you will need to take on more staff.'

'I need them already,' Fay said ruefully and glanced at the clock on the wall. 'Maggie should be back soon.'

As if on cue, they heard the front door open and close and then Maggie's voice calling out, 'It's only me, Fay. Sorry I was so long, but I ran into James and stopped for a coffee.' James was an artist friend she saw sometimes. Maggie's arms were filled with parcels. 'I got those ground almonds you wanted for the petit fours... Hello, Rose. How are you and the family?'

'We're all well, thank you,' Rose assured her, smiling as she watched Maggie unload her bags. 'You have been busy.'

'This is only a part of it – I've already unloaded the stuff I bought for the restaurant. While we're closed it is a chance to look round the specialist shops and find different things we can use. When I'm busy in the kitchen, I have to send a list to Maureen and let her shop for me – unless I go to the wholesale markets very early.'

'That must be hard work, getting up before it is light in the winter to go to the wholesale food auctions in Smithfields and Covent Garden,' Rose said with a smile. 'I couldn't believe it when Peggy said that's what you'd done last winter.'

'Well, the meat and fish are so fresh,' Maggie said, 'and fishmongers can't always supply enough of what I want, so the best way is to go and buy it myself.'

'Rather you than me at that time in the morning,' Rose said with a little shiver. 'Oh, look at those prawns! They are so big. I don't think I've seen any like that before.'

'They were a special order,' Maggie told her. 'I think we were lucky to get them, but Fay wanted the best, so I got in touch with my supplier. We're going to do a champagne mousse and a huge platter of them.' She glanced at Fay. 'I think I need to freeze them to make sure they keep; it's quite warm out. Is there room?'

'Not in the American fridge,' Fay said. 'You'll get them in the top of that one.' She pointed to a smaller fridge at the other end of the kitchen. 'I knew I should have had two large fridges when Dad had this one sent over from America...'

'I am having a big chest freezer in my kitchen,' Maggie said. 'Once that is running, you'll be able to pop stuff in there overnight if you need to.'

'Good,' Fay said and began rolling her special pastry. 'I need some of your coffee iced biscuits, Maggie. At least we won't need to freeze them.'

'Thank goodness for that,' Maggie retorted with a rueful look. 'I hope Jace is paying us well, Fay. I don't think we've ever done this much for anyone else.'

'Oh, the biscuits are not for Jace's party,' Fay told her with a grin. 'Freddie wants them to take away with him this weekend. He is very partial to them, as you know.'

Maggie's look softened. 'Oh, well, if they are for Freddie, I'll make a nice big batch, because he does love to munch them and I doubt if he will feed himself properly half the time. He never does unless we nag him into it...'

4

'So, this is your room; it's basic, but we all have the same. You'll find it is adequate,' the tall young man with jet-black hair and blue eyes said and grinned at Freddie, making him feel immediately at home. It was a small plain room at a boarding house the team used, but looked clean and had a bed, a chest of drawers and a wardrobe.

'It is fine,' Freddie said, dumping his bags on the floor. He moved his shoulder ruefully. 'I don't know what my sister packed in that rucksack, but it weighs a ton.'

'Perhaps she's packed all your belongings so you never go back?' His guide twinkled at him. Guy Forrister had met him at the station, bringing him to the boarding house in a blue van that had seen better days. It belonged to the Sussex Lifeguard Station, which covered many of the beaches in the area, and they all used it when necessary.

Freddie laughed. 'If I didn't turn up on time, my whole family might come looking.'

'You're close then,' Guy said with a nod of understanding.

'Well, I hope you enjoy your stay with us. You lived at the sea once, I understand?'

'We were in Devon,' Freddie said. 'I often went swimming in the sea there. The surf wasn't as high as it looks here when the tide is in, but the sea can be dangerous even when it looks calm. If youngsters swim too far out and get frightened or caught in a rip tide, they can easily drown...'

'You're perfectly right, Freddie – it is Freddie or do you prefer Fred? I told you my name, didn't I?'

'Yes, you did.' Freddie grinned. 'I called you, sir, and you said to call you Guy – and I'm Freddie. My family always call me that and I probably wouldn't answer if you called me Fred, if I wasn't fully aware.'

'Go off into dreams, do you?' Guy asked. 'Don't do it when you're on duty. When we have lots of visitors, we need to keep scanning the sea all the time, even when it seems calm. Quite often, the youngsters who float away on their rubber rings aren't aware when a wind comes up or a current catches them. Splashing about in the sea when it is warm can be fun but quickly turns into a nightmare on some of our beaches. We have quite a large team – thirty of us in all – and we rotate duties so that we all patrol different beaches up and down the coast. We recruit young people in the summer to train and help out when the beaches are crowded. It is a skill that you never forget and might come in useful in years to come.'

'No, I won't drift off when I'm on duty,' Freddie promised. 'I'm looking forward to it.'

'I should leave you to unpack then,' Guy told him. 'We have dinner at seven here and we have to let Mrs Phipps know if we don't want it. It is sometimes nicer to have fish and chips out, but breakfast and dinner are included in the tariff. It is up to you. I wouldn't say our landlady is the best cook, but she's not too bad.'

'I've been spoiled that way,' Freddie confessed. 'My mother, twin sister and my cousin, Maggie, are all brilliant cooks. I expect that is why my case is so heavy. Fay will have sent me loads of cakes and biscuits, just in case I don't get enough to eat.'

'Ah, I see.' Guy laughed. 'Afraid we'll starve you down here?'

Freddie shook his head. 'I'm known to forget about eating if I get interested in something – then I feel starved and eat whatever is in sight.'

'There's no need to go short here. Breakfast is good. There's always plenty and it's tasty,' Guy said. 'Most of us eat well then and buy something light in the middle of the day – bacon roll or something. Some of the others eat in every night, but I pick my days. Mondays are pie nights and they are quite good, also the roast on Sunday, but midweek they can be a bit stodgy – so you've been warned and now I really will leave you to unpack. You'll meet some of the others at dinner – and the rest of the team tomorrow.'

Freddie thanked him again for meeting him at the station and Guy left. For a moment, Freddie felt unsure. Had he done the right thing coming all the way down here for the few months until he started his course at university? It had seemed a great idea when he saw the advert, but now he wondered if he would have done better to stay in London. He could have used his time to teach local kids how to play football or cricket, but his father had suggested he try something different for a while.

* * *

'Once you get to university you will be busy, studying, taking exams. I know you'll probably go out at night with other students, but you're not into drinking a lot of beer. Knowing you, you will train hard and join all the sporting groups. Why don't you try working at something different just for a chance to have fun?' Freddie's father had said when he had been thinking about what to do next.

Freddie had taken his father's advice and looked for likely jobs and being a lifeguard on one of Hastings' beautiful beaches had appealed. He'd applied, not really thinking he would be asked to join the team for the summer months, but a letter came in reply to his and, after a brief interview on the telephone, he'd been accepted and sent all the information he'd needed. They'd stressed that training would be given, even though Freddie had told them he'd done a brief course on lifesaving when he was at school in Devon. Because he was a strong swimmer from an early age, his teacher had suggested it, so Freddie knew the basics. Obviously, the team he'd joined would have its own rules and way of doing things, but he couldn't see any difficulty in that regard. If all the team was as friendly as Guy Forrister, the experience should be a good one – why then did he suddenly have this feeling of unease? A feeling that his orderly life was about to be disrupted?

Dismissing his doubts, Freddie started to unpack, grinning when he saw the tins in his rucksack. No wonder it had felt heavy! He opened the first of three and discovered it was filled with Maggie's iced biscuits, the second one had a coconut cake in it and the third was crammed full of sausage rolls, fruit cake and jam tarts. How on earth did Fay think he was going to eat all this lot?

Freddie laughed. He would take some with him for lunch tomorrow and share it around. It was an easy way to make friends and he already knew that everyone would enjoy his sister's cooking. Had his mother not already left for the holiday in America, no doubt she would have packed him an apple pie for good measure.

Freddie wondered how his parents were getting on. It was more than time they had a really good holiday right away from the family. When Freddie's mother went to stay with Pip or with Janet – Freddie's half-brother and -sister – she was always working, helping with cooking or washing up or looking after children. Now she'd gone far away and Freddie hoped she was having a good time.

It seemed strange not to be able to just pick up the phone and tell his mother and father he'd arrived safely. He'd done that when he'd been to his football trial for Manchester United, but they hadn't been able to give him a number to ring in America, because they were travelling all over the place, going down to Texas by train and buses with stops for a few days, and then hiring a car to drive on to the deep south countryside his father had known as a boy. It was intended to be a long trip and meant the family could only hear from them if they telephoned the pub – or sent cards. Freddie expected his mother would send a lot of cards, views of the new places she was seeing. She always did when on holiday in Devon or Cornwall, but this trip was something far more exciting. Going to America was a huge adventure and one Freddie hoped for when he was older, but he knew it was costing his father a small fortune and would be something he would only do when he'd saved enough money.

Freddie would ring his sister soon, but she wouldn't worry. Fay was far too busy this weekend to think about her brother. She had a big party to cater for that very night and he knew she was nervous.

'Don't worry about pleasing Jace,' Freddie had told her. 'He will think it is all perfect. You know he normally grabs a ham roll or something.'

'He likes things nice,' Fay had retorted. 'He enjoyed what I made for our picnic, which is why he asked me to cater for his party – but it isn't really Jace I'm anxious about—'

'You're hoping this could make the catering business take off, aren't you?' Freddie had seen the anticipation, excitement and fear in his twin.

'I know Maggie loves having me around in the restaurant and I enjoy it – but I did so want to do special cooking for people who understand good food.'

'You will.' Freddie had given her a friendly squeeze. 'Just give it time, Fay. Don't give up too soon – the people you want to impress aren't the easiest ones to get in with; you have to be patient.'

'I'm not, that's the trouble,' Fay had grumbled. 'How can we be twins and be so different, Freddie? You're patient, thoughtful and sensible – and I'm the opposite.'

'I'm the tortoise and you're the hare,' Freddie had teased her then. 'You'll get there, Fay. Just don't be disappointed if it doesn't happen overnight.'

'I know...' she'd sighed. 'I'm going to miss you when you leave, Freddie – and Mum and Dad are away too. What do I do if I need help and advice?'

'You think things through carefully, but if you really need help, ask Maggie or Maureen. Mum and Maureen have been best friends for years. She will help if she can...'

'It's not the same,' Fay had retorted. 'Mum always knows what to do – and if she isn't sure, which isn't often, she asks Dad and he sorts it. I feel deserted... Oh, I know that is selfish of me. They deserve their time away, but I always rely on Mum...'

'We all do,' Freddie had agreed instantly. 'But it isn't fair to expect her to go on day in and day out without a holiday, Fay. I miss them too. I miss talking to Dad – but I'm old enough to look out for myself and so are you.'

Fay had laughed then. 'That isn't what you said when I stayed out late with Jace in France that time.'

'No – and I'd warn you about that again, if I thought you'd listen,' Freddie had said with a frown. 'He's all right as a friend, Fay – but I think he might hurt you if you got serious about him.'

'Well, I shan't because we want different lives,' Fay had told him crossly. 'You don't need to warn me off him, Freddie. I am only interested in him as a client and a friend.'

'That's all right then.'

Freddie munched one of Fay's savoury sausage rolls as he finished unpacking. They were tiny and very spicy, altogether different from the ones his mother made at Christmas. He wasn't sure he liked them as much. Sometimes he preferred plain fare, though he didn't tell his sister that, because she would pout and flounce off in a mood. Fay had protested she was only interested in Jace as a client, but Freddie wasn't sure it was true. He'd felt the disappointment in her when Jace had walked out of her life in France. He'd also seen the excitement when he came back and asked her to cater for his party.

What did Jace have in mind? Why choose Fay to do his cooking when there were other established firms who could probably have offered him more? Was it just that he'd liked her picnic and remembered it – or had he used it to get back in touch? Freddie knew she'd met him a couple of times, once in the morning and again in the evening, to discuss menus and various bits and pieces Jace wanted. Fay had returned looking as though someone had lit a candle inside her. Freddie didn't think that was just because she saw a chance for her business to grow. Ought he to have stayed in London to be there for her if all her excitement and hope for the future came crashing about her ears?

He wondered if the boarding house had a telephone he could use. He would have to ask Guy. Perhaps he would ring Fay in the morning if he got time. No use ringing her now as she would be busy preparing for the party. If there was a phone here, she could have the number and ring if she wanted to talk; if he wasn't in, he could always ring her back later.

Freddie pushed his vague worries to the back of his mind. Fay would find a way to come to him if she needed him, even if it was just through her thoughts. He'd known in the past when things were wrong – but whether that would work with him miles away he wasn't sure. Yet he knew she wouldn't thank him for fussing over her unnecessarily. He had to be there when she wanted him and leave her alone when she didn't; it had always been that way.

* * *

Shrugging his broad shoulders, Freddie went downstairs. He could hear voices coming from the sitting room, male and female, laughing. As he walked in, the laughter stopped and they all looked at him, then Guy smiled.

'Listen, everyone – this is Freddie. He's our newest member and we'll be starting his training tomorrow. This evening is the time to get to know each other – Freddie, this is Muriel, George, Steve, Jill and Mark – they will be training with you. Our more experienced members will join us on the beach in the morning. Most of them live here all the time and have their own homes. I hope to one day too as I intend to make Hastings my base in future – but the rest of you girls and boys here this evening are down for the summer season. It's the time when we need to be vigilant and require more of you. We don't get so many swimmers in the colder months.'

Freddie moved forward to greet the others, his hand outstretched. They all smiled and nodded, but no one offered to shake hands and he let his hand drop to his side, feeling slightly foolish. He was the youngest of them, he could see that just by looking at their faces.

'Hi, Freddie,' the young woman Guy had named as Muriel indicated a vacant seat on the sofa next to her. 'What made you want to spend your summer down here? I'm here to earn some extra money. I'm going to set up a hairdressing salon when I go home. I thought I'd have a bit of fun and earn some money before I start. What will you do after the summer?'

'I am going to university to train as a sports teacher,' Freddie told her. 'I thought this might be good experience... helping people in trouble.'

Muriel laughed and took out a packet of cigarettes, offering it to him. He shook his head. 'Very wise. I smoke too much. I doubt you'll be called on to rescue anyone from drowning, Freddie. Our job is to patrol the beach and make sure the kids don't do anything daft. If someone does get into trouble, we alert the real lifeguards and they do the rescue.'

'What if we need to act swiftly to save someone?' Freddie questioned. 'Isn't it better to just go in and grab them and bring them back rather than trying to alert a more experienced guard?'

'That is a good question, Freddie,' Guy interjected from the other side of Muriel. 'The best procedure is to alert the other lifeguards with the whistle, but if you are patrolling further down the beach and you think there isn't time to wait, then you would blow the whistle and go straight in. It should alert others to come and help you with the rescue – but you need the training first, of course. Trainees are told to alert the other guards because they might get into trouble themselves if they don't know the tides or what to do.'

Freddie nodded. 'That makes sense. I've done basic training at school. I know how to hold someone and how to tow them back but not much more.'

'That's why we give training. If you do the school training, the person you rescue just goes along with it. In reality, drowning people often fight the person trying to rescue them – that's why we always have more than one lifeguard on duty. A drowning person will be terrified and struggle; it needs strength and determination to overcome that natural fear.'

'Being a lifeguard is mostly coping with minor injuries,' the man introduced as Steve said with a confident look. 'People leave bottles buried in the sand and others cut their feet on them. They get stung by bees and wasps on the beach – or pecked by gulls... we direct them to the first-aid station or take them there if they are really in distress. Sunstroke is another thing we have to watch for. People flock down for a rest in the sun and don't realise that they can burn on a day that doesn't seem over-warm with the sea breezes washing over them. It's just looking after folk, I reckon.'

'All I've had so far is someone asking where the nearest toilets are,' Jill laughed. 'Even a bee sting hasn't come my way.' She was a tall blonde girl, perhaps in her early twenties. 'Perhaps I don't inspire confidence...' She fluffed out her long hair and made flirtatious eyes at Guy.

'You'll get your chance one of these days,' he said, smiling at her. 'We won't get through the summer without having to go in after someone. I just hope we won't have any fatal accidents this year. Two years ago, some fishermen out with crab pots found the body of a young girl... she'd gone missing from the beach. A search was made, but no one had seen her in the water – that's why we tell you to keep watching the water. If a young child enters the sea and looks vulnerable, go after them before something happens. No need to frighten them – just make sure they doesn't go out of their depth and aren't going to get caught by a current from a breakwater.' He looked up as the door opened and a woman with a white apron over a printed dress entered. 'Ah, I think dinner is ready, everyone. Thank you, Mrs Phipps, we'll all come now.'

She nodded to him and looked at Freddie. 'You'll be Freddie Ronoscki then? Do you speak English?'

'Yes. My father is an American, my mother a Londoner.'

'Ah – it was just a strange name,' she said and nodded. 'I was busy in the kitchen when you arrived – but Guy looked after you?'

'Yes, he did,' Freddie agreed and smiled. 'Thank you, Mrs Phipps. I was wondering, do you have a telephone here I can use if I need to?'

'Calls in but not out,' she said. 'Family can ring and leave a message – there's a phone box just down the road if you want to ring home.'

'Oh, that's fine,' Freddie agreed instantly. 'If I can give my sister the number, she could use it if she needed to.'

'Right. I'm ready to serve.' Mrs Phipps nodded abruptly. 'It's sausage and mash with cabbage and peas, bread and butter pudding for afters.'

'Miserable old thing,' Muriel said when the landlady had gone. 'As if it would hurt us using the phone. We could pay for the calls.'

Freddie shrugged. 'It doesn't matter – I just wondered about emergencies, if my sister should need me – my parents are in America at the moment.'

'How exciting,' Muriel exclaimed.

'I haven't heard from them yet,' Freddie said. 'My sister is a cook. I've been eating her sausage rolls. I wish I hadn't now.'

'I'll bet they were nicer than our dinner. If it is stodgy, I'll leave it and buy some chips later.'

Freddie nodded. The smell of slightly burned sausages was strong in the dining room. He frowned as a plate was served to him by a young girl. She gave him a shy smile.

'Sorry, they are a bit burned – Aunt Edith left them to me to finish and I forgot them.' She looked anxious. 'She will be so cross if no one eats them...'

'They will be fine,' Freddie replied. He smiled at her, determined to eat all his supper because if too many of them left it, the young girl might be in trouble, but the idea of fish and chips was undoubtedly appealing.

5

The party was in full swing, spilling out of the rather grand house into the large gardens behind. Fay had been impressed when she and Maggie had arrived earlier that afternoon to prepare. The kitchen was modern, despite the age of the house, which must have been built in the eighteenth century. It was large and cool, ideal for the work they had to do, and the house was furnished with what looked like priceless antiques.

'This is the kind of house I'd like to live in,' Maggie had said, looking round with approval. She'd smiled at Fay. 'Maybe I will one day...'

That had been several hours ago. Now they'd finished all the cooking; the food was all set out in the long dining room and being eaten with evident approval.

Fay took some extras in and collected plates and glasses on her tray, feeling grateful that she didn't have to wash most of these herself.

'Fay, can you spare a moment?' Jace caught Fay's arm as she was about to disappear into the kitchen. 'I just wanted to thank you – that cake was fantastic; everyone clapped when you brought it in.'

'I wanted to surprise you.' And she had, the little ripple of applause well worth the time it had taken to make.

'It was a wonderful surprise.'

'I'm glad you're pleased.' She'd worked hard over the past few days to make the party a success for him and it seemed she'd succeeded.

'Are you leaving immediately?' Jace's question brought Fay back to the present. She could hear the laughter from the large conservatory and the garden and some shrieking from one of the girls she'd noticed earlier. She was with Jace's entourage and travelled everywhere with him and the band, and she had a tendency to become very loud when she got excited. Jace had introduced her as Mitsy. 'Why don't you stay now your work is done and have a few drinks?'

'Thanks, but it has been a long day,' Fay replied with a smile. 'I'd love to have a drink some other night, Jace, but not this evening – besides, Maggie wants to get off. She has to get up early in the morning.'

'All work and no play makes Jill a dull girl,' Jace said, a look of annoyance passing over his handsome face. 'I thought we could catch up, Fay. It's been a while—'

Another burst of wild laughter nearly drowned out his words and the door from the sitting room opened as Mitsy burst through into the hall. She looked at Jace, crooking her finger to summon him, a mischievous look in her eyes.

'What is it, Mitsy?' he asked, a flash of impatience in his blue eyes.

'You're missing all the fun.' She glanced at Fay with a look of dislike. 'Why are you with the hired help when you should be with your guests? You have to mix, Jace. These people are important to your career.'

'Mitsy is right,' Fay said, blithely ignoring the other girl's spiteful remark. After all, she was the hired help for that evening and she knew that his guests consisted of well-known agents, a representative of Decca Records and some famous names from the world of music and film. 'Give me a call, Jace. I have to finish up and leave. Goodnight, Mitsy. Enjoy your evening.'

Fay enjoyed the dumbfounded look on the other girl's face as she walked away. She heard Jace speak sharply to her, but she didn't turn back. Mitsy was clearly jealous and thought Jace her property... Perhaps they were together.

Smothering faint pangs of regret, Fay entered the kitchen and put down the last of the dishes she intended to fetch. Jace's staff could do the rest of the clearing up in the morning.

Maggie had finished packing their saucepans and cooking tools in the large baskets they used for the purpose, along with various spices and jars of oil and sauces they had brought with them in the little van they'd bought for the business.

'Ready to leave?' Maggie asked. 'Or do you intend to stay on for a while?'

'Jace asked me to stay for drinks, but I said no,' Fay replied. 'I'm tired. I just want to get home, have a bath and go to bed.'

Maggie nodded her agreement. 'I feel the same and we have quite a drive back. It was a lot of work today. You really pushed the boat out for this one – a lot of fiddly bits and pieces.'

'I wanted to impress and I think I did. Several people asked who did the cooking; they can get details from Jace if they need them. Hopefully, it may bring in more trade for us.'

'It certainly went well,' Maggie agreed. 'Carla and Ruby left as soon as we finished setting up the buffet, so it's just us. That basket is heavy. Do you think we can manage it between us? It took three of us to lift it into the van on the way here.'

'It had more foodstuffs when we came,' Fay said but frowned as the two of them struggled to carry it. 'Maybe I can find someone to help us get it on the van...'

Even as she spoke, the door of the kitchen opened and Mitsy entered, looking as if she'd been chastened, though there was a glint of smouldering anger in her eyes.

'Jace said I was rude calling you the hired help,' she said, reluctance in her tone. 'I have to apologise.'

'Doesn't matter. I am the hired help,' Fay told her. 'But you could give us a hand to get this basket in the van if you will?'

'Is it heavy?' Mitsy said and moved forward, testing the weight, and then she bent her knees and picked it up in her arms. 'Show me where the van is...'

'I meant to carry it between us,' Fay said. She went to help, but Mitsy shook her head.

'I'm used to shifting stuff on the road with the van...'

Maggie shrugged at Fay and led the way. She'd fetched the van to the back of the kitchen, so it was only a short distance and she undid the back door, giving Mitsy easy access. She slid it in and stood back, a look of satisfaction on her face.

'That's why Jace asked me to be his roadie,' she said, looking pleased with herself. 'I train with weights and I've won medals for it.'

'You are very strong,' Maggie said and smiled in a friendly manner. 'We could do with someone like you at times. If you get tired of travelling come and see us.'

'Oh, I shall never get tired of being with Jace. He's my man...' Mitsy said and she was looking meaningfully at Fay. 'Jace and me – we're together.'

Fay nodded, understanding that she was being warned off. She wasn't sure that Mitsy's claims were true because Jace had made it clear he wasn't the marrying kind – but perhaps they did have an understanding.

'Well, good night and thanks for your help,' Maggie said. 'Come on, Fay. We have everything now.'

'It was good food,' Mitsy said suddenly. She produced an envelope from her back pocket. 'Jace said to give you this.'

'Thanks.' Fay took the envelope and opened it. It was thick and filled with five-pound notes. 'Thank Jace for me.'

Mitsy nodded and stood back. 'We're going back to America when this tour is over – and we'll be on the road for the next six weeks; it's all booked.'

'Enjoy it.'

Hiding a faint pang of disappointment that she wouldn't be seeing more of Jace, Fay climbed into the front seat beside Maggie. They waved to Mitsy, but she turned her back on them and went into the house.

'That young woman is jealous of you,' Maggie said. 'Does she have good reason?'

'Only in her head,' Fay retorted. 'Oh, Jace gives me the eye sometimes. If I'm honest, I like him more than I should – I aways did – but he doesn't want the things I want.'

'Which are?'

'Oh, you know...' Fay stared straight ahead. 'To be successful at what I do and build a good business – and one day to have a home of my own, not too far from my family. Jace just wants to travel the world, singing, having fun and making friends.'

'Doesn't sound too bad a life if you loved him?'

Fay shook her head. 'I could have gone with him last year when he got that American record contract, but I refused. It isn't the life for me, Maggie.'

'I'm glad you decided that for yourself,' Maggie said. 'We should all miss you if you went off to the other side of the world, Fay – but it has to be your choice. Granny Peggy wouldn't stand in the way of your happiness. You must know that?'

'Mum would insist that I wait for a while if I said I wanted to go with him, but she would also want to know when the wedding would be...' Fay laughed, letting go of her disappointment. 'It was a good evening. We may have made five hundred pounds out of that party tonight...'

'That's far more than I expected,' Maggie replied, looking thoughtful. 'Did he give you extra money then?'

'Yes. There is five hundred pounds in this envelope – and I'd already been paid more than enough to cover our expenses; it's twice what it should have been – and I charged full price, Maggie.' Even though Maggie looked after the restaurant and Fay the catering, the business was all one and they pooled the profits.

'Perhaps he made a mistake,' Maggie suggested. 'You can telephone him tomorrow and ask.'

'Yes, I ought to just check,' Fay replied. 'He paid me cash the first time so perhaps he forgot he'd paid two hundred and fifty pounds in advance...'

'Or he just earns so much he doesn't care,' Maggie said. 'I've been told they earn hundreds of thousands of pounds, those popular singers. He probably doesn't know what to do with his money. He ought to invest in property even if he doesn't use it often. One day his records might not sell as well as they have in the past.'

'I'll pass on your advice when I telephone,' Fay told her with a smile. 'I think I am going to stay in bed all day tomorrow.'

'No, you're not,' Maggie replied. 'Tom said they would have the bar finished today, so tomorrow we'll be cleaning it and getting it ready to open. We can get the bar up and running while they are still working on the extension at the back...'

'Slave driver,' Fay groaned, but she knew Maggie was right. If they left it closed for too long, the regulars might find somewhere else to drink. 'I'm so tired, I could sleep for a week.'

'Serves you right for choosing such a complicated menu for the buffet,' Maggie quipped. 'Next time a friend wants a party, keep it a little simpler, please.'

Fay laughed. 'I suppose I did go over the top with all those French pastries and the canapés, didn't I?'

'They seemed to eat them all. The lead drummer found his way to the kitchen to see if there were any more of your pastries, Fay. He said they don't get food like that wherever they go and asked who made them.' Maggie giggled suddenly. 'When I told him you did, he looked astonished, said you were too beautiful to be that clever, and asked if I thought you would marry him. I said I didn't think so but he could ask...'

'Oh, Maggie, you didn't!' Fay exclaimed.

'I think he had drunk something or...' She shook her head. 'I don't know if Jace and his band smoke that stuff... you know, marijuana?'

'Oh, pot,' Fay said with a nod of her head. 'Jace doesn't, I know that – he told me once that he thought drugs were daft, but members of his band might. I don't know. I wouldn't touch it with a bargepole.'

'I tried it once,' Maggie confided. 'James offered it to me. He's not an addict, but he smokes it now and then. Just one puff I had – but it made me feel awful, so never again.'

'I've friends from school who do,' Fay told her. 'They all say it makes things more fun, but I tell them they are mad to use it – it only leads to hard drugs and then you're hooked. Dad warned Freddie and I when we were at school, so I never fell for it when I was offered a dodgy-looking cigarette, but a boy I knew did and he got into lots of trouble because of it, ended up spending months in hospital.'

'Well, I needn't worry about you then, infant,' Maggie quipped and Fay would have punched her if she hadn't been driving.

'Don't call me that,' she muttered. 'I'll start calling you old lady if you do.'

'Heavens forbid,' Maggie laughed. 'Seriously, you made some wonderful food today, Fay. That course in France wasn't wasted; I ate two of those French pastries, the ones with the custard in. I couldn't resist them.'

'You'll get fat,' Fay teased. Maggie was as slender as she was, which was amazing because they both tasted their food as they cooked, but perhaps they were usually too busy to eat much of it. 'They were delicious, though I say it myself.'

They talked for a bit longer and then fell silent as they drove through the night that was lit by both tall street lamps and shop windows, displaying all kinds of goods. Fay was thoughtful as she looked at the mannequins in a popular dress shop when Maggie paused at the traffic lights. There was a striking shirt dress with red and white stripes that she liked. She had some very smart leather winklepicker shoes she'd hardly worn in a bright red leather that would go with the striped dress.

Fay thought she might shop there if she got time the next week. For work she always wore comfortable slacks and shoes, and a cool blouse with her apron over the top, but there were times when she enjoyed wearing a dress. When Jace visited the kitchen she'd half-wished she was wearing a slinky dress like some of his guests, but it wouldn't have helped her work.

A little sigh escaped her, wishing herself back at Jace's party for a moment. Maybe he would suggest meeting somewhere for a drink when she rang him to make sure he'd meant to give her all that money...

* * *

Jace rang Fay the next morning as she was helping Maggie clean the new bar and set it up with bottles and sparkling glasses. Maggie answered and handed it to her with a little smile. 'It's Jace for you...'

'Jace,' Fay said, slightly hesitant. 'I was going to ring. I think you gave me too much cash last night.'

'That was Mitsy,' he said. 'She told me this morning that she had paid you. I wanted to be sure she gave you enough.'

'Yes, she paid me nearly twice as much as you owed. Do you want me to send it back?'

'No. You were worth every penny. Everyone was impressed and a couple of people wanted your number. I think you might get the chance to tender for a society wedding – the younger brother of an earl was there last night and his daughter is getting married. He was very taken with both you and the food.'

'Oh – well, I hope you gave him the number?'

'I haven't yet. I shall, but watch yourself if you agree to do the job. The Honourable Terrance is a bit of a... He throws some wild parties. Just a friendly warning.'

'Okay, fine, and thanks for giving me the chance to impress at your party.'

'Several of the men wanted to know where you'd gone,' Jace went on, sounding a bit odd. 'Including my drummer, Keith. He kept telling me he wanted to stay here and marry you.' Now there was definitely a hint of jealousy in his voice.

'Yes.' Fay trilled with laughter. 'I believe he said something like that to Maggie last night. I think he was a little drunk.'

'Keith is nearly always a little drunk; he plays best like that,' Jace said with a harsh laugh. 'I told him you were only interested in becoming a famous cook and he said that's okay; he'll help you by trying all your dishes.'

'Just the sort of husband, I need,' Fay teased. 'Mitsy said you were off today – on tour for the next few weeks?'

'Yes. We've just stopped to get petrol and I'm ringing from a phone box. That's why I wanted you to stay last night – so that we could catch up before I had to leave for my tour. I was looking forward to spending time with you.'

'Sorry. I was just tired after working all day. Will you be back in London before you return to America?'

'Yes. I've just been told we've got two weeks at the London Palladium. I'll get you tickets – for you and your cousin – and then we can have a drink after.'

'I'd enjoy that,' Fay told him. 'I love to hear you sing. I've got all of your records.'

'I've been working on an LP while I was in London this time,' Jace said, sounding pleased. 'I've also got another recording session when we come back and then it will be released when I go on tour in America.'

'That must be exciting for you?'

'Yes, it is great. The first two singles went straight up the charts to the top five. I am hoping the LP will make it to number one.'

'I'll keep my fingers crossed for you – and tell all my friends and customers to buy it.'

'Great. I have to go now. Mitsy is calling me. It has been nice talking to you, Fay. I'll be in touch when we get back...'

The line went dead abruptly and Fay felt a slight sense of loss. Jace was always in a hurry to get somewhere and he probably aways would be. It wasn't the life for her, so there was no point in letting herself like him too much. They might meet briefly when he returned to London and then he would be off again – and if she was daft enough to care, it could break her heart. No, she was better off here, doing the work she loved and living close to family and friends.

'Come on, Fay,' Maggie's voice summoned her from her dream. 'I want to get this finished today so that we can open the bar. I promised Granny Peggy it would open as soon as Tom had finished it. She was worried that all her regular customers would find a new place to drink.'

'As if,' Fay said scornfully. 'Most of them come here to flirt with her and talk about old times – and she gives them free drinks and apple pie sometimes too. I don't know how she ever made a profit.'

Maggie laughed. 'She certainly never made the kind of profit on one night that you did last night... He did say we could keep the extra money?'

'Yes.' Fay laughed. 'I think these record companies are paying him well and he's doing personal tours all the time, earning lots more that way. When he booked the party, he said one night's work would more than pay for it.' Fay shrugged. 'He must keep a lot of cash around if Mitsy can just help herself and pay me without him actually knowing until after.'

'Is that what she did?'

Fay nodded and Maggie looked thoughtful.

'She wanted to make sure you didn't see him again. I told you she was jealous of you.'

'Well, it didn't work. Jace is sending us tickets for the London Palladium, Maggie. We can watch the show and meet up afterwards.'

'That sounds like a fun evening,' Maggie agreed. 'It was nice of him to offer me a ticket too.'

'He is nice,' Fay replied, a little too promptly. 'The only trouble is he doesn't want the kind of life I do...'

'I know what you mean...' Maggie sighed. 'James is a bit like that, too. I never know whether he'll turn up if I agree to meet him one evening. If he gets lost in his painting, he just forgets...'

James Morgan was a brilliant artist. He often forgot to eat when he was working and Maggie had got to know him when she'd taken him some food. He was a tenant in a property that Maureen and Gordon owned and Maureen often took him food she'd made, because she was afraid that he might starve. Maggie had taken something when Maureen was unable to visit and he'd immediately wanted to paint her. Fay knew that she visited his studio occasionally and believed the portrait to be finished long since; she also knew that they went out now and then, but she didn't know if Maggie was serious.

'Are you in love with James?' she asked now and Maggie looked startled.

'What a question,' she protested. 'The honest answer is that I don't know, Fay. I like him a lot – but I've promised myself I won't marry until I'm thirty at least. I want to give this business of ours a good go...'

'Me too,' Fay said but gave her a wistful look. 'I think I might be a little bit in love with Jace, though – at least when he is singing...'

'He does have a lovely voice. I've heard you playing his records,' Maggie agreed and then gave a gurgle of laughter. 'We're a right pair! You with your rock singer and me with my artist. Neither of them is good husband material.'

'No, they aren't,' Fay agreed, smiling. 'Which is just as well as we're too busy to be wives.'

'Agreed,' Maggie said and stood back to look at her handiwork. 'Do you think Granny Peggy will be pleased with it?'

'It looks exactly the same as it always did,' Fay replied. 'Tom has just moved the whole lot and given it a spruce up.'

'Yes, that was the idea for the bar,' Maggie agreed. 'All the regulars have to do is use a different door for the time being – but the restaurant will be different. Modern and trendy.'

'Trendy.' Fay giggled. 'Yes, I like the sound of that.'

She was interrupted by the ringing of the telephone and picked it up, half expecting it to be Jace again.

'Missing me?' her twin's voice on the other end made her smile.

'Freddie! Is everything all right – what is the food like?' She asked knowing her brother enjoyed good food.

'A bit burned last night, otherwise it's all fine,' he said. 'Thanks for all the food you sent. I've eaten most of it. How are you doing?'

'We're just setting up the bar the way it was,' Fay replied. 'We're okay – you've only been gone a day.'

'I know. Was the party all right?'

'Yes, great,' Fay said. 'We haven't heard from Mum and Dad again yet. I expect they are having a wonderful time and are too busy.'

'So I should hope,' Freddie said. 'Have you got a pen there – I could give you a number to ring for emergency only. I'm using a phone box.'

'No pen,' Fay replied. 'Write to me, Freddie. Give it to me then – you know what I'm like. I'll write it down wrong or lose it, but I keep your letters.'

'Right then,' he said. 'Need to dash – training today. Take care of yourselves and love to Maggie.'

'Well, that was short and sweet,' Fay said as the line went dead. 'Freddie is the same as always – checking to see I've not done something stupid and burned down the kitchen.'

'He cares about you,' Maggie said. 'I like Freddie. You can rely on him.'

'Yes, I was just joking really,' Fay said. 'Freddie is the marrying kind one day. The girl that gets him will be lucky.'

'He has a lot of studying to do first if he is going to be all he wants to be,' Maggie replied. 'But you don't need to worry about him. Freddie is the sensible one...'

6

Freddie enjoyed the limbering-up exercises they all did on the beach first thing in the morning, before the holidaymakers began to arrive for the day. He'd been a bit unsure for a start, but his first week had been fun and he'd soon got to know the others. It was still May, early in the season yet, and the sands were not crowded as they would be once the schools broke up for the long summer holiday. At the moment they had time to look around and to have a bit of fun playing ball games, though much of the time so far had been spent training. The training was more complicated and stricter than he'd thought, a lot of the rules seeming either straight forward or common sense to him, but now he realised there was more to it than he'd realised.

'Take your breaks when they are offered and stay out of the sun except when you are patrolling the beach,' Guy told them that morning. 'It can get hot at midday and it's a long day. You need to drink plenty and keep a flask of water with you. Put some ice in it if you can. If you get hot and bothered, you won't be alert.'

'We're not children,' Muriel moaned and made a face at Freddie. He didn't respond. Guy was telling them for their own good, as well as that of others. Freddie wanted to listen and learn.

'Don't get distracted by nice-looking girls – or boys – and don't get into arguments. Don't join in children's games on the sands either...' That raised a few grins, but Freddie knew there was a good reason behind it all. 'You will all get plenty of free time, so when you're on duty, keep your eyes on the water, as well as being watchful for accidents on the beach. It only takes a few seconds for something nasty to happen.'

'If someone is nearly drowned or swallows a lot of water, what do we do when we get them to the beach?' Freddie asked. 'They showed us at the swimming pool when we had lessons with our school – but you might have better ways.'

'The first thing is to make sure nothing is in their mouths or obstructing the throat, and then turn them on their side. Mostly they will bring up a lot of water and just breathe again on their own, if you've got them in time. If they swallowed too much, you may need to do a bit of compression work to bring them round – but for those of you who are new to the job, it is best left to us regulars. We'll be with you and can take over.'

'Can you show us, just so we know?' Freddie persisted. 'I think I know what to do if someone isn't breathing, but it can happen anywhere – even if it isn't through nearly drowning.'

'We call it chest pumping or CPR,' Guy said. 'I will show you all tomorrow, but I want to concentrate on the towing methods today. There are three different tows, but the best is to grab them by the sides of the head and hold it, face upwards of course, as you swim backwards. That makes sure you keep their head above water. You can place your hands under the arms and over the shoulders, or there is the arm around the body – but I like to make certain their head is floating on top of the water. By holding the head, you can do that easier, but some lifeguards use the other methods.'

'What about if they struggle and fight?' Muriel asked. 'It's all very well to talk about textbook rescues, but we all know a drowning person is going to fight you.'

'Some lifeguards do render the victim unconscious in that case,' Guy said, 'but I don't find that easy. Personally, I talk to people and try to calm them – but that is why we work as a team. The more of us there are, the better it is. In a swimming pool, one lifeguard is normally enough, but in seas like ours here in Hastings where the surf can get very high, we prefer to be a team. Most people will cooperate once we get them and give them something to hang on to, but they all need support to keep their heads out of the water. No good towing them to the beach if they're under water the whole time. Could well be too late when you land them.' He grinned at their shocked faces. 'I know I sound as if I'm talking to you like kids, but it's surprising the way it sticks if you get it into your head. I find repetition works. Otherwise, when something happens it is easy for you to panic.'

'That's why we need training,' Freddie said. 'The more we go through it, the more it becomes a routine.'

Guy nodded. 'Freddie has the idea. I know you can all swim at least a hundred and fifty foot without stopping because you wouldn't be here if you weren't strong swimmers. You all look capable of swimming out and grabbing a drowning man, but it is remembering to alert the others so that if you get into difficulty, someone else is there to help, making sure you have your float to hand and not left back at the hut.'

'I was a relay champion,' Muriel muttered. 'I'm not likely to need help.'

'None of us can say that,' George contradicted. 'The sea isn't like a pool – there are currents and tides and jellyfish.'

'Yes, that's another thing we have to watch out for; it's a part of the job,' Guy told them. 'We don't get some of the hazards they do overseas. I worked in Australia for a while and there you have to watch for sharks as well – but even our jellyfish, which are mild compared to those in some seas, can give a nasty shock and painful sting. If we spot them, we can warn people where they are and save them a ruined day and maybe more.' He looked around at their faces. 'Who wants to attempt to save me then?'

Everyone answered in the affirmative, but he picked Freddie and George.

'You two will work well together. 'I'll swim out a few yards to deep water and then call out and tread water. Come and get me...'

Freddie looked at George and grinned. He liked the young man who came from East Anglia and worked as a car salesman but was looking for a change of lifestyle. George said what he thought but wasn't forever moaning, the way Muriel did. Freddie was glad he hadn't been teamed with her for this first try.

They waited for Guy's signal and then raced each other to the water, plunging straight in, though the cold took Freddie's breath. He hadn't expected it to be that cold and was a second behind George as they swam out to Guy as fast as they could, arriving almost at the same time. Guy was splashing and yelling as if he was in trouble, dipping under the water.

'Calm down, mate,' George said. 'You're safe now. We've got you.'

Guy hit out at him as if in terror, but Freddie went behind and took hold of his head, placing a firm hand each side. 'Take him by the body, George and I'll take his head.'

Guy struggled a bit, but they pushed a float under one of his arms and he calmed and then, between them, they towed him back to the shore. He lay as if unconscious and they summoned the others and four of them carried him up the beach.

'Turn him on his side,' Freddie said as no one moved. 'Okay, Guy, you're safe now.'

Guy sat up and grinned at them. 'Not bad. I swallowed quite a bit of water on the way back, though. You need to lift the head a little more, Freddie, but you've got the idea, both of you. You'll do as a team. I'll be putting Sarah with you and you'll patrol this beach.' He looked at Muriel then. 'Right, you next with Steve and then Jill and Mark – but you can save Freddie this time...'

Freddie got up obediently and swam out to roughly the same distance as Guy had. He went through the same motions, calling out and splashing about as if in trouble and the two swam out to him, Muriel beating Steve by several strokes. Freddie splashed some more but didn't test her by attempting to struggle. He simply lay back in the water and allowed them to tow him back as he had for the school training.

When they got to the beach, Muriel turned him expertly on to his side and Guy came to watch. He nodded. 'If I said he's not breathing, do you know what to do?'

'I've seen CPR done,' Steve said, 'but I haven't done it.

'I may as well show you now. Cross your hands over like this,' Guy showed them all. 'Now press down on his chest but gently. This is just an exercise and it can bruise badly – for real you would need to press harder, of course.'

Steve struggled to do as he was shown and Muriel elbowed him out of the way and gave them an expert demonstration. She got a bit enthusiastic and Freddie groaned. 'Steady on, that hurts.'

'Sorry. I did my training on a dummy,' Muriel apologised and flopped down on the sand beside him.

'It's okay,' Freddie said and smiled. 'I didn't know you'd had the training.'

'I did a first-aid class,' Muriel replied. 'A friend of mine collapsed and died at college; she was only eighteen. They said CPR might have saved her, so I went to classes.'

'Good thinking,' Guy said and turned away. 'Steve, your turn to be rescued by Jill and Mark... the rest of you can take a break.'

* * *

Freddie and Muriel left the others and started walking up the beach.

'Come on, I saw a nice café just up the beach, let's get a coffee and a sandwich. My treat,' Muriel said, blinking rapidly.

'I'll buy some fish and chips tonight,' Freddie said, feeling a rush of sympathy for her. Most of the other trainees were a year or two older than Freddie and Muriel must be in her mid-twenties. He'd thought her a bit bossy but now saw that she had reason and was clearly upset by the sudden death of her friend. 'Tell me what happened to your friend – if you like?'

'I don't talk about it much,' Muriel said as they set off towards the little café. 'She was lovely – it was her heart, so they said... I wasn't there, but no one knew what to do and by the time the ambulance came it was too late.'

'I am sorry. It's sad; she was so young,' Freddie said and Muriel nodded. 'I was frightened when my sister nearly died of a burst appendix. I don't know what I've had done if she had.'

'Cindy was like a sister to me...' Muriel bit her lip and then shook her head. 'It's daft to get upset. I suppose it was doing the CPR...'

'You cared about her,' Freddie said. 'Is she the real reason you came down here to do this job?'

'In a way,' Muriel admitted and looked at him. 'You're a very caring person, aren't you? I think you'll do well here. I saw how confident you were earlier.'

'Not really,' Freddie laughed. 'I just did my best... will you teach me how to do that chest compression? Guy says leave it to them, but you never know when you might need it.'

'He should teach you as part of the training, but if you'd like I can help...'

* * *

Freddie saw the young girl who had served him burned sausages as he entered the boarding house later that day. She was polishing a piece of furniture in the hall and looked pale and miserable. He was about to pass her and then something made him stop.

'Are you all right?'

She sniffed and shook her head. 'Aunt Edith is cross with me. She says everyone is eating out this evening because I keep burning everything...'

'It isn't because of that,' Freddie told her kindly. 'We're having fish and chips as a treat, that's all.'

She nodded and looked wistful. 'Did you have a good day at the beach?'

'It was good, but it was hard work too,' Freddie said. 'Guy keeps us on our toes. He says we need to be fit and we spent a lot of time exercising. Not many people on the beach because it was a bit cool. It's still only May, I suppose.'

'It's often lovely here in the spring,' she told him with a shy smile. 'Not that I get to the beach often. I have to work when the weather is nice because that's when we have more guests.'

'Yes, I suppose so,' Freddie agreed. 'You must get time off, though?'

'I get one afternoon a week – usually a Saturday – and then I'm free until the evening.'

'What about Sunday?' Freddie frowned. 'You don't work every Sunday, do you?'

'Mostly,' she said. 'Aunt Edith goes to church and I have to prepare lunch. She does lunch on Sunday, not an evening meal. I get a couple of hours after three...'

Freddie detected a note of hope in her voice and nodded. 'Well, I'm not sure what days I'll be working once I start proper – but I'm free this Sunday. Would you like to go to the beach with me?'

'Oh, you don't have to...' she hesitated, then, 'Yes, I should like to go if you don't mind?'

'Of course I don't – but you ought to tell me your name...'

Her shy smile peeked out at him. 'It's Greta... my father named me for his mother and she was a German, but she married an Englishman during the First World War.'

Freddie nodded. The name sounded German, but she looked like an English girl with her dark hair and pale complexion and she didn't have an accent of any sort, not even a Cornish one.

'My father works abroad. He builds bridges.' Greta's pale face came alight with pride. 'My aunt says it is important work. He asked her to look after me when my mother died.'

'I'm sorry your mum died,' Freddie said. 'I have to go up and change now – but I'll see you for a trip to the beach on Sunday. I'll be in tomorrow for dinner anyway.'

Greta nodded. 'Thank you,' she whispered as he walked away. 'Thank you, Freddie...'

He didn't look back, his thoughts already elsewhere. Freddie was enjoying his time in Hastings – the freedom and the fun – but he was also looking forward to his time at university. He'd spoken to Maureen's daughter, Shirley, about it and she'd told him she'd had a great time, even though she'd had to study hard to become a doctor.

Freddie admired Shirley for what she did. He had considered taking up medicine once but knew that his heart wasn't in it as hers was and he preferred to be outdoors. A sports teacher was what he intended to be and there were other things he could do to help youngsters who needed it. The things he was learning on the beach might not be entirely relevant to his future, but they would help him grow and mature into the kind of man his father would approve of.

He hoped his parents were having a wonderful time in America. They were sure to send letters and cards when they got around to it, though it was a bit strange they hadn't been in touch since that first call... which reminded him, he ought to write to Fay...

7

'Hello, Mum,' Shirley's voice on the other end of the telephone made Maureen smile. 'How are you? Have you heard from Peggy and Able yet?'

'I'm fine as always,' Maureen said. 'No, I haven't had a card from Peggy yet; it's not like her not to send one, but it takes ages for them to come from overseas sometimes. When you and Ray were on holiday last winter, I didn't get your card from Switzerland until you were home again.'

'I know. It's hardly worth sending them really, but everyone likes doing it – it's what you do on holiday, send a view from somewhere posh and a comic one if you're at the sea.'

'Like that naughty one you sent your dad when you were in Cornwall for a week last summer?' Maureen laughed. 'Freddie is in Hastings now. Fay said he rang once but not since. She is expecting a long letter. Apparently, he is good at writing letters and she keeps them all.'

'Well, they are twins,' Shirley replied as if that explained everything. 'So, how is Dad? Are you coming over for dinner on my day off next week?'

'Yes, of course,' Maureen told her. 'We went to Rose and Tom last Sunday and this weekend I'll cook – you two can come if you'd like?'

'We're off to a medical conference in Brighton,' Shirley said. 'You didn't say whether Dad's all right?'

'He's the same as usual,' Maureen replied. 'He gets a bit tired sometimes, but he hasn't mentioned chest pains or anything recently, so I just keep my fingers crossed.'

'There's been some experimental work done on what they call a bypass operation,' Shirley said. 'It isn't available for humans yet, but I'm sure it will be one day.'

'Are you saying that's what your dad needs?'

'Maybe. One day... Ray says there are other treatments – so keep me in touch with how he is, Mum.'

'Of course I will.' Maureen sighed. 'He seems all right to me, but you know your dad – doesn't complain much.'

'Yes, I do. Let me know if you need me,' Shirley said. 'I don't get to see you as much as I'd like, Mum, but my work keeps me busy. If we're not in theatre operating on a patient, I'm at the clinic and in the evenings, we like to eat out when we can. This conference is important, but I'll see you next week. You can come early and help me cook dinner so we have more time together.'

'We'd like that,' Maureen told her, 'but we understand work comes first, Shirley. You and Ray are both so dedicated to your job and we're proud of you.'

'Thanks, Mum. I'll pop in as soon as I can. Love you. Give my love to Dad and tell him I'll ring him one evening if I can.'

'You do that,' Maureen said as she heard the little click at the other end. She knew that Gordon had hoped to see more of his daughter once she finished university and came back to the East End to work, but she'd married her mentor, a man some years older than her, and now they were both caught up in their work.

Ray was a brilliant surgeon and Shirley was his assistant in theatre and took clinics at the children's hospital, as well as giving her free afternoon to another clinic in the East End. It treated the homeless and those who didn't have a doctor or a job or family – in some cases they didn't even have hope and the clinic was the only place they felt able to attend.

Even Ray hadn't been able to persuade Shirley to give up the extra work that she did without pay, despite it having put her in danger a couple of years previously. She'd gone to see a patient at the derelict warehouse he and other homeless folk had been using as home and was attacked on her way back. Fortunately, one of the homeless men had saved her and nothing like that had occurred again, but Shirley was more careful these days and didn't walk alone in rough areas.

Maureen heard a little click and a thud on the doormat. The afternoon post had arrived and she went to investigate, hoping that it might be a card or letter from Peggy. However, it was a magazine that Gordon took regularly to keep up to date with what was happening in grocery marketing and a bill for the electric. Maureen bent to pick them up. She missed Peggy and Able, and she missed working in the kitchen at the Pig & Whistle with the girls.

She felt a flicker of anxiety. Was Peggy all right? Something nagged at her, a feeling of impending doom. She shook her head. No, that was daft. Of course, her friend was fine. She was just too busy travelling to write yet – but that wasn't like her. Perhaps the girls had received a card. She would go over and ask them later.

* * *

Maureen had been to look at the new bar, which was open, and had smiled when she saw that Tom Barton had faithfully recreated the old one, just making it look smarter and fresher. Work was still going on for the new restaurant rooms, but Maggie and Fay were cooking meals for consumption in the bar, fairly simple things like hot pies, sausage rolls, apple pie and custard and cakes. Fay made lovely cakes now. Maureen had to admit they were better than anything she or Peggy had produced when they were running the cake shop – but they used a lot of fat and cream and must contain a huge amount of calories. So Maureen resisted buying them most of the time. Gordon was satisfied with her plain Madeira or a light fruit cake and she wouldn't indulge her sweet tooth if he couldn't share. It was better for her anyway and helped her keep her slim figure.

Maureen hadn't been asked to help out while the restaurant was closed but knew she would be needed for a few hours now and then when it opened again. It suited her to go in two or three mornings a week and she was lucky she didn't have to worry about money these days. She decided to go shopping and was just about to leave when the telephone rang again. She stopped and a shiver went down her spine. Something bad had happened! Her heart raced as she picked up the receiver.

'Maureen, it's Janet,' Peggy's eldest daughter's voice was breathy and anxious. 'I've just had a telegram from Able; there has been an accident and Mum is badly hurt. I'm trying to arrange to fly out there as soon as possible, but I need to get a passport from the post office. I've been ringing round for ages and Pip says there is a seat on a plane next week he can wangle free for me. His boss at the aircraft factory is flying to America on business; he's taking some staff and one has cancelled so I can have his place. Ryan says he'll pay my expenses out there – but I wondered if you would look after my son. Ryan can't manage him alone with his work. Sheila and Pip would have him, but Ryan doesn't want him to go down there...'

'Peggy is badly hurt?' Maureen hardly heard the rest of what Janet was saying. 'Oh no, Janet! How bad is it – and what happened?'

'I don't know the details yet,' Janet said. 'Able just told me Mum is hurt and asked if I could come out. I think he might have been hurt too, because otherwise he would have rung – but perhaps not as badly as Mum.' There was a break in her voice and she gave a little sob. 'If anything happens to her—'

'Pray God it won't,' Maureen said, but her heart was beating wildly. Peggy was her best friend and she couldn't imagine a life that didn't include her. 'Calm down, Janet. Tell me what you want to do...'

'Ryan is driving me to the airport and then he will bring Jon to you later this week. I don't know what else to do, Maureen. I know it's a great deal to ask, but Ryan has a lot of work on just now.'

'I'll have Jon for you,' Maureen said. 'Ryan will need to bring his things and tell me what I need to do for him...' Janet's son had been injured in a road accident, running in front of a vehicle, and though he'd made a good recovery in the years since, he was still a bit fragile. He sometimes fell over, because his balance wasn't right. Janet had spent a long time at home looking after him and only recently been able to start working again. Her dreams of a business renovating property had been put to one side when Jon was hurt and she now did a few hours a week serving in a dress shop while Jon was at school. 'What about his schooling?'

Jon attended a special school that Ryan paid high fees for, because of his extra needs. It meant that Ryan's idea of living on a smallholding had also fallen through. He'd taken an office job, similar to one he'd given up but not as demanding, and was home at six every evening, giving him more time with his family. Peggy had offered to have Jon with her and sometimes he stayed with his granny for a week or two; he seemed happiest with her, but Ryan wouldn't let it be a permanent thing. However, they now lived in Southwark and that meant Jon saw his granny most weekends.

'I've telephoned the school and explained and they've said he can just work on some projects at home.' Janet sounded tired and strained, as she added, 'Why did it have to happen? Mum was so looking forward to this holiday...'

'I know,' Maureen said, feeling sick with worry but wanting to hide it for Janet's sake. 'Try to keep calm, Janet. Have you told Maggie and Fay?'

'Pip is going to talk to Maggie...' Janet said. 'I know she is my daughter, but I couldn't tell her. I'm not sure how to let Freddie know.'

'I think Fay has an emergency number or she will have when Freddie writes to her. I am sure she has an address.' Maureen took a deep breath. 'Someone should go down there. Freddie adores his mother... You all do.'

'We had a bit of a tiff before she went,' Janet confessed and Maureen could hear the tears in her voice. 'If she doesn't... Oh, I'm sorry. I have to go. Ryan will bring Jon tomorrow...'

Maureen swallowed her tears as the phone went down at the other end. Janet was clearly very distressed and Maureen was too. Abandoning her idea of shopping that afternoon, Maureen decided to visit the pub. Maggie and Fay would be upset and frightened and she must do what she could to help them.

She felt the sickness swirl inside her, because losing her best friend would be like losing a part of herself and the whole family would be devastated. Peggy had been the heart of her family – no, she was! Maureen pushed the rogue thought away. Peggy wasn't going to die! She mustn't!

8

Maggie replaced the receiver and looked at Fay, horror and grief in her face as she tried to make sense of her Uncle Pip's words. Granny Peggy hurt and in hospital fighting for her life? It couldn't be true! It just couldn't!

Struggling against her tears, Maggie wondered how she was going to tell Fay that her mother was badly hurt. Pip had told her that her mother was flying out to America, but Janet hadn't asked Maggie if she wanted to go with her. For a moment that stung, but then she realised that it was too much for her mother to even tell her, let alone ask if she wanted to go with her. Maggie's mother was an up-and-down sort of person, one minute laughing and joking and the next quiet, reserved and depressed. Maggie thought she must take after her father, because she wasn't like her mother.

'Something bad has happened – is it Mum or Dad?' Fay said in a small voice that wasn't a bit like her usual confident tones. 'Tell me, Maggie. I'm not a baby.'

'I know you're not,' Maggie said quickly. 'Your mum has been badly injured in some kind of accident and I think Able may be hurt too, but not as badly.'

Fay gave a little cry of distress, her face working. 'Is she in hospital? How bad is she?'

'I don't know. Apparently, the telegram just said, "Peggy badly injured in hospital. More news when available. Sorry, also injured, Able." So he may not even have sent it himself but was allowed to dictate it.'

Fay bent her head as the tears came. 'No, not Mum and Dad,' she cried, her shoulders shaking with her sobs. 'I can't bear it...' Her head came up all at once. 'Can we go out there? Please, Maggie... let's go...'

'My mother is flying out early in the morning,' Maggie said. 'Pip didn't think the rest of us should go. He says it would be too much for them if we were allowed to see them and far too expensive, even if we could get seats. Janet only got one because of Pip's connections with the aircraft industry. He says Mum will telephone us as soon as she can... Able must be stuck in hospital too or he would surely have rung us rather than send a telegram.'

'No!' Fay cried, the fear growing inside her that her mother wouldn't ever return and was fighting her tears when someone knocked at the door and then Maureen entered.

'I see Pip has told you.' Maureen must have seen it in their faces. 'I hoped to get here first, because bad news is always worse on the phone. I am as upset as you both are, girls, but we have to keep positive. I am going to look after Jon while Janet goes out to see what is happening, but I'm here for you both. We have to pray and believe that Peggy will return to us when she recovers.'

'She will recover, won't she?' Fay asked, her face wet with tears. 'I do love her so much. I know I am a pain in the neck at times and I ask for too much, but I know how lucky I am. If I didn't, Freddie would soon...' Her mouth trembled. 'Freddie! How can we tell him?'

'Don't you have an address for him – the boarding house?'

Fay shook her head. 'Not yet. He was going to give me a number for emergencies, but I said he must write it down for me in a letter—' Her face creased and the tears ran again. 'I thought he was checking up on us and I dismissed it...'

'He must have had letters about the job he took,' Maggie said. 'We'll look in his room. If we can find the lifeguard's headquarters we can ring them and get an address – and then one of us has to tell him. If we'd got address, I'd go tonight.'

'If I were you, I'd wait until Janet gets out there and gives you more news,' Maureen suggested.

'And if the news is bad?' Maggie asked, her head up, eyes flashing with determination. She had never forgotten how it felt to lose her father to the war. 'Freddie would hate us if we kept this from him.'

Maureen nodded. 'Yes, I suppose you are right. It seems such a shame when he's just started that training course.'

'I want him to come home,' Fay spoke loudly. 'I couldn't bear it if anything worse happened and he wasn't here.'

'I'm going to look in Freddie's room,' Maggie said.

Fay sniffed back her tears. 'I know where Freddie keeps his things. Let me go.'

Maggie nodded and looked towards Maureen as Fay left the room. 'Mum is asking a lot, parking my brother on you. He can be a little devil at times, but he's my brother and I love him, so I am glad he's going to be with you. He loves his granny too and if he hears about this, he may play up, but he must be told. You will explain it to him, please?'

'Yes, I shall. If his parents haven't already told him, I will.'

'I doubt if they have. They wrap him in cotton wool since the accident and I swear it makes him worse. When he's with Granny Peggy, he is a different boy. Ryan should let him live with her, but he refuses to hear of it.'

'Perhaps that is for the best,' Maureen said softly. 'We don't know how this will affect her... how ill she is and if she will recover completely.'

Maggie inclined her head, her eyes moist with the tears she'd held back while Fay wept. 'Yes, I know you are right. I can't imagine Granny Peggy being anything but her normal self. It is too awful to think about.'

'I refuse to consider it,' Maureen said. 'The Peggy I know will fight this, whatever it is.' She hesitated, then, 'I'll leave you to yourselves – but you know where I am if you need me at any time.'

'Yes, thank you, and I'm sure we shall. I think we have to try to carry on as best we can...'

'It is what Peggy would expect.'

Maureen left, but Maggie just sat at the table, feeling too shocked to get on with anything, and then Fay returned with a letter in her hand.

'There is a telephone number we can ring in the morning – and they should be able to give us a number or an address.'

'Yes, Freddie will want to know.'

'I need him here – just in case. I couldn't face it alone if—' Fay faltered and Maggie put both arms around her. 'Oh, Maggie...'

'I know,' Maggie said and now her eyes were wet, too. 'We've got that dinner party tomorrow night – shall we cancel it? And we could postpone the reopening of the restaurant.'

'What would Mum do?' Fay asked and Maggie nodded, both of them speaking together: 'She would carry on, no matter what, so we should too.'

'Let's get cleared up here then. I have to go and fetch a wine order from the merchants. I'll take the van and be back in an hour or two at most. Or do you want to come with me?'

'Rose asked me to babysit for her this evening. Tom is taking her to a dinner dance. I can't let her down, Maggie. You take your time. I'll be back about midnight.'

'Tom will walk you back – mind you, I suppose you're safe enough in the lanes. We haven't had anything horrid happen here for years.'

'Oh, don't tempt fate,' Fay cried. 'I wish I could telephone Freddie this evening – but the lifeguard station closes at four.' She glanced at her watch. 'It is nearly five o'clock, Maggie. I think you need to leave or that wine merchant will be closed.'

* * *

Maggie drove to the wine merchant, which was situated down a small lane running adjacent to Oxford Street. It had taken her much longer than she'd expected to complete her order and the merchant had invited her down to the cellar, showing her some rare wines and letting her taste one. She thought he might have been showing off a little, but she'd known him for a couple of years now. He was an acquaintance of James, her artist friend, who liked good wine when he had time to think about it, and always did her a better deal if she went in the evening. A man of more than sixty years, he enjoyed sharing his vast knowledge with her and she always found it useful. However, that evening, her thoughts had remained with Granny Peggy and when he asked after her, she'd struggled to hold back her tears. Those same tears were hovering as she drove away.

How was her grandmother? Why hadn't Able phoned them? He must be in hospital, too. It was so worrying to think of them both ill all those miles away...

As she emerged from the poorly lit lane into a road blazing with light, her eyes misted with tears, Maggie somehow missed the car passing the entrance to the lane and almost went into it, skidding away at the last moment to hit a lamp post with her left front wing.

She sat for a moment, engine still running, feeling dazed, and then a man pulled open her door and yelled at her.

'What the hell do you think you were doing?' he demanded. 'Turn the damn thing off!' He reached into the car and switched the engine off.

Facing him, still dazed, Maggie found herself looking at a man in a hood. His manner was threatening and she shuddered, feeling a shaft of fear – and then, to her dismay, burst into tears.

'Have you been drinking? This van stinks of wine,' he demanded.

'I tasted a special wine but only a sip,' Maggie said indignantly through her tears. 'I bought wine for the restaurant and some of it must have broken...'

'No point in crying over spilt wine. Your insurance should cover it and the damage to your front wing.'

'I'm not—' Maggie shook her head. He was leaning towards her and now she noticed the terrible scarring on one side of his face. 'My grandmother has been hurt and...' She sniffed and raised her head. 'I have to get home. Fay will be waiting and she is so upset...'

'You're bleeding.' He reached towards her, touching her forehead. 'Come on, I'll take you home. You are in no condition to be driving... I'm not sure you haven't had a drink...' His voice softened slightly.

'Just a sip...' Maggie assured him. 'I can't just leave the van here.' She saw a policeman approaching. 'Oh, no. If he thinks I've been drinking, I'll lose my licence and I need it...'

'Leave it to me.' The man in the hood turned as the policeman came over. 'We're all right. It was a cat and this young woman swerved to avoid it. I'm helping her.'

The policeman looked at him and nodded, before glancing at Maggie. 'Is that right, miss?'

'Yes,' Maggie lied firmly. 'I'm perfectly fine, officer. It was just a silly mistake.'

'Very well. I'll leave her to you, Mr Hayes – no need to report this.'

'Thank you, Constable,' her rescuer replied and turned to Maggie. 'Come on, get out.'

'Do you know him?' she asked as the police officer walked away.

'Yes. He is a friend. We know each other from some charity work we both do... Are you going to be all night?'

'I need to transfer some merchandise to your car – if you could do that for me?'

He hesitated and then nodded. 'Okay – and I'll move the van to a safer spot. I'll ask someone I know to come and collect it for you.'

'Thanks...' Maggie managed. She gave him the key to the back of the van and collected her handbag. He opened the back door and lifted out two cases of wine.

'I'll carry these – my car is the one you almost hit...' He indicated the green Jaguar he'd parked a short distance away. 'It isn't locked. Get in.'

Maggie found herself obeying. She wasn't sure why she trusted him; she just did. Her initial reaction on seeing him had been fear, but that was the hood, but as soon as she noticed the scar, she'd realised why he wore it.

He carried the wine boxes back to his car for her, locking them in the small boot. Sitting beside her, he turned to face her.

'I'm sorry if I was hard on you. My name is Greg.' He touched his cheek. 'I got this in a racing car accident and didn't fancy another one.'

'I'm sorry; I'm Maggie. Perhaps I was too emotional to drive this evening – but it seemed best to carry on.'

'You're lucky it was me,' he told her. 'I managed to swing away from you before you swerved – otherwise we might have collided, but we didn't, so we'll forget it.' He glanced at her forehead, smoothing it with his fingers. 'It's just a scratch. You must have bumped it on something...'

'It's all right,' Maggie said. 'You're going the wrong way. I live in Mulberry Lane in the East End.'

'I'll take you there shortly,' Greg told her. 'My London apartment is just around the corner. You are obviously too upset to drive this evening. I'll see to that cut and telephone my friend to fetch your van – and then I'll take you home, OK?'

Maggie hesitated and then nodded. 'Yes, all right, thank you... but I should warn you, I can fight like a she-wolf if I'm provoked.'

He heard the teasing note in her voice and laughed. 'I'm no axe murderer, Maggie. I wear the hood because I hate people looking at my face and either turning away in horror or looking at me with pity.'

'It's not that bad,' Maggie said. 'It was the hood that scared me, not the scar. I'm not frightened now.'

Greg shot a glance at her and then laughed. 'Brave girl, aren't you, Maggie? I like that.'

He didn't look at her again but soon drew up in front of an impressive building.

'My apartment is here. You can come up or I'll fetch my first-aid box down...'

'I'll come,' Maggie said. 'And thank you... it does feel a little sore.'

9

Freddie was reading an article in the newspaper about the future wedding of Prince Edward Duke of Kent to Katharine Worsley at York Minster which would take place on the eighth of June. He'd just finished his breakfast when his landlady came into the dining room. He wondered what he'd done wrong as she summoned him with a flick of her hand, her expression unreadable but also unsmiling.

'Someone on the phone for you, Mr Ronoscki,' she muttered. 'I told them to wait – though I don't hold with private calls; this is a business...' She gave a little sniff and went off, leaving Freddie to go through to the sunny front parlour.

Freddie's heart raced. He hadn't given this number to anyone, because he'd only sent his letter to Fay the previous day, having left it in his jacket pocket and forgotten to post it for ages, and it surely wouldn't have got there by now. He picked the receiver up and heard voices, instinct picking out his twin's instantly. Something must be badly wrong for her to have found out how to contact him. 'What's wrong, Fay? How did you get this number?'

'Oh, Freddie,' Fay said. 'You've got to come home – Mum is hurt bad, Dad too perhaps, and I can't bear it. I need you here.'

Freddie's stomach clenched. 'Slow down and tell me what exactly has happened?'

'We don't know,' Fay said and he could hear the cry for help in her voice. 'Janet got a telegram and she asked Pip to ring us – he says Dad is hurt too but not as bad. Please, you must come – just for a couple of days until we know more.'

'Yes, I'll come,' Freddie said. 'I'll have to catch a train – not sure when I'll get there, but I'll come straight away. Just calm down and try not to worry. Mum will come through, she always does.'

'Yes, I know – but I'd rather you were here...' Fay's tone was pleading.

As Freddie replaced the receiver after promising to catch the first train, he turned and found Guy looking at him.

'Something wrong?' he asked.

'My parents have been hurt in some kind of an accident over in America. My sister got this number from somewhere and wants me to go home for a few days – until we know more.'

'She probably rang the lifeguard station; they normally open early. Yesterday was their early closing.' Guy was thoughtful. 'Yes, you must go, Freddie – but I hope you'll return to us when you can?'

Freddie promised he would. He took the stairs two at a time and threw a few things into his rucksack. If he hurried, he might just get the earlier train, otherwise it would be nearly evening before he even left Hastings...

* * *

Fay turned from the phone to see Maggie standing behind her. She sniffed and wiped her eyes. 'Where did you get to last night? I was home by ten, because Tom had a stomach ache and they came back sooner than expected – but you didn't get in until nearly midnight—'

'You managed to get Freddie then?' Maggie didn't answer the question. 'Sorry if I woke you...'

'You didn't. I couldn't sleep anyway – but I was glad when I heard you come in.' Fay looked at her. 'It didn't take you that long to buy two cases of wine...'

'There were three, but I had a slight accident with the van – it's in the garage and some of those bottles were broken, so Greg left them.'

'Greg who?' Fay asked, surprised.

'Greg Hayes. He is, or was, a racing driver and I almost ran into him. He was kind and took me to his house to bathe a small cut on my forehead – and he had steaks, so it seemed only fair to cook him dinner...'

'You nearly ran into him?' Fay asked shocked. 'Are you all right? Did you go to a doctor?'

'No, I was just shaken and banged my head on something in the front of the van, that's all.'

'Oh, Maggie. As long as you weren't hurt, it doesn't matter about the van – though I'm not sure how we'll manage that dinner party.'

'We can take Able's car; he won't mind,' Maggie said. 'Greg said he would take us, but I said no.'

'Why? Is he horrid?'

'No, he is very nice...' Maggie hesitated. 'He might pop round one day, just to make sure I'm all right.'

'I like the sound of him,' Fay said and hugged her. 'He was your knight in shining armour, Maggie. I can't see James coming to your rescue like that.'

'No, perhaps not,' Maggie agreed, 'but James doesn't drive. He hates cars.'

Fay nodded, her thoughts going back to her main worry. 'Freddie is coming straight home. He says he'll be on the next train.'

'He'll be here this evening then,' Maggie said. 'You needn't have asked him, Fay. He will just sit around worrying.'

'I need him – and he would want to be here anyway.'

* * *

Freddie arrived late that evening and the three of them had supper together. He was waiting for them when they returned from the dinner party they'd catered for and hugged them both, told them he was sure everything would be fine and then ate a plate of ham sandwiches and half an apple pie.

'You're going to get fat,' Maggie warned, but he just grinned.

'I haven't eaten since breakfast. I—' Whatever he was going to say was lost as the front doorbell rang. 'I'll answer it,' Freddie said. 'You two stop here.'

Maggie and Fay looked at each other in anxiety. Who could it be? It was gone eleven at night and they were not expecting anyone. Freddie returned with the answer a moment or two later.

'Mr Hayes has called to see you, Maggie. He has brought your van back...' Freddie frowned. 'You didn't tell me you'd had an accident?'

'It was nothing much,' Maggie replied. She looked at Greg and smiled. 'That was kind of you. You should have let me know and I would've picked it up.'

'I wanted to be sure it was fit to drive – and to make sure you were all right. No after effects of that knock on the head?'

'I'm fine,' Maggie told him. 'Would you like something to eat or a cup of coffee? We've just had supper, that's why we're still up. Freddie came back from Hastings to be with us for support.'

'Have you heard anything more about your grandmother?' Greg asked, his eyes meeting Maggie's across the room. 'I've been thinking, if you knew the name of the hospital, I'd probably be able to find out more. I have several friends out there...'

'Thank you, but for now we just know she is in hospital and Grandad too,' Maggie told him. She hesitated, then, 'How are you getting home?'

'I thought I'd ring for a taxi?'

'I'll take you,' Maggie began, but Freddie cut in.

'No, I'll take Mr Hayes. You're tired, Maggie. I've done nothing but sit on a train all day – besides, I'm a fan of motor racing and you're not.' He'd recognised him instantly despite the scarring.

'I think Freddie is right,' Greg said and nodded to him. 'You can drive me – and you can call me Greg.' His gaze returned to Maggie. 'I'm going to a charity dance this weekend – if you're free?'

'I wish I could, but it is the reopening of the restaurant,' Maggie said regretfully. 'I have to be here.'

'No problem. I'll call you another day.'

Fay looked at her as they went out and the front door closed behind them. 'Well, I'd say you've made yet another conquest, Maggie.'

'Don't be daft, I've only met him twice...'

'Ah, but that's all it needs – love at first sight.'

Maggie laughed ruefully. 'He was very angry with me at first, but so kind when he realised, I was hurt a little.'

Fay nodded and smirked in a satisfied way but said no more.

'I'm going to bed,' Maggie said. 'So don't look at me that way.'

She was just about to leave when the phone rang. Fay stared at her in alarm and ran into the hall, snatching up the receiver. She recognised the voice as Janet's immediately, even though it sounded strange and far away.

'Janet, how are they?' she cried. 'We've all been so worried...'

* * *

Freddie had forgotten all about his date with Greta until he was driving home from dropping Greg off at his apartment. He hadn't gone in, because it was late and he needed to get back, but had been invited to meet some of Greg's motor racing friends for lunch at the weekend. He frowned as he thought of Greta's reaction to his neglect to tell her he was leaving. In the rush to get home, he just hadn't given her a thought – and that wasn't like him, but then, he'd never known his mother to be desperately ill before.

Freddie parked the van in the yard at the back and let himself into the kitchen with his key. He saw that lights had been left burning and switched them off as he went into the hall. As he started up the stairs, he heard Fay call and then she came rushing from her room and flew down the stairs to greet him, throwing herself against his chest.

'Thank God you're here,' she said and he could see that her eyes were red from crying. 'Janet just rang us long distance from the hotel a few minutes ago. Dad is getting better physically, but he's devastated, because Mum... she is still in a coma. The doctors say there may be brain damage and they're going to do lots of tests...'

'It's like when Pip was in a car accident,' Freddie said in a choked voice. 'Did Janet say what happened?'

'It wasn't a car accident,' Fay related tearfully. 'Dad told Janet that there was a march for civil rights by a large crowd of coloured people when they were out sight-seeing. Someone called Martin Luther King was making a speech at a church in Montgomery, Alabama, and a large crowd of his supporters had gathered outside to hear him. The police were supposed to be protecting the large number of Freedom Marchers, who were riding buses and trains across the country in support of their demands for equal rights, but had disappeared. Mum stopped to watch what was going on. Dad says someone threw stones at the church windows and a woman in the crowd was hurt in the turbulence. Mum went to help the woman who had been knocked down and... Dad says some rough types in the crowd attacked her, knocked her down and kicked her, in the chest and the head...'

'No! That's evil,' Freddie cried, his fists clenching at his sides. 'All she was doing was trying to help someone. How could they be so vicious?'

'Dad went to her as soon as he saw that fighting had broken out, but he was set on too, though not badly hurt. He isn't talking to Janet much at the moment; he just sits in Mum's room, holding her hand and speaking softly to her. Janet says he's blaming himself for not being quick enough to save her.' Fay's eyes filled with tears. 'Janet says the Freedom March is something to do with civil rights for coloured people... apparently there was a riot with tear gas and there was so much chaos and confusion... Why did Mum get involved?'

'Have you ever known anything or anyone to stop Mum doing what she thinks is right? Look at the way she brought that girl she found fainting in the market home a few years back, and the trouble she caused us all...' Freddie said and his twin nodded her agreement. They both knew Peggy would have gone to help the injured woman, whatever Able said to warn her against it.

'I didn't like that girl Mum brought home – Gillian – but Mum wanted to help her. She always helps everyone – it isn't fair, Freddie? Why would they attack her like that?' Fay's voice was caught with emotion.

'I don't know, but there are racist troubles out there; coloured people are segregated and not allowed to do things we take for granted – perhaps whoever it was that hurt Mum didn't like her helping a coloured woman.'

'Then they are horrid and deserve to be locked up for life. I hope they hang them! If anything happens to Mum—' A sob escaped her. 'Mum is very ill, Freddie. Janet thinks she may die.'

Freddie looked at her hard. 'Did she say so – or are you just thinking that?'

'She didn't say it, but she sounded upset, sort of defeated – as if she didn't know how to bear it.'

'Don't cry,' Freddie coaxed and put his arm around her shoulders. 'Mum will get better – she has to...'

Fay just shook her head at him and ran upstairs. Freddie started after her, but at the top of the stairs Maggie came from the bathroom and cautioned him.

'Let her cry for a while, Freddie,' she suggested. 'It's no good bottling it up.'

He looked at her and saw she'd washed her face, but the red around her eyes gave her away.

'We have to believe she will come through, Maggie. We can't just give in to our fears.'

'I know and I will carry on and open the restaurant, just as she'd want,' Maggie said. 'I just couldn't help crying when Fay told me...'

'Yes, you carry on as usual,' Freddie agreed and then grinned. 'Even if your refusal of his invitation did disappoint Mr Hayes, he tried not to show it... I think he quite fancies you, Maggie.'

'Don't...' she said and gave him a watery smile. 'He doesn't know me.'

'If he did, he would love you, as we all do,' Freddie told her. 'Go to bed, Maggie. I'm going and we'll all say our prayers and hope things look better in the morning.'

10

'Eat your egg,' Maureen coaxed as Jon sat looking at his breakfast stubbornly. He'd been with her a few days but still hadn't settled properly. 'I thought you liked a nice soft-boiled egg? Your father said that was your favourite breakfast.'

'It's too runny,' Jon said sullenly. 'Don't like it that way.'

'Oh, I'm sorry, is it?' Maureen exchanged her egg for his. She'd cut the top off and it was just right, but Jon pushed it away.

'I'm not hungry. When is Mum coming back?'

'I'm not sure,' Maureen told him. 'You know she had to fly out to America because Granny Peggy isn't well? She will come home as soon as she can.'

'Will Granny Peggy die?' Jon asked and Maureen saw the fear in his eyes.

'I hope not,' she said, her heart catching with grief at the idea. 'She is my friend too and I love her dearly.'

Tears welled up in Jon's eyes. 'Granny Peggy is the only one who loves me,' Jon gave a little sob and rubbed at his wet cheeks.

'Your mother and father both love you, Jon,' Maureen told him and leaned over to take his hand. He flinched as if he would take it away, but, perhaps, he sensed that she cared and he let it lie within hers, though he didn't respond. 'Maggie loves you, too – and Gordy, and me and Gordon; we love having you here with us, don't we?' She looked at her son Gordy, who hesitated and then grinned at Jon.

'Yeah, we like you all right,' he said. 'Do you want to play football in the garden?'

'Yes...' Jon was off his chair and halfway to the kitchen door when Maureen called to him.

'Do you want a rock cake to eat instead of your egg, Jon?'

'Yes please.' Jon's smile flashed out and Maureen opened the cake tin, giving him one of the small cakes she'd baked the previous day. He took it eagerly. Seeing Gordy's look of hope, she gave him one too, even though he'd eaten a good breakfast.

After the two boys had gone outside to play, Maureen cleared the table and washed up. She frowned as she was about to put Jon's uneaten egg into the wastebin. Changing her mind, she put it in the fridge instead. It would make a sandwich later. Maureen hated to waste good food, because she remembered being without eggs in the war, when all they could get was the powdered stuff. In those days, Jon would have thought it a treat to have a fresh egg, as they all did then.

Her face creased with grief, both remembered and present as her war memories made her think of Peggy. How was her best friend faring? Maggie had told her how the accident had happened and Maureen thought it was typical of Peggy to get involved. If only she'd ignored what was going on instead of trying to protect a stranger, but that was Peggy and one of the reasons they all loved her.

Glancing out of the window, Maureen saw the lads playing happily together. Jon was running about after the ball and laughing in the early-morning sunshine. He seemed not to have any disability and she wondered if the balance troubles were put on for his parents to elicit sympathy or a nervous thing. If he truly believed that his granny was the only person who loved him... yet, surely, he couldn't feel his parents didn't care? Janet spent most of her life looking after him and was haunted by guilt because he'd nearly died in that accident. Maureen knew her marriage was going through a bad patch, which was mainly due to what had happened to Jon.

Ryan still blamed himself and he'd taken a back seat in the child's life. He was there if needed, but he clearly didn't show his son how much he loved him. Maureen wondered at that, because Gordon had always been a kind and loving father to their children, expressing his feelings in ways that made them feel wanted and precious. Did Ryan know what his attitude was doing to his son? Did he care how he was faring?

As if in answer to her thoughts, the telephone rang and when she answered it was Jon's father. 'Ryan, how are you?' she asked.

'I'm all right. How is Jon? Is he settling with you?'

'He's playing football in the garden with Gordy at the moment. Would you like to speak to him? I can call him in...'

'No, let him play,' Ryan said. 'Janet rang me and she is going to stay on out there for a while. Are you all right keeping Jon with you? I have asked for leave, but I have a conference this coming week that I must attend. After that, I will take some leave and I'll fetch him home.'

It was on the tip of Maureen's tongue to say that she didn't mind keeping him for as long as Janet needed to be with Peggy, but then she realised that perhaps it was what father and son both needed, to be forced into each other's company.

'I think that is a good idea, Ryan,' she told him. 'Jon is feeling a bit insecure at the moment. He is worried about his granny – and he told me she was the only one who loved him. I know that isn't true – but perhaps you need to show him your love a bit more? You could take him on a special holiday, just the two of you. Is there anything he likes to do in particular?'

'I'm not sure...' Ryan sounded thoughtful. 'Perhaps a beach holiday. We haven't had many of those.'

'Teach him to swim if he can't or build sandcastles and play football on the beach,' Maureen said. 'He needs to be loved and to know he is loved.'

Ryan was silent for a moment, then, 'I know. I have tried, Maureen. At least I did at first – but Janet so obviously blamed me and I felt guilty. Jon was a healthy little boy before the accident. It was my fault and I can't forgive myself so I stood back and let her take care of him. She is better at it than I am.'

'That isn't true,' Maureen said. 'He needs you both. You were so good with Maggie. She loves you as a father and you never made her feel anything else but your daughter, even though she was Mike's child. Why can't you show your own son the same love?'

'I can... I try to,' Ryan gave an odd laugh. 'I wish I could talk to Janet as easily as you, Maureen. It's as if we both freeze if we try to talk about Jon.'

'You are both hurting inside,' Maureen told him. 'It is hard to take that first step, Ryan, but if you don't, you could lose both of them. I am certain you don't want that.'

'No, I don't,' he admitted. 'I suppose I am stubborn and my pride is hurt.'

'Jon is pretty stubborn too. I wonder where he gets that from?'

Ryan gave a shout of laughter. 'I'm glad we've talked, Maureen. I was feeling close to despair when Janet just took off like that; I understood her need, of course I did – but she didn't ask me to go with her and that stung. I do love her and Jon very much.'

'You should be telling her this,' Maureen said. 'If I were you, I'd take an extended leave. First you need to win Jon back and then, if

Janet is still out there, why don't you both go out to join her? You could go by sea.'

'How did you get so wise?' he asked.

'Age and experience,' Maureen quipped. 'So, will you fetch Jon next week?'

'The conference can go hang,' Ryan replied, laughing out loud. 'Please tell Jon I'll be there in the morning, Maureen. I'll make some arrangements today and pick him up at about ten.'

'Good. That is what you need, both of you.'

Maureen heard Ryan chuckling at the other end of the line as she hung up. She turned to see her husband smiling at her.

'Who have you been flirting with?' he teased.

'It was Ryan. He rang to see how Jon was and I gave him a few home truths – in the nicest possible way, of course.'

'Of course,' Gordon said. 'I came home early, my love, because I thought we might take both the boys to the zoo and have a meal out. We don't get out enough and, well, I thought Jon would enjoy a family outing.'

'That is just what I've been telling his father. He is going to take him away for a few days and then, if Janet isn't back and needs to stay on, they might go over on a ship.'

'That will be an experience for Jon. He hasn't ever been on a ship, has he?' Gordon looked thoughtful. 'I'd like to take you and Gordy somewhere nice, but I'm not sure I'm up to going to America, even on a luxury liner.'

'No need. We can have a lovely beach holiday here, Gordon. That suits me fine.'

Gordon put his arms around her. 'That is what we will do then. I have a good manager these days at the shop. Toby can be trusted to look after things for us and he is very honest. He found a half crown on the floor last week and gave it to me. I told him to put it to one side and if anyone asked if they'd dropped money in the shop to give it to them – but if no one claims it in the next two weeks, then it is his.'

'He is still only nineteen,' Maureen said with a smile. 'I remember years ago, if the lads round here had found half a crown most would have kept it.'

'Not all,' Gordon told her. 'Tom Barton would have given it back if he'd found it on the shop floor.'

'Yes, Tom would – but his brother wouldn't.' A look of fleeting sadness passed across her face. 'Poor little lad was killed on a bomb site... looting, they called it, digging for what they could find. Tom tried to get him away and was injured himself but his brother died.'

Gordon nodded. 'Yes, they were some hard times, love. You've been thinking about Peggy, haven't you?'

'Yes, I have,' Maureen admitted. She sighed deeply. 'I can't do anything but pray, Gordon. I can't change anything.' She smiled as he put his arm about her. 'I am not going to spoil our day. Come on, let's get ready.'

'I'll go and tell the boys,' Gordon said. 'You put on something nice – and make sure your shoes are comfortable.'

Maureen laughed and went upstairs to change into a pale linen skirt and a short-sleeved jumper. She would take a light jacket with her, though if the sun kept out, it would be warm. Smiling, she ran a brush through her naturally wavy dark hair. It was cut short and flicked about her face. She hadn't been sure about the new style for a start, but Gordon said it made her look younger so she was pleased with it now.

She was so lucky to have him. Maureen smiled. She was glad she'd spoken out to Ryan. Perhaps it was all he needed to get him going...

* * *

Ryan had picked up the telephone again as soon as he finished speaking to Maureen. He leafed through his book in which all the important numbers were stored and spoke to the secretary at his office. When she answered, he told her he wouldn't be in again for at least three weeks.

'But the conference...?'

'This is a family matter and I shall have to forgo the conference this time. Please cancel all my appointments for three weeks, May. I know it is inconvenient, but my wife's mother is very ill and she had to go out to America. I think I am needed at home more than at work just now.'

With that, he replaced the receiver and smiled. It was the first step and he was determined that he would make things better. Ryan knew that the awkwardness that had grown between him and his wife was partly his fault. He'd been too willing to accept the blame for Jon's accident, but the boy was much better now and could lead a normal life. Ryan had to stop feeling guilty. He just needed to let his family see that he loved them.

He began to look through his book again. There was a nice little cottage that he and Janet had stayed at in Cornwall once before they moved up to Scotland. He would see if it was available for the next week, but if not, he would ring Pip and ask if they could stay there...

11

'Well, that is finished,' Tom Barton said and looked around at the restaurant. Finished in pristine white and duck egg blue, it looked clean and appealing. 'I hope it is what you expected and wanted, Maggie?'

'It is beautiful, modern and fresh,' she replied, smiling at him. 'I know Granny Peggy will be really pleased when...' Her words tailed off. 'When she comes home.' She lifted her head and looked at him. 'She will come, I know she will.'

'Have you heard anything more?'

'No...' Maggie's lower lip quivered and she bit down on it. 'They say no news is good news, don't they?'

'Let's hope so,' Tom agreed. 'I can't imagine Mulberry Lane without Peggy.'

'I don't want to,' Maggie replied with a catch in her voice. 'Oh, Tom, I couldn't bear it if...' She shook her head. 'No, I'm not going to think about that possibility. I have a restaurant to open so I'd better start getting ready. We have all new dishes, cutlery and tablecloths. I'm going to open this evening.'

'Good. That will keep you both busy. Is Freddie around?'

'Yes, I think so – why?'

'I have a job he can help me with if he will,' Tom said. 'He has been mooching around since he came back. There isn't enough for him to do here when he'd expected to be in Hastings.'

'He should go back,' Maggie said decisively. 'We have a number for him now so we can let him know... when she is better.'

'I'll take him out of your way for a while, Maggie – and I'll persuade him to go back.'

'Yes, he will probably listen to you,' Maggie agreed. 'Once we open, Fay will be too busy to be with him anyway. What do you want him to do?'

'Knock down a derelict building,' Tom said promptly. 'I always find it a good way to get rid of anger, aggression or worry.'

'I think Freddie is feeling worried and upset,' Maggie said. 'He rarely gets angry, but it will do him good to do something physical.'

'My thoughts exactly. He is a big strong man and he'll be better working than sitting around waiting for the phone to ring.'

* * *

Freddie watched as the wall began to tumble; it gave him a feeling of satisfaction to know that he'd knocked it down, easing the tight knot of tension inside him. They hadn't been able to use a wrecking ball, because it was a mid-terrace house of three and the machine would not have had room to manoeuvre; also, they had to shore up the adjoining walls. It was a case of men using big hammers to do the necessary work.

Tom and Able owned the whole row of empty terraced houses and this one was beyond repair, so he was tearing it down and would build on to the house it left exposed so that became a larger property. Tom was also going to extend the end terrace cottage so that they would have two nice-sized homes for someone rather than three cramped houses.

'These old back-to-back houses should have come down after the war,' Tom told Freddie as they worked side by side. 'It was a wonder they didn't get bombed or swept away in one of the slum clearances, but they were well built and somehow held on. It is time they were modernised. When they're finished, they will double our investment – but we'll probably just let them. Able and I think property will continue to rise so we're building for the future.'

'I know Dad likes property,' Freddie agreed. 'He says it is for Fay and me and our futures.'

'You haven't considered coming into the firm?' Tom asked him. 'I think you would be good at it.'

'No. I want to teach,' Freddie said. 'Maybe I've had it too easy, Tom, but I'm not much interested in making a lot of money. I want to give something back to society. I'll do that by helping kids through sport – and those with disabilities too in my spare time.'

Tom nodded. 'Yes, I see. It's a pity in a way, but I can understand how you feel. I know your dad is proud of you.'

'They are wonderful parents, Tom. I want to help kids who don't have a family like mine.'

'You are just like your mum,' Tom replied. 'She helped everyone in the lanes during the war – and she did a lot for me. She is a fighter, your mum. If anyone can come through, she will.'

'Yeah, she will,' Freddie said and started to knock down a chimney piece. 'Mum won't give in if she can help it.'

'Then don't you think you should go back to that job you took for the summer?' Tom asked. 'Peggy would expect it of you. We can let you know what's going on.'

'Yes, I suppose I should,' Freddie agreed. 'When Fay told me, all I wanted to do was to get home, but I'm not doing much good here, am I?'

'You're not doing a bad job,' Tom told him with a grin. 'But if it isn't what you want to do with your future – go back to something that is more in your line.'

'Thanks, Tom,' Freddie said. 'I've been twiddling my thumbs the past few days, not knowing what to do – I shall return to Hastings. I'm letting the team down by not being there and that isn't fair, is it?'

'No, it isn't,' Tom agreed. He looked about him as the last bit of chimney piece crumbled and fell into a pile of rubble. 'I'll send a gang into clear this lot in the morning. What do you say to a pint of the best down a little pub I know?'

'Good idea,' Freddie said and laughed. 'You didn't need me for this at all, Tom – but thank you just the same. It was just what I needed.'

'I thought it might be,' Tom grinned. 'Come on, I can do with a pint and a nice ham roll with pickles.'

* * *

'You're going back in the morning then?' Fay said as they sat drinking a coffee on Freddie's return. 'I'm glad you came, Freddie, but there isn't much for you to do. I'm busy and so is Maggie. You'll be best with your friends and doing a job you enjoy.'

'Are you sure you are all right if I go?' Freddie considered her. 'You know how to contact me now – but I'll ring you every evening. What time is best?'

'Either before we start service or half-past ten or later.'

'I'll try to ring about half-past five in the afternoon,' Freddie agreed. 'You will be getting ready but not actually in the throes of cooking then.'

'Good – but remember, if there is real news, I'll ring you,' she said. 'I don't care about your landlady. I'll just leave a message for you to ring back.'

'I'll know if something is wrong, Fay. I was uneasy that morning before you rang me – and I'll know and I'll ring home.'

'She will be all right—' Fay broke off as they both heard the telephone shrill. Her face went white as she looked at him. 'It has to be Janet at this hour...'

They both went to the head of the stairs. Maggie had answered and was listening, her face tense; then she looked up. 'Freddie, Fay, it's Able. There is news. He wants to speak to you...'

Freddie was the first to the phone. 'Dad...' he was breathless with anxiety. 'Mum...'

'Your mum has woken up,' Able said. 'She is alive and everything works but... she has what they call amnesia.' Able took a deep breath. 'She has forgotten me, which means she can't remember you or Fay either.' There was a break in his voice. 'She thought she'd been injured in the war back in England when she woke. Janet was familiar to her, but she was puzzled by the way she looked. We told her it was 1961 but she thought it was 1940 and it took her a while to accept that things had changed...'

'Dad, that must have been awful for both of you,' Freddie said. 'I am so sorry. Does she know you now?'

'Janet explained who I was and she accepts it as truth – but no, she still doesn't know me, properly.' There was a catch in Able's voice. 'It will take time.'

'Will her memory ever return?' Freddie questioned.

'The doctors say it should, but they can't be certain. It is the head trauma she suffered; it could have been much worse – but we have to be thankful that she will live, Freddie. That is all that matters for now. She is a little shaky and—'

Fay was pulling at his arm, desperate to speak to their father. 'Fay is here, Dad. She wants to talk to you now...'

Freddie handed the phone to his twin and heard her asking questions as his father repeated the news to her. 'She doesn't remember me or Freddie?' Fay sounded and looked stunned. Tears sprang to her eyes and she thrust the phone at Freddie, who took it as she ran off.

'She is crying,' Freddie told his father. 'You were saying Mum is a bit shaky still. Can she walk and talk?'

'Just about,' his father told him. 'The doctors say she will relearn it, but we have to be patient. We're staying on out here for the time being, because I dare not leave her and they think it is too soon to move her...' Able hesitated. 'At the moment, I am not sure she trusts me enough. She is clinging to Janet for the time being.'

Freddie could hear the hurt in his father's voice but made no comment; there was no point in telling him it would come right when they both knew it might never be the same.

'Are you all right for money, Dad?' Freddie asked, sticking to practical things. 'I have the money you put into my college fund account. I can send you that if you need it and take another job for a while, postpone my teaching course.'

'No, don't do that,' Able told him firmly. 'I will make arrangements for any bills myself – but I've been told my hospital bills have been paid. I don't know who by, but I have an idea it might be the father of one of the youths who turned on your mother. I'd got a new camera and was taking photographs and I think I may have pictures on it that prove what happened. Of course, when I saw it was Peggy they were kicking, I stopped filming and rushed to help her – not that I could do much with one arm. However, an older man stepped in and ordered one of the youths to go with him. I've since learned that he is a wealthy American. He may have paid the hospital bill in the hope of keeping me quiet...'

'Have the American police asked you what you saw?'

'Yes, but I wasn't well enough to answer. I hope to get the film developed and give it to them if there is evidence...'

'You must,' Freddie agreed. 'We can pay that bill if you're uncomfortable with it being paid for you.'

'I shall,' Able said. 'But unless I know who paid it, I can't repay it and the hospital authorities won't tell me at the moment.'

'If I were you, I'd just hand that film to the police there and let them get on with it, Dad.'

'I think you are right,' Able replied. 'I'd better go now, Freddie. This call is costing a fortune. I'm in a hotel now, but I'm visiting your mum later.'

'You won't give up on her, Dad?'

'Never. You, the same – even if she doesn't know us for a while. We still love her, right?'

'Always. Love you too, Dad,' Freddie said and replaced the receiver. He had tears streaming down his cheeks when he turned and found Maggie at his side. She opened her arms to him and he went to her. She held him tight for a few moments.

'She is going to live, Freddie,' she said. 'It is enough for now.'

'Yes, it is,' he said and wiped the back of his hand over his cheeks. 'I'd better go and pack. I have an early train to catch.' Maggie let him go. At the top of the stairs, he turned to look at her. 'Thanks, Maggie. If you were not my cousin or aunt or whatever, I'd marry you.'

'Don't be daft,' she said and laughed as she saw his cheeky grin. 'I love you too, but not like that; I've got other ideas.'

'Oh, I just bet you have,' Freddie riposted. 'I saw him. Lovely apartment, smashing car – E-type Jaguars cost well over two thousand pounds; he must have lots of money. I wonder what James will say when he finds out you have another man friend?'

'Neither of them is mine,' Maggie retorted. 'I do not intend to marry for years.'

'Until you're old and past it,' Freddie replied cheekily and ran along the corridor to Fay's room. He could hear sobbing from inside, but when he tried the handle, it was locked. 'Let me in, Fay. I want to talk.'

'Just let me be, Freddie. I'll be up in the morning before you leave.'

'If that's what you want,' Freddie said and walked on to his own room. Fay was breaking her heart, but perhaps she needed to cry. He'd needed it too, but they should be glad – glad their mother was alive and would get better, even if she didn't recognise her husband or remember her twins...

It was going to be very hard for all of them if Peggy couldn't remember anything since the beginning of the war, but worst of all for her. Freddie thought she must feel very lonely and perhaps fearful. She'd always been such a brave, caring person and it wasn't fair that some hooligan had done this to his mother.

Freddie felt a surge of rage against the men who had done it. He hoped his father would go to the police despite the obvious attempt to bribe him by paying his hospital bills. Those bullies deserved to be punished for what they'd done, to his mother and to the woman Peggy had been trying to help...

12

Freddie was so brave and so likable and both the twins had their father's way of teasing. Maggie allowed herself a little smile as he disappeared along the corridor.

Returning to the kitchen, where she had been planning a new menu for the next day luncheon, Maggie found her mind wandering. If Peggy had forgotten Able and the twins, she wouldn't remember that Maggie was grown up and in charge of the new restaurant. Would she be upset when she saw what had been done to the Pig & Whistle when she got back? Maggie knew her grandmother had been a little reluctant to make the changes, but she'd done so for them, because she loved them and wanted them to succeed. If she'd forgotten them...

Maggie shook her head. There was no point in dwelling on things that could not be changed. A smile tugged at the corner of her mouth as she recalled Freddie's cheeky remarks about Greg and James. Little did he know how close he had come to the truth. It was stupid to let the memory of a man's smile into her heart. The look in Greg's eyes when he'd understood that she truly wasn't revolted by the scar on his cheek – humility, hope and gratitude –

that's what she'd seen. He must have been hurt badly by someone – a girl or woman who had made it plain she was disgusted by the brown markings on one side of his face. The scars had faded from what they must have been and he'd told her he was considering treatment, but Maggie doubted any skin grafting could completely restore the good looks he must once have had. It didn't matter to her and wouldn't to anyone who really liked him, and she did like him a lot.

She was daft even to think of him, Maggie told herself. She had no intention of having an intense relationship and marriage meant children and a home to care for. Besides, there was James, and she liked him, too. They had an on-off sort of friendship that suited them both. Maggie might not see James for weeks when he was working frantically on his paintings or away on one of his tours to America. A gallery over there had bought several of his best paintings, including some that he'd done of Maggie. James had debated whether to let them be hung in the gallery, but Maggie had told him she didn't mind.

'You can paint me again whenever you like,' she'd offered with a smile and been surprised by his answer

'I can paint you as you are now, Maggie, but some of the early ones will never be replicated. You've changed – grown up more, become more worldly.'

'Is that a bad thing?' she'd asked, still amused.

'Yes, in a way,' James had said, his eyes searching her face. 'You had a wonderful look of innocence and expectation that I loved. It has gone now. You are still beautiful, Maggie, but I see something different now when I look at you. I'm not sure I want to paint you again.'

Maggie's smile had faded then. His careless words had hurt her and he didn't even see or understand what he'd said to her. 'Do what you like with your paintings,' Maggie had thrown at him as she'd left. 'I'll be busy for a while so I shan't be round. You will have to remember to feed yourself...'

She wasn't sure he'd even heard her, because he was off in one of his dreams, but he'd telephoned her later that evening to ask her to the theatre.

'I meant to ask when you were here,' he'd said, 'but you know what I'm like, Maggie.'

'Yes, I do know what you're like,' she'd replied. 'I'm sorry, I can't accept your invitation. I have something else to do...'

'Are you angry with me because I said I wasn't sure if I wanted to paint you again?'

Maggie had hesitated, then, 'Not angry – but I was hurt. I felt devalued in some way, which was stupid of me.'

'It was silly. You know I adore you and I think you are lovely – but I'm not certain I could capture the look you have now. It is not you at fault, it is me. I'm not sure I could do you justice, Maggie.'

'I accept your apology.'

'Good. The last thing I want to do is upset you.' He'd been silent for a moment. 'I have another big show coming up in America. I'm going to take the early stuff I did of you, but only to be shown not sold.'

'That is plain daft,' Maggie had objected. 'If you get a good offer you should sell. I shan't be offended.'

'Well, I suppose I might,' he'd agreed. 'I'll see you when I get back then?'

'Yes, of course. We'll have dinner together. You can take me somewhere nice...'

'That's a promise,' James had replied and they'd ended the call. That had been two months earlier. Maggie knew he was due home any day now. She would go out with him as promised, because they were friends. Despite his frequent declarations of love, Maggie had never taken them seriously. If she'd agreed to marry him, he would probably leave her standing at the altar because he was painting and had forgotten. No, James wasn't the kind of man Maggie would marry, but she didn't know who would be. Someone kind and thoughtful – or someone who sent little shivers of pleasure down her spine?

Shrugging, Maggie returned to the menu she was preparing. She'd kept Granny Peggy's shepherd's pie on the lunchtime menu for years, but was it time for a change? A sigh escaped her as she pencilled in a chicken casserole and the shepherd's pie; let the customers decide for themselves. New wasn't always better and Peggy's apple pie was a favourite with everyone, so she would keep that as well as her chocolate mousse and the praline ice cream and pear dessert she'd recently perfected. Decorated with a swirl of chocolate sauce and a shaving of dark chocolate, it would pass muster at any of the fancy dinner parties that Fay catered for but was also popular with her customers.

Maggie sat with her pen poised as she considered her almond and mascarpone pudding. It had raspberry jam at its heart and was one of Fay's favourites. Nodding, she put that on the list. Fay would need some cheering up for a while and she'd make sure that there was a couple of slices left for her friend and partner. Now she had best get to bed...

* * *

Maggie was halfway through service the next evening when Carla came to tell her that Greg wanted to speak to her on the telephone. She looked at her in surprise and some dismay.

'Now? Did you tell him I was cooking for a restaurant that is nearly full?'

'I did, but he said he has to talk to you and won't keep you long.'

'Go,' Fay said and gave her a little push. 'I can manage for ten minutes, but don't be longer.'

Maggie left what she was doing and went through to the hall, where Carla had left the receiver off the hook. 'Hello,' she said. 'Is that Greg? What can I do for you?'

'I have some people coming over from America. I shall meet them in London next Friday lunchtime – can you cater for eight of us in the evening at your restaurant, say at seven-thirty?'

'Oh…' She felt vaguely disappointed. 'Yes, I am sure we can. We've only just reopened, so we're getting more people drift in rather than book at the moment. Are you looking for anything special?'

'Surprise me,' he said. He hesitated, then, 'I'll be going back to America with someone the following day and I'll be away for a while. This was a chance to see you before I go.'

'I'll cook something special for you,' she told him. 'I must go; we're busy this evening.'

'Yes, of course. I'll see you next Friday at seven-thirty then.'

'Yes, thank you for thinking of us…'

'You'd be surprised how often I think of you,' Greg replied and replaced the receiver.

Maggie found she was smiling as she returned to the restaurant. She was curious about the friends he was bringing to her restaurant and decided she would do an extra-special menu. Greg need not have brought his friends to her restaurant; there were many others that could provide special food. He'd wanted to see her – so why not ask her out? Would she have gone if he had? Maggie wasn't sure.

'Everything all right?' Fay asked as she returned to the kitchen and started to prepare the tiny cheese and onion tarts that they were serving as a starter that evening. They would be hot and were cooked in little ramekins and served on a saucer with a frilly serviette and a salad. 'These are fiddly to do, Maggie.'

'I set them up in a row and can just whizz down them if we get a big order,' Maggie replied.

'Well, table number six all want them and so does table number nine, eleven and twelve,' Fay said, 'and that is twenty-four altogether.'

'Gosh, I didn't think we'd need so many,' Maggie said, feeling pleased.

'You are in a good mood,' Fay said, suddenly looking at her. 'What did Greg want then?'

'He's bringing some friends to dinner in the restaurant next Friday, eight of them altogether. So I'll book his table out...'

'Oh, is that all?' Fay turned away to get on with the starters. 'Someone wants your prawns and avocado. Very posh! Are they in the fridge?'

'Yes. You only need to add the fillings and sauce to them,' Maggie said. The slightly different menu seemed to be going down well this evening. 'I thought we'd try hot dogs tomorrow in the lunch period.'

'Mum would have a fit,' Fay said and then stopped, looking at Maggie in horror. Her bottom lip trembled, but she clamped down on it firmly.

Maggie nodded at her. 'We'll have her home soon, Fay. Once she sees the old bar just as it was, only better, she will remember everything. You'll see. It's just because everything it strange out there. When she gets home, she will be fine.' Maggie could only pray that her words would prove true. It would break Fay's heart all over again if her mother didn't know her.

'I wish she hadn't gone now,' Fay said fiercely. 'I thought it would be a lovely holiday for her and now...'

'It's not because we all said she should go and have some fun,'

Maggie told her. 'It's because Peggy being Peggy couldn't just stand aside when she saw someone being hurt. If she'd seen it happen here, she would have gone to the victim's rescue just the same. It could have happened in our own lane, Fay. Don't blame yourself; it is just an accident of fate. Besides, we all agreed it would do her the world of good to have a long holiday.'

Fay nodded, but looked miserable as she fetched out various starters and put them on the service trolley for Carla and their new waitress, Alice, to fetch and take through. 'I know,' she said, drawing a shaky breath. 'But it is too awful, Maggie. I thought she was going to die and I know it's wonderful that she will live – but supposing she never remembers us?'

'She will,' Maggie assured her, though she wasn't as confident as she made herself sound. 'Granny Peggy is a strong lady and if anyone can make herself get well it is her. Besides, once she sees you and Freddie, she is bound to love you. She won't be able to help herself...'

Fay shot her a look of gratitude just as Carla returned.

'Everyone is ordering those cheese tarts,' she announced. 'I hope you've got plenty, Maggie, because one customer has eaten his and wants it again, it is so good!'

Maggie laughed. 'I made plenty of them, because I like them myself.'

'Don't forget to save me one of those; they smell delicious,' Carla said as she picked up her tray and departed once more. At the door of the kitchen, she stopped and looked back. 'There are more flowers in the hall – and I've had twenty people ask me how Peggy is this evening. What shall I say?'

'Just that we don't know much yet,' Maggie advised, 'and thank them.'

Carla nodded and went out.

Fay swallowed hard. 'I wish people wouldn't...'

'What – be kind? Don't be silly, Fay. Granny Peggy is liked – even loved – in these lanes. We're not the only ones to be upset over it...'

Fay nodded. 'I know – I'm just being silly...'

'No, you're being very brave and I do understand that it hurts,' Maggie sympathised. 'But her friends are all anxious too. As Tom said to Freddie, Mulberry Lane wouldn't be the same without her.'

13

'I wasn't sure you would come back,' Guy told Freddie when he arrived at the boarding house the following evening. 'I told Mrs Phipps to keep the room, so I'm glad you did.'

'I telephoned your office as soon as I knew when I'd be coming,' Freddie said. 'I couldn't let you know any sooner, because I didn't know if I'd be able to get back for a while.'

'How is your mother?' Guy asked, looking sympathetic. 'An accident is bad at any time, but to happen over there is worse somehow...'

Freddie nodded his agreement. 'I thought Fay and I might go out together, but it wouldn't help. Mum recovered consciousness but...' He shook his head. 'It seems she can't remember my father or us... though she does remember our half-sister who is several years older.'

'That is rotten for your father and you, of course – but he is her husband. It must be a terrible time for him, for both of them.'

'Yes, it is,' Freddie confirmed. 'They've always been so close, and Mum – well, she's just the best...'

'I expect we all think that of our mothers,' Guy said, 'but I do understand and if you need to leave in a hurry again – well, just let me know in time to change the rota.'

'I hope I won't have to,' Freddie's voice was apologetic. 'I rushed off for my twin's sake, but there wasn't much I could do to help. They have a couple of numbers they can reach now – the life-guards' office and this boarding house. So if they need me, they will ring. I'll pop home on the train if my mother gets back – or when, I should say. She will expect to see me...' Freddie's voice caught with emotion. 'I have to be thankful she came through it all.'

'Do you know what happened?' Guy asked and frowned as Freddie explained. 'That makes it even harder to take – being attacked for trying to help someone.'

'Mum always tries to help anyone in need,' Freddie said. 'It isn't the first time she has been attacked for it, but previously she wasn't badly hurt.'

'Your mother does sound a rather special lady.' Guy looked thoughtful. 'One day I should like to meet your family, Freddie – but for now we have to talk about tomorrow. You missed some important training so I'll go through it with you when we've finished. If I forget, remind me that I need to show you the correct way to breathe when affecting a rescue and when resuscitating.'

* * *

Freddie had missed the evening meal so didn't see Greta before he went to bed. He'd eaten on the train down and had some cakes and biscuits that Maggie and Fay had given him, so he nibbled one in bed and read a few pages of his Agatha Christie novel, smiling as he thought he had guessed the ending. Putting the book down, he switched off his light and settled down to sleep, but not before sending a little prayer on its way for his mother's complete recovery.

In the morning, Freddie took his place at the breakfast table after helping himself to some cornflakes. He looked up as someone approached the table.

'Do you want the cooked breakfast? It is scrambled egg on toast or two boiled eggs with bread and butter.'

'I'll have the scrambled egg and toast please, Greta.' Freddie smiled at her. She did not return his smile and he remembered that he'd broken their date. 'I'm sorry I left in such a hurry – I didn't get time to tell you...'

Greta looked at him then but didn't answer, moving on to the next table to take the order from Muriel and Steve, who were chatting and laughing. Muriel waved at him, but Steve just nodded. Freddie felt a little excluded, but then Jill came and sat at his table.

'I'm late down,' she said and sighed. 'I didn't sleep well last night. I keep getting headaches. I think it's called a migraine.'

'Oh, that's not good,' Freddie said. 'My twin gets them sometimes and she goes to bed with the curtains closed and takes an aspirin. Do you have pain now? I think I have a strip in my bag upstairs.'

'Thanks, but I took one before I came down,' Jill replied. 'I expect it will go when we get to the beach and into the fresh air...' She glanced over her shoulder. 'I think it is the disinfectant Mrs Phipps uses – it is very strong and makes me gag a bit. Probably gave me the headache. She'd been splashing it about last night... someone was sick in the bathroom, but no one had owned up to it.'

'Are you sure you're not coming down with something?' Freddie looked at her in concern because she was pale. 'I am sure Guy would understand if you needed to visit the doctor.'

'I'll be fine once I'm out in the air,' Jill assured. 'Are you having the cooked breakfast? The scrambled egg was burned again yesterday. I think I'll stick to cornflakes and toast today.' She got up and went to the serving table, where she found both items and returned with her tray. 'The toast is cold, but I'll ask Greta for some coffee...'

Freddie nodded as Greta returned with his scrambled egg on toast and a pot of coffee. The cups were already on the table and there was milk on the serving table.

Freddie thanked her, but again Greta didn't return his smile, so he gave up and looked at his breakfast, half expecting the toast to be burned, but it was all fine and tasted nice when he ate it. Greta was clearly annoyed with him for letting her down, but his breakfast hadn't suffered because of it.

* * *

After breakfast, the little group made its way to the beach, armed with bottles of drink and packed lunches, as well as towels and sun cream. It looked like being a warm day and they spent long hours on the beach so needed to be prepared.

'We're going to do some more rescues this morning,' Guy said. 'Most of you seem to have got the idea, but, Jill, I think you need to do another rescue and practise your hold. You nearly choked me the other day. Freddie, it's your turn to be the swimmer in peril, so pair up with Jill. Muriel, you don't need another lesson so you can be another swimmer in distress. Steve, you can rescue her. George, you are with me this time... Mark, you are with Sarah.'

Freddie smiled at Jill encouragingly. Her colour seemed to have returned a bit now they'd left the smells of the boarding house behind.

'I'll swim out until I can't touch the ground,' Freddie said to Jill and smiled. 'Don't worry, I shan't give you too much trouble.'

'Thanks. I'll be okay,' Jill replied, giving him a faint smile.

Freddie ran into the sea. The water was cold and he swam briskly until he thought he was at the right depth, then he called out and started splashing the water as if in trouble. Jill waved and came running down the beach and into the water. She swam towards him confidently as he trod water and waited for her, but then, all of a sudden, he saw her stop swimming and she sort of flopped beneath the surface.

Instinct took over. Jill hadn't seemed well earlier and he was sure she was in trouble. He quickly reached the spot where he'd seen her just sink and could see her body just beneath the surface. She must have her feet on the sand but couldn't seem to move.

'It's all right, Jill,' Freddie said. 'Don't panic. I'll get you back to the beach and we'll get help.'

Grabbing her by the shoulders, and making sure her head was above the water, Freddie towed her to the safety of the beach. Once they reached the edge of the water, he stood up and heaved her body up and over his shoulder, calling out for help as he walked up the beach. Everyone else from the team was in the sea, either being rescued or rescuing someone.

Freddie gently positioned Jill's body on the sand and turned her on to her side, going through the procedure to help her bring up the water she'd swallowed. Water came from her mouth, but she gave no sign of life. Quickly lying her on her back, Freddie opened her mouth and looked for an obstruction, which he'd forgotten to do, but could see nothing.

'I'm going to start chest compression, Jill,' he said to her. 'Please try to respond.'

He was starting the compression when Guy came up to him. 'I

thought I told Jill to... My God! What happened?' he demanded as he saw that she wasn't breathing.

Freddie didn't stop what he was doing as he answered: 'She was swimming out to me when she suddenly seemed to flop under the water. I knew she hadn't felt well at breakfast, so I went straight to her and brought her in. I told her to take the day off, but she thought she would be all right...'

Jill's body suddenly shuddered and she was violently sick, some of it landing on Freddie. Her eyes were now open and staring but she wasn't seeing them properly.

Steve came pounding up the beach to them and looked down at Jill. 'What happened?'

'She had some kind of seizure in the sea, I think,' Freddie replied, wiping himself with a towel. 'We need to get an ambulance...'

'I've already phoned,' Muriel said, coming up to them. 'They said they will be here in ten minutes.'

'Keep her warm,' Guy instructed, handing Freddie a blanket. He wrapped it around Jill, whose eyes were closed again. She was breathing but unconscious. 'She should have told me she wasn't feeling well. The silly girl could have drowned out there.'

'I think she took something last night,' Steve told them, looking worried. 'We went out for a drink and met some people. I'm fairly sure at least two of them were on some kind of drug and they may have given Jill a tablet.'

'Would she have been daft enough to take it?' Guy asked. 'Surely, she knew she couldn't do this job and take drugs?'

'She was worried about her stamina,' Steve replied. 'She told me the training was harder than she'd expected and she may have thought it would help her. Some of the tablets these drug pushers sell you are lethal, all kinds of rubbish goes into them, not just heroin or cocaine. The people who pedal this rotten stuff don't care what lies they tell or what it does to their victims.'

'You didn't see her take anything?' Guy asked.

'No – but she went to the cloakroom and she could have taken it then.'

'Were they local – the people you thought might have given her drugs?'

'No – Birmingham, I think by their accent. Just down for a fun weekend, so Jill told me.' Steve frowned. 'I should have warned her to be careful...'

Guy frowned. 'Not your fault, Steve. If Jill took a tablet she bought or was given, she has probably done it before...' They heard a siren in the distance and Guy looked at Steve. 'You must tell the ambulancemen that she might have taken something dangerous. It might save her life.'

The ambulance arrived and both the driver and his assistant came hurrying on to the beach. They asked for details and Freddie told them what he'd seen and Steve added his part of the story. The ambulancemen looked at each other and nodded.

'This is the second case of a mysterious collapse this morning – well, one was in the early hours. We think it is possibly drugs.' A look of anger passed across the driver's face. 'If you see these men again, sir, please inform the police. Whatever they are selling is dangerous and costing lives – our earlier patient died on the way to hospital. This batch of drugs has something harmful in it, not just an opiate. One case we had recently actually found traces of arsenic when the autopsy was done. If this young lady lives, it will be due to the fact that you knew what to do to help her start breathing. We just have to hope the damnable stuff hasn't affected her brain...'

There was silence amongst the little group on the beach as Jill was taken away in the ambulance.

* * *

Guy looked at the faces of the lifeguards and made a snap decision. 'We'll call that it for training this morning. Freddie, you need a hot drink, something to eat, and maybe a bath. Return to the boarding house. I'll speak to you later.'

'I'm all right,' Freddie told him, though another dip in the sea wouldn't hurt. 'I stink...'

'Do as I say,' Guy ordered. 'Steve and George, you are on patrol duty with me, Mark too. Muriel, go back with Freddie and make sure he does as I told him.'

'Come on,' Muriel said, smiling at him. 'Do as Guy asks, Freddie. You've had a shock. We all have. I could do with a hot drink and a drop of something in it.' She urged him to pick up his things. 'Just put your shorts and pullover on, Freddie. You can change back at the boarding house.'

Freddie nodded and obeyed. He was feeling shocked. Rescuing Jill had been fine, but the realisation that she'd nearly drowned because of some vile tablet she'd bought to make her feel better distressed him. She must have found the training much harder than the rest of them. What must have been going through her mind to make her take an unknown drug? Didn't she understand how dangerous that was?

Freddie's father had warned him and Fay never to take anything dubious from friends or strangers. 'Swallowing something you don't know anything about could ruin your lives,' Able had told them both when they were still at school. 'It isn't clever; it's stupid.'

It was hard to think that a young woman like Jill might have done herself irreparable harm – might even die. The thought made him sad and it reminded him that his mother was still very ill.

'Hot cocoa will do me fine,' he told Muriel as they walked the short distance to the boarding house. 'I do feel shocked though – stunned might be a better word. Did you know that Jill was struggling with the training?'

'Well, I thought she might be,' Muriel admitted. 'She looked tired and strained a couple of times. I asked if she was all right, but she insisted she was fine.'

'I told her not to train this morning, but she said the same,' Freddie told her. 'Guy won't have her back after this, will he?'

'No. She would be a weak link – besides, he hates drugs. Can't tolerate the sellers or the users. No, Jill is out of the team.'

'That is a shame. I imagine she bought the tablet to try to improve her strength or fitness. I'm sure she had no idea what was in it.'

'Yes, perhaps – or just for the hell of it,' Muriel frowned. 'Don't let on that I told you – but Guy's mother was a drug addict, on heroin I think, though I'm not certain of all the details. It's the reason he hates any form of illegal drugs. He won't even take an aspirin when he has a headache, for fear of addiction.'

'What a rotten thing to happen,' Freddie said. 'How do you know?'

'Someone told me,' Muriel said. 'I was supposed to keep it to myself, but I know you won't talk about it.'

'I wouldn't dream of it and I shan't speak of it to him unless he chooses to tell me,' Freddie assured her. 'It is very sad, but I know it happens. At home, I've been doing a bit of work, helping children from broken families... just a couple of evenings a week. I teach them to play football or cricket. I've heard the same sort of story from some of their guardians.'

Muriel nodded. 'I was sorry to hear about your mother's accident, Freddie. I wasn't sure you would come back?'

'I wasn't doing much good sitting at home worrying,' Freddie told her. 'I'm glad I was here this morning. If I hadn't noticed Jill was unwell earlier...'

'She might have died in the sea,' Muriel agreed. 'It is your first real save, Freddie. Are you proud of yourself? You should be.'

'I haven't thought about it,' Freddie replied. 'I was just glad when she started breathing – but I'm not sure how I'll feel if she is brain damaged. It must be awful to just lie there and not know...' He choked back a sob and then shook his head. 'Sorry, just me being daft.'

'No need to be sorry,' Muriel said. 'You're a decent sort, Freddie. Go and get changed. I'll bring up some cocoa to your room, if you like.'

'I'll just have a quick bath,' Freddie told her. 'I'll be down in twenty minutes for that cocoa.'

'Okay, whatever,' Muriel said and turned away. 'I'm going to have something right now...'

Freddie wondered if he'd offended her, but he didn't think their landlady would approve of her bringing him hot cocoa to his room. He liked Muriel, but she wasn't the sort of girl he wanted when he did start courting. Freddie wasn't sure what kind of girl would suit him, but he wasn't ready to get serious yet anyway.

* * *

Freddie went downstairs dressed in a pair of fawn slacks and a navy-blue open-necked shirt. Muriel wasn't in the sitting room, so he ventured to the kitchen and knocked. The door was opened by Greta.

'I am sorry to disturb you,' he said apologetically. 'I wondered if I could have some cocoa, please?'

For a moment, he thought she would refuse and then she burst into tears. 'I'm sorry for being so horrid to you earlier,' she said between sobs. 'I didn't know about your mum and Muriel told me you just saved Jill's life... I hope she's all right.'

'We all feel the same,' Freddie said. 'But I should have found a way to let you know I was leaving, Greta. I was just so worried over Mum that it went out of my head.'

'I know...' She smiled through her tears. 'Come into the kitchen and tell me how you like your cocoa. My aunt is out shopping and she won't be back for ages. I've got to make some pastry and bake pies, but I'm not very good at it.'

'What sort of pie – apple?' Freddie said hopefully.

'Beef and kidney and... I could do an apple pie for afters,' she said. 'I'm not quite sure how to cook the filling...'

'Mum showed me how she does hers,' Freddie told her. 'I'm not a cook like Mum and Fay and Maggie, but I know a little bit. How about I help you?'

'That would be lovely,' Greta said and smiled happily. 'Even better than the beach.'

'We can go to the beach this Sunday,' Freddie replied. 'I'll show you how to cook the apple pie and then think how pleased your aunt will be...'

'She is never pleased for long,' Greta sighed. 'I wish my father would come home so I could live with him. I hate it here...'

'What would you rather do?'

'I don't know,' Greta said. 'I'm not very good at things unless someone shows me again and again until I get it right and then I sometimes get distracted. My head is full of stories and I get lost in them...'

'Do you write them down?'

Greta stared at him. 'How did you know?'

'I didn't – but I'd like to read one of your stories, Greta.'

'They aren't very good when I write them down,' she replied

sadly. 'In my head they live and breathe, but when I write them, they are dull.'

'Practice makes perfect,' Freddie teased. 'If you want to write stories, you should go to evening classes to learn. Don't give up your dreams, Greta. Everyone needs to dream a little.' He grinned at her. 'I dream of apple pie – so come on, let's make a big one...'

14

Maggie debated what to wear that Friday evening. Her usual workwear was dark slacks and a white cotton blouse, covered by a large white apron: practical and washable and sensible and dull. Yet she could hardly cater for a busy service in a black cocktail dress and high heels. In the end, she decided to stick to the tried and tested. Greg would have to take her as he found her; it was her cooking that would be on show that evening, not her.

The fresh salmon and cucumber mousse for starters would be served with a small side salad and was easy once the mousse was made and set in the fridge. Maggie had decided on beef Wellington or chicken in wine and mushroom sauce for the main course, but she'd also done a light cheese flan that could be served with new potatoes and salad or the same vegetables as the meat dishes. For dessert, there was Fay's lemon drizzle pudding or Maggie's milk and dark chocolate delight with cream swirls.

'I love the little almond biscuits you serve with those,' Fay had said when Maggie tried them out on her, 'and I love it that you mix milk and dark chocolate in your crème desserts; most cooks do just the dark chocolate kind and sometimes it can be bitter and not at all what you want for afters.'

'You have a sweet tooth,' Maggie had teased. 'I've warned you before, you will get fat.'

Fay had laughed because she was slim and light and she'd danced off knowing that she'd stay that way.

Maggie smiled to herself. In ten minutes, she would go down to the main kitchen to start preparing the meal for Greg and his friends. She was looking forward to seeing him later, though in all probability it would only be for a few minutes after the meal.

* * *

The restaurant was busy that evening. Carla told them in the kitchen that all the tables were full and they'd had to turn away some disappointed customers.

'That will teach them to book,' Fay said with a smile of satisfaction. 'It shows that people like what we serve anyway.'

Maggie nodded her agreement. She'd half hoped they wouldn't get quite as much trade that evening so that she could concentrate on the meals for Greg and his friends, but they'd asked Rose to help in the kitchen and she'd agreed. Maureen was too busy and had told them she was taking Gordy to the cinema that evening to see a film called *Carry on Constable*; it was a comedy and they were looking forward to it. However, they had Alice, who had previous experience in a restaurant, which meant that both Fay and Maggie could put all their efforts into the cooking, with Rose helping to prepare the vegetables.

'I wish Mum was here to see this,' Fay said as she served up the delicate soup she was responsible for as an alternative starter. It was a consommé with tiny pieces of cauliflower, carrots, cabbage and beans in it and it had a delicious clean taste. 'She would never believe I could do it...'

'Oh, Granny Peggy knows you're a good cook,' Maggie assured her as she worked on her pastry case for the beef. 'I just wish she was here helping us... It always makes me feel safe when she is with us, if you know what I mean?'

They looked at each other in agreement, fear and tension just below the surface. Able hadn't rung for a couple of days, but Janet had talked to Maggie. She had said he'd been having some treatment himself and there was no change in Peggy's condition.

'She is bored with lying in bed and wants to go home,' Janet had told them. 'The doctors won't let her travel yet, but she may leave hospital at the end of next week. Able says they will stay on for a bit longer, which means I shall have to stay too, because she is clinging to me still. She remembers me but not Able. He is very upset because she is treating him politely but as she would a stranger. He tries not to show it, but you can see the hurt in his eyes. I don't feel I can just abandon them.'

'Oh, Janet,' Maggie had said. 'How will you manage for money?'

'Ryan says I can stay as long as I need to. He offered to bring Jon out, but I told him there's no point. I need to be with Mum at the moment. He said he understood, but I'm not sure either he or Jon is happy about it.' She sighed deeply. 'We just don't get on as we used to...'

'I'm so sorry,' Maggie had sympathised. She knew her mother's relationship with Ryan wasn't always one of complete accord and Jon might become troublesome if his mother was away too long. 'If I can do anything to help?'

'Thank God you don't throw tantrums. I think you must take after your father rather than me.'

'Yes, we're not much alike, are we? Perhaps I am like my father

– Jon is more like you, up and down. I love you, Mum, but I don't need you around all the time; he does, I think.'

'Yes, perhaps,' Janet had agreed. 'Ryan told me he is making time to take him places. I think they went to a cricket match the other day, after they got back from the sea – he took Jon and Gordy to the game. Jon spoke to me on the phone; he said it was good fun. Apparently, on a part of the ground, the younger ones were allowed to have a go at batting and bowling...'

'That sounds like fun,' Maggie had laughed. 'Well, keep in touch and give my love to Granny Peggy and Able. I'll take Jon out somewhere next Sunday.'

They'd ended the call there and Maggie had related the bits that mattered to Fay. Each time a call came, it made them both sad and reflective, but they'd agreed that they would just get on and work as hard as they could.

Maggie and Fay both missed Peggy when it came to the busy service. She had always been there for them, often taking something from the oven at just the right moment. Her presence was a comfort and they needed her that evening, more than they might have expected. Peggy usually did the straightforward pies and prepared a lot of the vegetables, leaving them to the fancy cooking they both enjoyed; it was harder work without her. Without Peggy they would have to get more staff. Rose was helping, but more with preparation and tidying the kitchen than with the actual cooking, and she could only stay for two hours, which wasn't truly long enough.

'I need to be home by nine-thirty,' she'd told them. 'Tom has to get up early and if I'm out late he can't rest.'

'It's good of you to come, Rose,' Maggie had told her. 'I know we need some regular help. I stuck a notice in the window and in Maureen and Gordon's shop – but my newspaper advert doesn't go in until next week. I had expected Granny Peggy would be home...'

'Yes, I'm sure you miss her.' Rose had looked thoughtful. 'She may not be able to help as much in future, Maggie. Peggy is into her sixties now and after this accident…'

Maggie knew she was right, but she didn't want to admit it. She'd liked the way they'd worked together: Maggie, Fay, Peggy, sometimes Maureen or Rose helping out; they were a proper team. It amazed her that Granny Peggy had run the pub almost single-handed for years during and after the war. It hadn't been anywhere near as busy then, but Maggie knew that her grandmother had worked long hours, cooking and serving in the bar. A lot of what she'd cooked had been prepared and then eaten cold or just warmed up, but some dishes had been served fresh and hot. How on earth had she done it all?

Maggie prayed constantly that her grandmother would recover fully and come home to her family. It didn't matter if she couldn't do much; just having her there would be enough.

* * *

Maggie's thoughts returned to her work as they became busy serving up the main courses. Greg's party all ordered the beef, but a lot of other customers ordered the chicken casserole. Two ordered the cheese flan and salad with hot new potatoes. Then they were on to the desserts. Most of them were prepared earlier and just needed setting out nicely, either with fresh cream or ice cream. Greg's party, all of them men concerned with the world of motor racing, had either the lemon drizzle pudding or the two chocolate mousses with biscuits and whipped cream, done in a tall glass like a knickerbocker glory. The almond tart sat in the fridge looking sad and lonely until the last minute when four customers ordered it.

Carla returned to the kitchen laughing. 'I hope you've done

plenty of that chocolate one, because the men at that racing driver's table all want seconds.'

'Another eight?' Maggie looked at her in dismay. 'I think we might have four left – but there is some coffee and walnut cake that Fay made, if they will try that instead?'

Carla went off to inquire and came back grinning. 'They have agreed to that, Maggie. Four slices of coffee and walnut cake with ice cream *and* cream and four of your chocolate delights.'

'That's a relief,' Maggie said and breathed again. She looked at Fay and then they both started laughing at the same time. 'I've never known a whole table to ask for two desserts each before.'

'You shouldn't make them so delicious,' Fay said and pulled a face. 'I was hoping to get one of those when we'd finished.'

'Too late now,' Maggie returned with a grin. 'You can cut me a piece of your cake though, before that is all gone...'

Several minutes later, Maggie had just sat down with a cup of coffee and a slice of the delicious sponge cake when the kitchen door opened and Greg entered.

'That cake is delicious too,' he said. 'Your waitress, Carla, said it was all right to come through, Maggie. I just wanted to thank you for that wonderful meal you gave us. Two of my friends are staying over for a couple of weeks on business and they both intend to book for another meal here – but the others are flying back to the States on the same flight as me.'

'I'm pleased you all enjoyed it,' Maggie said. 'I thought sportsmen had to watch their diets?' Her eyes sparkled at him.

'We do but none of us are in training at the moment so that's why we ate like pigs – those desserts were to die for.' He chuckled. 'Not literally but wonderful.'

'We aim to please,' Fay quipped. 'We do private parties sometimes... or I do. Maggie will be too busy here now.'

'I'll pass the word on,' Greg promised. 'You should work in America – you'd get lots of private commissions there.'

'This is where we want to be based,' Maggie said firmly. 'At least for the foreseeable future.'

He nodded, his gaze narrowing. 'Well, I just wanted to thank you in person, Maggie – and you, Fay. I'll be away for a while, several weeks I imagine.' He lingered for a moment, as if wanting to say more, then, 'We'll talk when I get back, Maggie. I'll ring you… all right?'

'Yes, please do…'

He smiled at her, his eyes meeting hers for a moment. It seemed they were full of meaning, but she wasn't sure just what he was saying and then he walked out of the kitchen.

'That was short and sweet,' Fay remarked when the door had closed behind him. 'I thought he would ask you to go for a walk or have a drink with him or something…'

Maggie turned to look at her, her disappointment showing. 'I thought so too…'

'And you went to so much trouble this evening…'

'Just another service,' Maggie answered dismissively. 'It was good of him to give us his custom. He didn't have to… Besides, I suppose he has to look after his guests.'

'You hoped for more. I know you did,' Fay said. 'Freddie told me he thought Greg was keen on you.'

'How could he possibly know something like that? We've only met a couple of times,' Maggie said sharply. 'Yes, Greg was kind and helpful when I had the accident, but that doesn't mean anything.'

'He got the van done and brought it round,' Fay reminded her. 'We haven't had a bill for it yet.'

'No, I should have asked about that,' Maggie admitted. 'Well, whoever did it will send it when they want the money.'

'Unless he paid it himself?'

'He wouldn't... would he? I never thought to ask. I'm an idiot.'

'No, you're a clever chef and I love you. I'm just peeved because he didn't ask you out.'

'Don't be,' Maggie replied. 'Greg probably means to spend his life in America and that wouldn't suit me at all. It may be for the best if I don't see him...'

She admitted to herself that she was a little hurt, but it was her own fault for reading too much into Greg's decision to bring his friends to their restaurant that evening. Maggie knew that it could never work, even if she did like him more than she was ready to admit. His life would be spent travelling the world for his racing career, and hers was here in Mulberry Lane – or England anyway – and that meant any relationship was bound to fail. Better then, that it never really got started...

15

Freddie looked at Greta as they left for the beach that Sunday morning. It was warm, but there was a faint breeze, so it wouldn't be too hot. They both had towels and he carried a picnic basket containing the sandwiches, cakes and cans of drink he'd been out and bought that morning. The cans were icy cold and would keep the sandwiches cool in the bag for a while; he'd decided not to ask Greta's aunt for a picnic, because Greta didn't want her to know what she intended to do with her day off.

'Aunt Edith doesn't know that you helped me with the apple pie,' she'd told him when they met that morning. 'She was surprised how well I'd done it. She doesn't like me to get too friendly with the guests. She thinks it doesn't do...' Greta gave a little giggle. 'She thinks I'm going for a long walk on my own.'

'Well, what she doesn't know can't hurt her,' Freddie replied. He thought Greta should stand up to her aunt more. It was only reluctantly that she was allowed out on Sundays instead of having to clean and help in the kitchen at the boarding house. 'It isn't right that she treats you like that, Greta. This is the nineteen-sixties, not the nineteenth century. You should have far more freedom and time off than you do. You need at least one evening off every week, as well as a free day. It's only right that you should have some fun.'

'Yes, I know,' Greta agreed. 'If I wasn't such a coward, I'd run off and find a new life for myself, but I'm not trained for anything and I'm not sure I could earn enough even to live in lodgings.'

'You should start by asking for one evening off a week other than Sunday,' Freddie urged. 'As I suggested before, you could enrol at night school and learn something useful – typing and shorthand perhaps. Maybe a writing class too, if there is one. You could at least type your stories then and you might sell them to a magazine. Mum buys women's magazines – *Woman* and *Woman's Own* and *The People's Friend*; she likes the stories in them. She doesn't have time to read a book, but she reads magazines. Glossy fashion ones, too, but I think she gets them for Fay really. My twin likes her clothes and tries to look like the models. Mind you, she could easily be one – but don't ever tell her I said so.'

Greta looked at him shyly. 'Do you really think I could learn something like that at night school? I could do secretarial work then and write in my spare time.'

'Yes, why not?' Freddie replied, encouraging her. 'You never know unless you try, Greta. I love football. I like to play and to teach it to younger boys and girls. I'll never play in a big team like Manchester United, but I enjoy what I do. You should enjoy your work and your life. You're only young...' His eyes went over her. She looked much younger than Fay.

'I'm nearly nineteen,' Greta told him. 'I know I look younger, but I am nineteen in July.'

'That's next month.' Freddie was surprised. She was older than she looked, but she was thin and pale and her hair needed a proper cut instead of being clipped back all the time. Perhaps it was just her nervous manner and the puzzled little looks she gave him sometimes, as if unsure of herself and her place in the world, that made her seem younger. 'We'll go somewhere nice that day, Greta.'

'If my aunt will let me...'

'Don't be afraid of life, Greta. Learn to stand up for yourself – and if your aunt is unpleasant to you, tell her you are leaving. She may realise then that she can't treat you like a skivvy all the time.'

'You're really nice,' Greta smiled up at him. 'I wish I was brave like you, Freddie.'

'I am lucky to have a good family,' Freddie admitted. 'I've had all the advantages my parents could give me. That's why I want to help kids that may not be as lucky as I was...'

'Tell me more about it,' Greta said as they approached the beach and then gave a little gurgle of delight. 'We have all day to ourselves...'

* * *

It was a good day on the beach. They swam and splashed about in the sea, though it was still chilly in the water, and they sunbathed, eating their picnic before it spoiled and then buying ice creams, followed by a big bag of fish and chips, which they shared.

Greta's pale skin turned a little pink and Freddie rubbed his sun cream into her back and shoulders, letting her do the rest. His own skin already had a pale tan and he never burned, though he always applied the cream if he was sitting out in it long without a shirt.

When they'd had their fill of lazing on the beach, they walked along the promenade to the amusement centre and Freddie changed some silver into pennies so that they could play the slot machines. When that had disappeared, they went to a little café and ordered a pot of tea and some toasted teacakes with butter and jam.

'Strawberry or… I think it is pineapple?' Freddie said when the food arrived.

'Oh, I love pineapple jam,' Greta said. 'My aunt won't buy it; she says strawberry is cheaper and more people like it.'

'I like strawberry best, so we shan't fight over it,' Freddie laughed as her eyes lit up. He realised that this was probably his first real date with a girl. He'd always thought he'd do it in style, a meal at a fancy restaurant, dancing or the theatre, but it hadn't seemed that important when he'd asked Greta to the beach and she was happy with simple things.

As if reading his thoughts, Greta gave him a shy smile. 'I've had a wonderful time today, Freddie. I can't thank you enough for everything.'

'A few sandwiches and a bag of chips?' he teased. 'You should demand dinner at the Ritz at the very least – well, you can when you're famous and your stories are in all the magazines.'

'I'm going to ask for Monday evenings off,' Greta told him earnestly. 'I know I can have typing lessons on a Monday. My aunt won't be pleased, but I'm going to ask her – starting next week, not this…'

'You do that,' Freddie agreed and, then, seeing their friends, gave a little wave. 'Look, there's Guy and Muriel over there at that table. They've seen us… Guy is coming over…'

* * *

As Guy approached their table, he looked very serious. 'I've just heard,' he said without preamble. 'I'm sorry if it spoils your day, Freddie, but Jill died this afternoon. Yesterday they thought she might come to herself because she moved her lips as if asking for something, but then this afternoon she—' He shook his head. '—I can't believe it. She was so full of life... Muriel was in tears. I took her for a walk to get her out of the house and we ended up here...'

'That is terrible news,' Freddie said, shocked. 'I hoped Jill would pull through. My God, what did she take that did such harm to her?'

'The police say they've found a batch of tablets and they are contaminated with a poisonous substance. They are liaising with the Birmingham police and hoping for an arrest – and I hope they lock them up for life when they get them!'

'I agree,' Freddie said. 'How did Steve take the news?'

'He was devastated, because he blames himself for taking Jill to that pub. He went storming off. I think he knows where one of the men Jill was talking to is staying. My fear is that he will attack him if he gets him.'

Greta gave a sniff and tears ran down her cheeks. 'You saved her from drowning, Freddie, but she still died...'

He handed her his handkerchief. It had traces of sun oil on it, but she wiped her face and put it in her jacket pocket.

'I'll wash if for you,' she said in a low voice and he nodded.

'What about Jill's family – do they know what happened?' Freddie asked Guy and he shook his head.

'I don't think she had anyone much... no one who cared anyway. The hospital tried to contact someone from her records but got no answer.'

Greta was paler than ever as Guy shrugged and walked back to Muriel. 'She had no one to care for her...' she said tearfully. 'I suppose my aunt is better than being on my own.'

'Not necessarily,' Freddie cautioned, but he could see that she was reconsidering asking for time off. Their lovely day out had ended badly and now Greta had lost her new-found courage.

'Well, you've got friends who care about you,' Freddie said and she looked at him blankly.

'Have I?'

'I'm your friend now – and I'm sure Guy and the others would care if something happened to you...' Even as he spoke, Freddie knew that his words were empty. Guy had shown some sympathy for Jill, but he probably hardly knew Greta, except as someone to bring in his breakfast. 'I still think you should try to change your life, Greta.'

'You're nice, Freddie – but the others...' She shook her head. 'I don't think they would miss me. My dad would, I think, but he's always away since Mum died...'

'I'm sorry you lost your mum,' Freddie said and reached to touch her hand. 'I understand that hurts. It is bad enough just knowing that my mother is ill, but losing her...'

'It's the worst thing that can happen,' Greta said and sniffed into his handkerchief. 'I should be used to it, but sometimes I feel so lonely. Mum was always there to cheer us up and she did, even when she was ill...'

'My mum is like that,' Freddie agreed. 'Always laughing, talking, always busy and she always helps everyone. She doesn't deserve what happened to her.'

'What did happen exactly?' Greta asked and Freddie told her. That made her head go up and her eyes flashed. 'Oh, those bad men! How could they? All she wanted was to help someone who was hurt. I'd like to give them a good bashing with my broom.'

Freddie stared at her for a moment. Charged with passionate anger, Greta looked entirely different from the pale mouse she normally was. Her skin had caught the sun and was a light golden shade, except for a patch of red on the end of her nose, her eyes a brighter green than usual. She wasn't beautiful like his cousin, Maggie, but she had her own kind of charm. He realised that she'd been used and kept down by her aunt and it had made her lose her confidence, but her righteous anger had given him a glimpse of what she could be like given a chance.

He found that he was laughing inside, though trying not to show it. 'That's the way,' he said. 'You give them a bashing with your broom, Greta – and do the same to life. If you let folk walk over you, they will – but stand up for yourself and things will improve.'

'You make me feel so much better,' Greta told him. 'I've had a wonderful day out and I'm not going to let anything spoil it, even though I'm sad for Jill. I will go to night school and learn to type. I might find a better job then.'

'I am certain you could – and perhaps those short stories will sell one day, if you keep trying.'

'It might be my handwriting...' Greta admitted. 'I did send one to a newspaper once. I got a nice letter back. The man said they didn't print fiction stories but would look at things with local interest, but only if they were typewritten.'

'Ah, I see,' Freddie nodded. 'Your scrawl is untidy, Greta, but perhaps that is because you get carried away when you write. I couldn't read every word but what I could I liked.' He'd thought she wrote vividly when she'd given him her story and would have liked to read more.

She laughed then and once again he saw the girl she could be. 'I knew you were lying when you said it was good.'

'No, I wasn't,' he protested. 'I could read bits and pieces and I liked them – but you do need to improve your writing, unless you type instead.'

'I'll learn and then I'll buy a second-hand typewriter. I saw one for ten pounds in a shop in Truro...'

'Make sure it works,' Freddie said, 'or you could waste your money...' He was thoughtful for a moment, then, 'I believe my cousin Maggie has one for typing her menus. I'll ask her where she got hers.'

Greta gave him a shy look. 'Your family sound so glamorous and talented. I should like to meet them.'

'Well, perhaps you will,' Freddie said vaguely. He would normally have invited her to his home for a weekend, because his parents had always welcomed his friends, but with his mother ill, he knew he had to be more careful. 'When Mum is better, you can come and stay with us...' Freddie had a sudden thought. 'Mum runs a boarding house as well as the pub... well, Maggie does most of that now... I know they are always looking for more staff. It isn't the kind of job you need, Greta, but you could start by working there until you've got your qualifications. Mum and her manageress, Pearl, are nice to work for. You would have your proper hours off and a decent wage, as well as somewhere to live...'

Greta stared at him in disbelief. 'How do you know they would like me or want me to work for them? My aunt says I'm not much use. I burn simple food when I cook and she says I'm lazy when it comes to cleaning...'

'Are you?' Freddie teased. 'Is there fluff under the beds?'

'No! I always go underneath,' Greta said. 'Do you really think your mum would give me a job?'

'She would if I asked... or she would have when she remembered who I was... but I am sure Pearl would take you on, Greta. Do you want me to ask her for you?'

Greta hesitated, then, 'I'd like to stay here until you leave at the end of the summer, Freddie. I'd like to be friends... if you would?'

'You are a friend,' he told her with a smile. 'I think that is a sensible idea, Greta. You enrol in that night school and start learning to type. If you want to come to London when I go – I'll take you and introduce you to my family. Fay and Maggie are always busy. They could give you a few hours helping with the preparation if they wanted or with the washing-up, but I am sure Pearl will have a place for you. Besides, you won't need it long, because once you can type, I think your stories will sell.'

'That would be wonderful,' Greta sighed. 'I've written some about holidaymakers. I think I'll write about the lifeguards next.'

'If you have a rescue in your story, make sure to give it a happy ending,' Freddie said. 'I think the people who read those stories would like that...'

Greta nodded and looked serious again. 'You did such a good thing rescuing Jill. It was a wicked shame that she died.'

'Whatever happens in your life, Greta – even if you are very unhappy – don't take pills people offer you in bars or nightclubs. You should only take what the doctor prescribes or something from a chemist.'

Greta nodded her agreement. 'I'll remember – and I'll remember what happened to Jill. Besides, she must have been very unhappy. I'm not.' Her eyes shone as she looked at him. 'I've got a friend I can trust...'

'Yes, you can trust me,' Freddie agreed, 'and I am your friend, Greta.'

Freddie saw the warmth in her eyes and wondered. He liked Greta and wanted to help her, but he wasn't looking for a serious relationship. Not just yet anyway. Freddie knew that one day he would want a home of his own and a wife and children – but he had a lot to do first... not least doing a worthwhile job here in Hastings for the rest of the summer. The season would be in full swing in another month, when the schools broke up, and then they would need to be on their toes...

16

Maggie answered the phone one evening towards the end of June. The past few weeks had been hard, worrying about Peggy and Able while trying to keep everything going at the Pig & Whistle. It was past eleven when the shrill tones summoned her; she'd done a full service at the restaurant and was feeling tired, yawning as she picked up. 'Maggie here...'

'It's me,' her mother said. 'I'm sorry. I know it is late over there. I just wanted you to know that we're coming back next week.'

'Is Granny Peggy better?' Maggie asked, hope rising.

'The doctors say she is well enough to come home,' Janet confirmed. 'She still doesn't know Able, but she is becoming easier around him and smiling more when he talks to her. She told me today that he is a nice man and she likes him a lot. I left them laughing together just now.'

'Thank goodness for that! He must be relieved?'

'He has been wonderful, Maggie. So patient and kind and generous... but then, Able always has been. She was lucky she found him. My father was a brute at times. Oh, not violent, but quick to blame and harsh to her, too. I know she loves Able so much; she just needs to remember all the good times they've had together.'

'And the twins,' Maggie said. 'She will need to get to know them all over again.'

'Yes, that is another hurdle for her, but you know how strong she has always been. Able suggested they stay on for a bit longer to give her time, but she said no. She wants to get back home and face whatever she needs to...'

'It is strange she remembers you but not Able,' Maggie said. 'Have the doctors given any reason for that?'

'They just say the memory can play tricks, but I know she is afraid she won't remember and I think that's why she wants to come home, to see if a familiar situation will help her to get the missing years back.'

'But it is all different,' Maggie reminded. 'We've had all that work done – though the bar is more or less the same, though in a different place. Don't tell her, Mum. It was supposed to be a surprise. She thought I would change everything.'

'Just as well there's something she might remember,' Janet said. 'I'd better go, this phone call is expensive. I'll let you know times of arrival when it's settled.'

Maggie stared at the receiver as it went down with a little click. It was good news that Peggy was now deemed well enough to travel, but why did any of it have to happen in the first place?

She glanced at the clock. Fay had gone for a little walk but would be back soon to hear the good news. It was too late to ring Freddie now, but she would in the morning, Maureen too...

* * *

'I'm so glad they are coming home soon,' Maureen said when Maggie spoke to her on the phone. 'Ryan rang me about half-past ten last night and gave me the news. Janet told him first because she knew he was thinking about arranging a passage for him and Jon to go out there, even though she'd told him not to.'

'Is Jon with you again?'

'No. Ryan took some extended time off work. I think they've been going out most days. Jon hasn't been to his school lately. Ryan has been helping him with his lessons at home, but they've done a lot of sightseeing – museums and stuff...'

'Poor Jon... Couldn't Ryan think of anywhere better?'

'Apparently, he loved the V & A and they've been to others; also, places of interest like the Tower and art galleries, as well as somewhere that had lots of mechanical things. I think Jon just likes it when his father takes him places.'

'Yes, perhaps that is it,' Maggie agreed. 'I'm glad Granny Peggy is coming home but a bit nervous too. She may hate what we've done and if she doesn't remember telling us to go ahead...'

'Able will have told her all the details,' Maureen assured her. 'I shouldn't worry too much, Maggie. Peggy has never been one to make a lot of fuss unless it is something she considers unjust. I am sure she will simply get on with it.'

'Yes, I hope so,' Maggie replied. 'I wish her accident hadn't happened.'

'We all wish that,' Maureen said. 'If you need help this weekend, I can come on Saturday, because Gordon is taking Gordy to a cricket match in Sussex and they are staying overnight at a hotel. I didn't want to go, because it is something for them to enjoy together. I'd rather help you and Fay.'

'That would be lovely. We have a full service on Saturday night and there will be a lot of prep to do, so if you could come about five and help us set up?'

'I can come for as long as you like,' Maureen agreed. 'I miss working with Peggy and Rose. We used to gossip and laugh all the time when we ran the cake shop.'

'It's a bit like that for us too,' Maggie said. 'I like working with Fay and Granny Peggy. I know she talks about retiring and leaving it to us, but I'd rather she was here – I'm not sure she will still want to help...'

'She has been through a hell of a lot, during the war and after – the way Laurie treated her – and then, thinking Able was dead, but she managed then and if I know her, she will now.'

'I pray you're right,' Maggie swallowed hard. 'We'll see you on Saturday then... Oh, I should have asked, how are Gordon and Shirley? I know Gordy is fine, he came around yesterday to see us; brought back something Freddie had loaned him and stayed for coffee cake and apple pie.'

'The monkey!' Maureen laughed. 'I try not to have too many sweet things in the larder, because it is hard on Gordon if he can't eat them. Gordon seems better recently – and Shirley is fine but busy. I see her once a week if I'm lucky, but she does telephone often.'

'Her job is very demanding, Maggie said. 'Give her my love when you see her and tell her I'd love to see her when she has a chance.'

'Her free time is mostly in the evening,' Maureen said. 'Perhaps she could come on a Sunday. You don't work Sunday evening, do you?'

'No. One of us does Sunday lunch and that's it until Tuesday when it all starts again. We have to have some free time or we'd burn out.'

'Until Saturday then...'

Maureen put the phone down and Maggie turned as Fay entered carrying a large cookery book and a tray of coffee and biscuits.

'I've been reading this French cuisine book,' Fay told her. 'I wondered if we might try a traditional fish pie one evening? '

'You don't mean the sort that has fish heads in?' Fay nodded and Maggie shook her head. 'I doubt our customers would like that – you can do one that just has nice fish but not that one...'

'It gives it a lot of taste,' Fay objected. 'The French cook all sorts of things we wouldn't use and so do the Chinese...'

'They can do as they please,' Maggie retorted. 'I think we can be innovative, Fay, but some things are a step too far.'

'Maybe you're right,' Fay replied and put the book down before picking up an almond crumble biscuit and nibbling. 'Jace sent me another postcard. He will be back in London the week after next and he wants to come and see me, says he has something to ask me...' She glanced at the postcard in her hand. 'Oh, I just remembered, there is a letter for you in the rack. I think it is from America, because it is airmail, that thin blue envelope – but I don't know the writing...'

'A letter for me...' Maggie went quickly through to the hall, glancing at the writing and then placing it in her apron pocket.

'Who is it from?' Fay asked and Maggie shook her head.

'I don't know – probably James.'

'I'd open it immediately if Jace sent me a letter. He never does...'

'He is always sending you cards, though, or telephoning.' Maggie's brows arched teasingly, because hardly a day passed without a call from Jace, even though most were brief. 'Can't he live without you?'

'Daft! He's just being friendly, that's all.' Fay laughed. 'I expect he wants another party – or a friend does...'

'You haven't had any requests for catering, have you?' Maggie looked at her speculatively.

Fay shook her head. 'No. I was disappointed, because several people asked and Jace said he would pass on my number, but we've been so busy in the restaurant since we opened again that it would have been difficult to cater for a large party without more staff. I can't take on more staff unless I get more orders.' She bit her lip. 'It isn't working out quite as well as I'd hoped, Maggie. I've done some small dinner parties and a wedding – but it isn't enough really.'

'Don't be disappointed,' Maggie told her. 'I need you in the restaurant anyway. I'd find it difficult to employ someone I like working with if you left me, Fay.' She hesitated, then, 'I've been thinking – if the catering doesn't pick up in say the next year or so, we could open another restaurant instead...'

'How?' Fay looked at her. 'We don't have enough money for that, Maggie. It will take years of hard work and saving money before we could do that.'

'Not if we got someone to back us,' Maggie went on thoughtfully. 'The Pig & Whistle was always just the start. I think when we're better known, we might be able to either borrow from a bank or get investors... sleeping partners. We might get a place up the West End then and that could be really good...'

'And you call me a dreamer,' Fay exclaimed. 'We hardly make a fortune now, Maggie. Sometimes we do really well, but supposing we have some empty tables or an unexpected bill? I thought the catering would bring in more money – and Jace's party did earn us quite a bit, but I didn't get the requests afterwards that I'd hoped for.'

'It is early days yet,' Maggie said. 'People don't always want a service like yours, Fay – but when they do, they may remember.'

'They might,' Fay twirled her hair. 'Aren't you going to open your letter?'

'All right, if you insist...' Maggie slit the thin envelope and read the short message in silence, then, 'It is from Greg. He says he may be away longer than he expected but hopes I'm well and the restaurant is prospering and looks forward to seeing me when he returns.'

'Is that all – no protestations of undying love?' Fay made a face as Maggie shook her head. 'Not much of a romantic, is he?'

'I told you – we hardly know each other.'

'You were disappointed that Greg didn't ask you for a drink after that meal you cooked for his friends,' Fay said, looking at her sympathetically. 'Are you in love with him?'

Maggie shook her head. 'I don't know him well enough, Fay – but I was disappointed. I like him and I hope he likes me.'

'It was a bit odd the way he just went off like that.' Fay looked thoughtful. 'When he visited the kitchen, I felt sure he wanted to ask you if you'd go somewhere with him – but then he just went...' She hesitated, then, 'It is your first letter, isn't it?' Maggie nodded. 'Jace keeps in touch with me, even though I turned down his offer to go on the road with him...'

'Maybe he is hoping you will change your mind, Maggie suggested. 'He is obviously still interested or he wouldn't phone you as often as he does.'

'I didn't expect him to, but he rings most days, even if it is only a quick hello and goodbye. His cards don't say much, just, "I'm here," or something of the sort.' A faint blush touched her cheeks. 'Sometimes he just draws a heart and puts a U in the middle of it.'

'It sounds to me as if Jace may be carrying a torch for you. He must have been thinking of you ever since you met in France.' Maggie looked at her thoughtfully. 'What would you do if he asked you to marry him and go and live in America?'

'I don't know...' Fay stared at her.

'You must have thought about it?' Maggie persisted.

'I haven't thought about it because it won't happen and even if it did, I couldn't go. My life is here, Maggie. You know it is... all the plans we made for a chain of restaurants one day.'

'They have them in America too,' Maggie said with a smile. 'I know when we started our cooking course and talked about the future, I said we should neither of us think about getting married for years and years – but if you wanted to change your life, really wanted it, I wouldn't hold it against you, Fay.'

'Mum would never let me just go off with him, even if I wanted to.' Fay swallowed hard. 'I shall be so glad when they get back.'

'Me too,' Maggie said. 'I know my mum said Granny Peggy was getting better, but I can't wait to see her and hug her...'

17

'I'll need to take a few days off when my mother gets home,' Freddie told Guy as they were walking back from patrolling the beach together at the end of the day. 'I know it leaves you short-handed, especially after losing Jill...' His voice faltered, because, although he'd hardly known Jill, it still felt so awful to speak of the young woman who had died in such tragic circumstances.

'I'm sorry for what happened to Jill, but she would probably have dropped out before the end of the season,' Guy replied. 'There are always some recruits that find it too hard, but I hope you won't, Freddie. You have the makings of a good lifeguard. As a teacher, you will get long summer holidays and you could make extra money by coming back each year.'

'Thanks,' Freddie replied with a half-smile. 'I intend and hope to come back in a few days anyway and I'll let you know. I can't see that I'll be needed at home. My father will tell me what he wants me to do, and I'm pretty sure he will say I should return to you – but I have to see Mum myself, just to know she is all right.'

'Of course. I wouldn't expect anything else,' Guy confirmed. 'If she was my mother, I'd feel the same. From what you've told me, you are lucky to have her.'

'She is great,' Freddie agreed. 'In normal circumstances, I'd ask you to come and meet her, but she may not know me…'

'That will be hard,' Guy sympathised. 'I'd love to meet your family at the end of the season, Freddie. Hopefully, things will be back to normal by then.'

'My twin is a bit of a firecracker at times,' Freddie told him with a laugh. 'She can throw a tantrum for no apparent reason, but she's fine really – Mum and Dad are the best and my cousin, Maggie, is a good sport.' He nodded. 'I am lucky. We have good friends living nearby too. Mulberry Lane is a close community.'

'I never had that.' Guy sounded a little envious. 'I definitely will come up with you at the end of season, Freddie. I'm thinking of leaving the service then. I've decided I need something more stable for the future.'

'You are giving up being a lifeguard?'

'I'm thinking so, yes,' Guy replied. 'I've travelled a lot, done all kinds of jobs, like being a steward on a liner, waiting tables, but I want to get on, buy a house of my own, so I ought to do something more substantial with my life.'

'Like what?' Freddie stared at him. 'You wouldn't enjoy being in an office, Guy.'

'No – but I might enjoy doing what you intend, Freddie. I did pass the right exams and I could have gone to college then, but I took time off to see the world. Now I feel as if I want a more settled life. It would allow me to be a lifeguard in the summer holidays too.'

'I think teaching is a good solid job,' Freddie told him. 'I wanted to be a professional footballer, but it didn't work out and I decided teaching sports would suit me better.'

'I was never that good at football, but I can play cricket and swim. I could teach physical fitness too.'

'Yes. You are already trained for that – and it is a part of a sports master's job,' Freddie agreed. 'I think you should do it. I could bring my stuff about college back with me – let you read the various brochures.'

'Thanks, Freddie. I think you've helped me to make up my mind. I shall enrol into a college if I can get a place.'

'You'll have to apply soon,' Freddie told him. 'It might be too late for this year, though it is easier to get on the teaching course than some others. Teaching isn't for everyone.'

'You'll make a good teacher.'

'You already are,' Freddie replied with a grin. 'Your experience as a lifeguard is bound to help you get in – and didn't you tell Muriel that you can row?' Guy nodded. 'You've belonged to a rowing club before so you'll fit right in at Cambridge. I'm going to join if they will have me – but I'll have to learn how...'

* * *

Fay rang that evening. Freddie was out and Guy took the call for him. Their landlady was not best pleased.

'The phone is there for my business not for pleasure,' she reminded him with tight lips.

'It would be nice if you had a pay phone in the hall,' Guy said as he took the receiver for her. 'We could all use it then without disturbing you, Mrs Phipps.'

'Whatever next?' she said and went off shaking her head at the very idea.

'Hi,' he said into the receiver. 'This is Guy – I work with Freddie.'

'I'm Fay, Freddie's twin sister.'

'He has told me lots about you, all good. I'm afraid he is out at the moment. I'll tell him to ring you back.'

'Hello, Guy. Freddie has told me how well you've looked after him. He needn't ring unless he likes. I just wanted to make sure that he hasn't forgotten our parents are coming home this week-end. He will be here, won't he? I am relying on him...'

'Yes, Freddie is coming for a few days,' Guy replied. 'I'll tell him you rang.'

'Thanks.' Fay replaced the receiver at her end.

Freddie turned up with their fish and chips a few moments later and Guy gave him her message. 'Your twin sister rang. She wanted to make sure you would be home when your parents got back.

'She knew I would,' Freddie said. 'I told her when she rang to let me know they were returning – but she's always like that.' Freddie laughed. 'She can be bossy and mercurial, but she makes the most delicious coffee cake you've ever tasted. Fay and Maggie are both cordon bleu cooks and have diplomas to prove it.'

'Talented girls.' Guy nodded his approval. 'No wonder you don't much like the food we get here.'

'Oh, I can eat most things,' Freddie said. 'Greta tries her best, but her aunt frightens her and makes her nervous, so she makes mistakes.'

'Like burnt sausages and toast,' Guy grimaced and then munched his fish and chips in silence for a while, before saying abruptly. 'Muriel fancies you, you know...'

His sudden change of subject made Freddie choke on a chip. 'Don't be daft,' he said when he'd stopped coughing. 'She is older than me – more likely to fancy you, Guy.'

'No, it is definitely you,' Guy replied. 'I was dating a local girl until a few weeks back, but we split up when she got a job offer as a travel courier for a coach firm. I liked her, but it wasn't serious.'

Freddie nodded. 'I haven't been out with anyone I felt I'd like to marry yet,' he said reflectively. 'I'm not ready for marriage for a few years yet. I want to have fun and then find a good job before I think about marriage.'

'What if you fall in love? I was in love when I was out in Australia; I took a job there for a couple of years after I left the liner I'd worked on as a steward. She found someone else. It took me a while to get over it...' Guy shrugged. 'I would have asked her to marry me, but this rich bloke came along and swept her off her feet.'

'She probably wasn't what you thought her,' Freddie said. 'When I do marry, I want a nice, honest girl who will be happy with the simple life.'

'Like Greta you mean?' Guy said. 'She is another one that fancies you, Freddie. The way she looks at you... anyone would think you were a god...'

'You're pulling my leg,' Freddie told him. 'Greta is just a friend. I don't think of her that way. She is a nice girl but more like a sister.'

Behind them, in the gloom of late evening, Greta stood frozen like a statue. She had come out into the garden for a breath of air, where they'd gone to eat their fish and chips, and overheard them talking. Tears started in her eyes, but she knuckled them away as she turned and went back inside the kitchen.

* * *

Before he left for London that weekend, Freddie sought Greta out in the kitchen. She was washing up, her back towards him as he spoke her name, but she didn't turn her head.

'I just wanted to tell you that I'll be gone for a few days,' he said. 'You have enrolled in that course at the night school, haven't you?'

'You know I have. I told you.'

'I just wanted to make sure you were actually going.'

Greta gave a little sniff and then turned to face him. He noticed her eyes looked a bit red and thought her aunt had been scolding her again.

'Has she been on to you again?'

'It doesn't matter,' Greta replied and sniffed again. 'I'm going to classes whatever she says.'

'Good. I expect to hear what you've been doing when I get back.'

'Why? Why should you be interested in me?'

'Because we're friends – aren't we? Remember I'll always help you if you want me to, Greta.'

For a moment, Freddie thought she would burst into tears, but then she gave him a faint smile and nodded. 'Yes, thank you,' she said in a low voice. 'We are friends. I hope your mum is better, Freddie.'

'So do I,' he replied. 'I'm a bit nervous about what she will be like...'

'When she sees you, she is bound to remember you,' Greta said. 'Anyone would love you, Freddie, and your mum is bound to once she sees you again.'

'Thank you.' He smiled at her. 'You are a nice girl, Greta. I am sure Mum would like you and I'll take you to her when she is better. Remember, you don't have to stay here forever.'

'I know...' She suddenly darted at him and kissed his cheek. 'Take care of yourself, Freddie, and come back when you can.'

Freddie hid his surprise at the kiss and smiled. 'I shan't forget you, Greta. I don't forget my friends...'

She had turned back to the sink. As he left the kitchen, he

thought he heard a little sob. Freddie almost returned to offer to take her home with him now, but he couldn't do that to his family. They had enough to cope with at the moment. He would take Greta on a visit once his mother was herself again... pray God that she would be, because she meant so much to them all.

* * *

Freddie arrived back home early on the Saturday morning, having travelled overnight. Fay was waiting for him at the top of the stairs, sitting there with a mug of coffee and a book in her hand. She smiled when she saw him and left the cup on the top stair as she ran down to greet him with a hug.

'I'm so glad you're back,' she said. 'I couldn't sleep, Freddie. I am terrified Mum will be different—' Her voice broke. 'If she doesn't know us – what will we do?'

'Just be normal and love her,' Freddie said and held her as she wept into his shoulder. 'Don't cry, Fay. We have to be strong for her sake. If she sees that we're watching her or very upset, it will make things worse for her. I don't know how Dad has coped with it since it happened – and it ruined their lovely holiday. He'd planned so much for them and now... I doubt she'll ever want to go there again.'

'I think she only went because she didn't want to be here while the bar was being renovated. We pushed her into making the changes, Freddie, so it's our fault – mine and Maggie's. She thinks the same...'

Freddie shook his head. 'Mum shouldn't have got involved when that woman was injured, but she always would, because that is her. It is one of the reasons everyone loves her. I think once she is home her memory will come back.'

'I pray it does,' Fay said and looked at him. 'Are you hungry,

Freddie? I can cook you some breakfast or there is a fresh apple pie in the fridge.'

'Apple pie and cream with coffee,' Freddie said, smiling. 'I'd love some decent food, Fay. I ate a sandwich on the train, but it was nearly as bad as Greta's cooking... No, I shouldn't say that; it isn't her fault she can't cook. No one has shown her how. I think you and Maggie – or Mum – could do that if I brought her here.'

'Who is Greta?' Fay asked, looking curious. 'Oh, I think you mentioned her in one of your letters. Did you take her to the beach?'

He nodded and smiled, reminiscently. 'My landlady is her aunt and she treats her like a skivvy. I've encouraged Greta to learn to type. She wants to write stories – well, she does already, but her handwriting is awful. No one would buy them like that...'

'Is there anything this Greta can do?' Fay asked and Freddie laughed.

'I think she can make beds, stuff like that – but she is a nice girl and she just needs a chance. You would look after her if I brought her here, wouldn't you?'

'Yes, if you asked me to,' Fay said, her eyes quizzing him. 'Are you serious about her, Freddie?'

'Serious... no, not in that way,' Freddie replied. 'I like her. She is a friend and she needs help, Fay.'

'Another of your lame ducks,' Fay said, laughing at him. 'Freddie! The poor girl will fall helplessly in love with you and you won't know it...' He looked a bit guilty and she gave a shriek of mirth. 'She already is – poor Greta!'

'Guy says she fancies me but...' Freddie shook his head. 'I haven't said anything to make her think I'm in love with her. She knows we are just friends, of course, she does.'

Fay's laughter stilled. 'Poor Greta and I really mean that, Freddie. I know you aren't ready for love and marriage, but I doubt if she understands. Be careful, love. Don't break her heart – it hurts too much.'

'Has someone broken yours?' Freddie looked at her through narrowed eyes. 'Not Jace?'

'No, he hasn't broken my heart,' Fay told him. 'I think Maggie's heart is aching though. She won't admit it, but I believe she is hankering after that racing driver.'

'Greg?' Freddie stared at her. 'I teased her about him. I thought he fancied her when I saw them together.'

'Well, if he did, he just went off to America for several weeks without even taking her for a drink – and that's after she went to a lot of trouble for him and his friends when they came here.'

'I hope he doesn't really hurt Maggie,' Freddie said. 'I'd be very angry if he thought he could play fast and loose with her feelings.'

Fay stared at him. 'What would you do if someone broke my heart?'

'Knock his head off!' Freddie said and laughed. 'But as far as you're concerned, I'm more likely to be comforting your latest victim...'

'Some brother you are,' she retorted and made a face at him. 'You just watch it or I'll put salt in your apple pie instead of sugar next time.'

'Maggie wouldn't let you,' Freddie replied serenely. 'So who has broken your heart then, Fay? Do you want me to put him to the torture?'

'Not yet,' she said, a mischievous glint in her eyes. 'Just as long as I know you would.'

'I'd kill anyone who really hurt you,' Freddie said, his smile vanishing. 'Just as I'd like to thrash those devils that hurt Mum.'

'Oh, I wish you could, but no one knows for sure who did it – at least that is what the police told Dad. He gave them the film from his camera, but they say it doesn't give a clear picture. It shows some men near Mum as she lay on the ground, but that isn't evidence that they harmed her. If he'd had a cine-camera it might have been different, but he can't work those properly, because of his disability, so he just has the one he hangs round his neck.'

Freddie paused, then, 'I read in the papers that President Kennedy has forbidden segregation throughout the States now – so at least something good came out of that civil rights march that ended in a riot.'

'Oh, Freddie,' Fay said and her voice wobbled. 'I'm so frightened that Mum won't know us, won't love us ever again...'

'Mum will love us,' Freddie replied with conviction. 'It might take her a while to get to know us, but when she does, she will love us just the same as she always did.'

Freddie comforted Fay, knowing that he shared her doubts and fears. He couldn't wait for his parents to get home, but he wasn't sure how he would feel if his mother stared at him as if he were a stranger.

18

'They are here...' Maggie called later that afternoon as a taxi drew up outside the Pig & Whistle. 'Keep your chin up, Fay. Smile when she comes in, don't burst into tears.'

Fay nodded but didn't say anything. Freddie put his arm around her; she was trembling. He gave her a quick hug and then the kitchen door opened and his mother walked in, followed by his father and Janet. His mother was wearing a smart new coat-dress he'd never seen before and red shoes; apart from that, at first glance she looked just as she had when they had left on their holiday. Then he noticed a small scar on the left of her forehead and realised that her face was thinner; she had lost weight all over and, now that he'd had time to study her, he saw that she was tired. His heart wrenched and he wanted to throw his arms around her as he normally would, but something stopped him. They were all waiting for Peggy to speak.

She looked around her and nodded and then smiled at Able. 'Yes, I do remember this,' she said. 'It looks different, but it is my kitchen...' Her eyes went to Maggie and she seemed to start and looked at Janet and then back to Maggie. 'You are my granddaughter Maggie, all grown up... and...' Her gaze moved on to the twins and she hesitated. 'Fay and Freddie? Yes, of course you are. Able and Janet have told me about you. I'm sorry I can't quite remember...'

Fay gave an audible sob and Peggy's face reflected her hurt.

'I am so sorry. I don't mean to upset you...'

'Mum!' Fay cried and burst into tears, running quickly from the room, overcome by her emotion.

'I'm sorry, Mum,' Freddie said and stepped forward. He felt Fay's pain too, but his mother needed his love and protection. He moved closer and then reached out to clasp her hand. 'It was too much for Fay. She loves you so much and has been on edge since the accident...' He leaned forward and kissed Peggy on the cheek. 'We all love you and we're so glad you're back.' He raised his eyes to look into hers. 'As long as we've still got you, it doesn't matter that you don't remember. You will remember in time, Mum. I know you will.'

'Freddie...' Peggy's cheeks were suddenly wet with tears as she too released the pent-up emotion inside her. 'I am sorry. Sometimes, I see pictures of two small children. I hope they are you and Fay and that my memory is returning.'

'Do you remember anything about Dad and marrying him?' Freddie asked, looking at his father. He thought how strained his father appeared and knew that he'd been worried sick. It couldn't have been easy for him these past weeks when his beloved wife lay ill in hospital, not remembering him and their life together.

'Not really,' Peggy said, but then she smiled at Able. 'I do love him, though. I know that much. At first, I had no memory at all and I was scared of everything, but then, when Janet came, I began to remember more – and Able is so good to me. If I hadn't loved him before, I would now.'

'Great! You will love us too, Mum,' Freddie told her, grinning like a Cheshire cat. 'Maggie and Fay have cooked a lovely meal for you. Come upstairs. We'll eat there when you're ready.'

'Able has told me everything has been changed. May I have a look around – it seems a bit strange, not as I remembered.'

'We had the restaurant extended and moved the bar,' Maggie said. 'Will you come and see, Granny Peggy – if you're not too tired?'

'I've done nothing but rest in hospital and on the plane,' Peggy sighed. 'I'd like to see just what you've done, if I may?'

'Of course you can,' Maggie replied. 'You let Fay and I take over and run it all, but it's still as much yours as ours, Granny.'

'Thank you, Maggie.' Peggy took the hand Maggie offered.

'I'll show you the bar first.' She led the way into what had once been a private sitting room. 'I hope you like it...'

Peggy walked in and then just stood and stared. 'It's the same,' she said in a voice barely above a whisper. 'It looks smarter, as if it has had a clean-up – but it's just the way it was in the war.'

'We just moved the bar,' Maggie told her. 'The regulars still come – but the restaurant is much bigger and we're busy all the time.'

'It hasn't changed, it is just better.' Peggy's face was wet with tears. 'Thank you,' she whispered. 'May I see the rest now please?'

'You don't have to ask, Granny Peggy,' Maggie said. 'This is your home and you are still the landlady of the pub. Everyone asks about you all the time.'

'Has Alice been in lately? She wasn't quite well...' Peggy broke off. 'No, she died. We had a big funeral for her...'

'That was years ago, Mum,' Janet said. 'Maggie, is it all right if I put the kettle on?' She sighed tiredly. 'It was such a long journey, the train to the airport and then the plane. I really need a cup of tea and something to eat – and then I need to get home...'

'Ryan and Jon are at Maureen's house,' Maggie told her. 'He

thought it best if they didn't come here – too many of us might have been too much for your mother.'

'I won't stop then.' Janet bit her lip. She looked at Peggy. 'You will be all right if I go, Mum? I won't stay for the meal, Maggie. Maureen will give me a cup of tea.'

'You go, Janet,' Peggy said. 'Thank you for all you've done for me.'

'It wasn't much, Mum,' Janet said and went to kiss her. 'You will be all right now you're home?'

'Of course I shall. You get home to your husband and son.'

Janet looked at Maggie apologetically. 'We'll talk later, love. I may pop round tomorrow when I'm not so tired...'

'You look tired,' Maggie said. 'Go and get some rest if you can, Mum. We will look after Granny Peggy.'

'Go, Janet,' Peggy said and sounded like her old self. 'I told you. I am fine now. Show me the rest of it, Maggie, and then we'll eat this meal you and Fay have cooked.' She glanced at Able. 'Can you get Fay to come back please?'

'Sure I will, hon,' Able said and then glanced at his son. 'How are you, Freddie?'

'I'm fine, Dad. I'll fetch Fay if you like?'

'No, I'll do it. You stay with your mother and look after her...'

'Yes,' Peggy said and smiled at him. 'You can come with us, Freddie. I want to hear how you're getting on in this job of yours. Able told me you are training to be a lifeguard for the summer, before you go to that job in Cambridge?'

Freddie nodded, swallowing hard. It was so difficult to know what to say. She still looked like his mother, and his father had obviously told her things she needed to know about her children, but she sounded like a polite stranger.

'Where should I start?' Freddie linked his arm with hers. He felt a tremor and understood then how hard this was for her. He and Fay had been worried how they would feel if their mother could not remember them, but, suddenly, he felt her pain inside and it was like a giant hand squeezing his heart. 'I've made new friends, Mum. Guy is in charge of our training and there are several of us helping out for the summer. A girl called Greta works at the boarding house, but she doesn't much like it. I'd like to bring her for a visit at the end of the summer, if I may...'

'Why shouldn't you? This is your home...'

Freddie looked at her. She'd sounded just the way she always did then – and he realised that the mother he loved was still there. She hadn't changed but she was a little more vulnerable, a little unsure.

'I told Greta you would say that – and Guy wants to visit too.' He smiled at her. 'You see, I've told them all what a wonderful mum I have and all about my family.'

'Thank you,' Peggy said softly. 'I'm glad I've been a good mother to you, Freddie, and I'm sorry I don't remember it.'

'It doesn't matter, Mum,' Freddie told her. 'You're the best mum in the world and we all love you very much. Don't worry about us. It will all come back to you when you're ready.'

'I do hope so,' Peggy replied. 'I feel as if I've lost so much – all the happy years. Able said they were good years and I know he wouldn't lie to me.'

'Dad loves you so much,' Freddie told her. 'Fay loves you too but... she has always been a bit up and down. I don't know where she gets it from, Mum. Neither you nor Dad is that way – and I'm not.'

'Your father told me his mother was a bit like Fay,' Peggy stopped and frowned. 'I don't know where that came from.' She stared at Freddie, fear in her eyes for a moment. 'My head is whirling. Can we sit down?'

'Sit here, Granny,' Maggie took her other arm and she and

Freddie steered her to a seat in the restaurant. 'Do you have a headache?'

'No...' Peggy closed her eyes for a moment. 'I saw pictures flashing through my head. Fay... Fay was ill, I think. She was crying and screaming and I couldn't make her stop. I had to leave her somewhere... I don't remember, but I saw her face as a small girl then...'

'Fay had trouble with her ear when she was little,' Maggie said. 'You did have to leave her in hospital once and she screamed when you left. You were very upset when you came home. I remember Mum telling me. I wasn't much older than Fay at the time.'

Peggy nodded, her gaze travelling round the restaurant. 'It's all right. I just feel a bit odd when I get pictures of things I don't remember. This looks very nice, Maggie. I can see you have a lot more tables now – and in the extension, too...'

'We have indoor toilets for the guests now,' Maggie said. 'In the old days, they had to go out in the yard... do you remember that?'

Peggy smiled wistfully. 'I can remember the war years as clearly as if it were yesterday, Maggie. It just seems to cut off about the time I met Able – which is stupid, because they were the happiest years of my life.'

'Why do you say that, Granny?' Maggie asked and Peggy shrugged.

'I just know I like being with Able – and I remember quite clearly that I was unhappy with your grandfather, Maggie. I was very young when we married and I think our first years were fine, but then Laurie got bored. He wanted so much more – and he went off at the first opportunity. After that, our marriage just disintegrated. I know that I met Able and we fell in love, because he told me everything. He says I was reluctant at first, because he is younger than me – but then we were together and happy...'

Peggy turned her head as Able returned with Fay.

Fay rushed to her and threw her arms around her. 'I am so sorry, Mum,' she said and pressed her wet cheek against Peggy's. 'I love you so much and I want you to love me.'

'I do love you,' Peggy replied. 'I know you are my daughter, because Able and Janet told me lots of things and I know they wouldn't lie to me. I also know that I love you, but I can't remember everything yet...'

'Mum just remembered when you were in hospital as a little girl,' Freddie told her. 'Little things come back to her in flashes. You have to help her all you can, Fay. I shan't be here all the time, but you will. You must tell her what you did together – what we all did and that will help her remember.'

Fay turned her tear-laden eyes his way. 'I know. I didn't mean to be selfish and silly, Freddie. I promise I won't do it again.'

'Good.' His smile bathed her in affection. 'I knew you would understand. You have to look after Mum for both of us...'

'How long are you staying?' Peggy looked at him. 'You shouldn't be here really, should you?'

'I've got a few days off,' Freddie told her. 'Guy was good about it. I needed to come home and see you, Mum – and Dad...' He smiled at his father, who was watching them all anxiously. 'Now I know you're here with the people who love you, I'll be able to go back to Hastings until the end of the season – but then there's university in the autumn, unless I postpone for a year.'

'You won't do that, Freddie,' Able and Peggy spoke together.

'Neither of us would want that,' Able told him. 'You have a career in front of you and we want you all to get on with your lives. I am here to look after your mother and she has lots of friends here. She will be just fine now we're home.'

'Yes, I shall,' Peggy said. 'I think I can smell something cooking. Had we better go up before dinner spoils...?'

'Oh lord,' Maggie cried. 'I made shepherd's pie and it must be more than ready…' She dashed off towards the kitchen.

'Let's go upstairs,' Peggy said. 'I know the way – unless that has been changed?'

'No, it is all the same upstairs,' Fay told her. 'We thought about having your bedroom decorated, but Maggie said that might be too much, so we didn't.'

'Tom did it for me—' Peggy said and then stopped and looked at Able. 'When was that?'

'It hasn't been done since we returned to the Pig & Whistle,' he said. 'It is some years now, hon. You've been talking about getting it done for a while but couldn't decide what you wanted.'

Peggy smiled at him, reaching for his hand. 'Thank you, Able. I'm sorry I have to keep asking you everything.'

'Just as well I have a good memory,' he said and leaned in to kiss her cheek. 'Ask away, my love. I'll do my best to fill in the gaps.'

Peggy nodded. Freddie saw her throat swallow and a little nerve flick in her cheek. She was so brave, but this was an ordeal for her. People didn't realise how frightening it was not to know the people you loved. When she first saw Able and was told he was her husband, it must have been bewildering and terrifying not to know him. Because of his deep love for her, which she had instinctively recognised, she had accepted him and now relied on him – perhaps more than in the past.

Freddie's heart ached for her. He wanted to wrap her in his arms and protect her, but knew that it wasn't possible. She was still the independent lady she'd always been and though she needed a little help and a lot of understanding, she hadn't lost her courage. She would battle through this and – pray God – she would win out in the end. Amnesia was a complicated problem and the doctors couldn't fully understand why it affected people in different ways.

Freddie wasn't sure she would ever completely regain her memory, but she was clearly remembering bits and pieces.

Maggie rescued the meal from the oven and it was golden and crisp on the top with just a little bit of brown at the edges. 'I wouldn't like to serve it to the customers,' she admitted as she handed round the plates. 'It isn't up to your standard, Granny Peggy.'

'I am sure it will taste fine,' Peggy told her. 'In the war, I had to do all sorts of things to keep the meals coming... but I expect I've told you that before...'

'I like hearing it,' Maggie said. 'You gave us all your old recipe books when we started running the restaurant. I think you were clever to make things the way you did with the rationing and shortages. Thank goodness we don't have any of that now.'

'Able says you're making a success of the restaurant,' Peggy said. 'I think we should have a little toast to that.'

'I'll get some wine,' Able said. 'But I think we should toast the landlady of Mulberry Lane being home again.'

'I'll drink to that,' Maggie said and smiled. 'I made apple crumble and a pear upside down cake for afters with custard or cream.'

'Ah, now we know we're home,' Able said and brought out the wine. He handed it to Maggie. 'You can do the honours. Opening wine is not my best thing.'

'I'll do it,' Freddie said and took the bottle from Maggie. He pulled the cork with ease and then poured a little for his father to approve before filling their glasses. 'To Mum coming home – and to the success of us all...'

'Yes,' his father agreed. 'Success for us all...'

19

Peggy lay beside her sleeping husband, listening to the familiar sounds: the faint rumble of traffic and a rustle in the old timbers in the roof; the sounds of home. They had been away for several weeks. Peggy wasn't sure how long, but they'd left England at the beginning of May and it was now July. The time between had been mostly a haze of pain and bewilderment for Peggy as she lay in that hospital bed, not even knowing who she was for a time. She'd been frightened, but too ill to think of anything, and then, when Janet arrived, she'd known her, yet so much remained shrouded in mist. Able had told her they'd been on a holiday, visiting his cousins in Alabama when they got caught up in the big freedom march that was sweeping across the country. There had been a riot and some coloured folk, were attacked. Peggy had seen a woman fall and instinctively gone to her rescue, when she was herself attacked and knocked to the ground. She didn't remember any of it and she hadn't known her husband, but, gradually, she'd come to trust Able, believing him when he told her that it was 1961 and related stories of their happy life together.

Peggy felt truly at peace for the first time since waking to a world that puzzled her and filled her with apprehension. A world filled with strangers and faces she didn't know. It had been a shock when they'd told her Able was her husband and he'd told her about the twins. For her, the world seemed to have stopped during the war – she remembered Laurie leaving to work for some secret organisation up in Scotland, but after that it all became hazy. It had been a complete blank for a while, but Able had visited her every day and sat with her quietly for so many hours that she'd lost her feeling of nervousness and looked forward to him coming.

Peggy had seen the hurt in his eyes when she didn't know him and that struck her to the heart. He was a good man. She'd sensed that almost immediately and gradually she'd accepted all that he told her, knowing that it was the truth even though she couldn't remember. He'd sat and told Peggy about the twins and Janet, her daughter Maggie, and her younger son Jon, and also about Peggy's eldest son, Pip, and his family.

'We don't see Pip very often, just when we visit for holidays,' Able had explained. 'He is married to Sheila and they have a son called Chris and a daughter—'

'Pip is just a boy...' Peggy had shaken her head. 'How can he have two children?'

'He's grown up now, Peggy.' Able had held her hand as she struggled to accept that the years had moved on. 'It is 1961 now, hon.'

'That means I'm almost sixty...' Peggy had looked at her hands and then touched her face. 'I can't remember those years...' Tears had trickled down her cheeks. 'I've lost all that precious time...'

'It will come back,' he'd said softly, holding her hand. 'I will tell you everything, all the little details of our lives – and in the end you will know it all, so even if your memory doesn't get completely better, you'll know how good it was.'

'Yes, tell me it all, as much as you can remember.' Peggy had looked at him anxiously. 'I want to be as we were, Able. I want to be that woman again – to be happy. I'm not happy where I am...'

'I know,' he'd murmured softly and kissed her. 'It wasn't easy for you back then. You went through a lot, my love. I wasn't there for you until after the war. I didn't know you'd had the twins. I came looking for you once, but I was told Laurie was back, so I didn't interfere – but then, when the war was finally over, I came back and you needed me and I loved you so much.'

'I feel that,' Peggy had told him. 'I feel your love, Able – but I need to know so much more. Please, tell me what happened when you came back to me... tell me how we met and fell in love...'

'I came into your pub for a drink with my general and you offered us apple pie,' he'd said and laughed softly. 'It was the best I'd ever tasted and I came back for more – but what I really returned for was that smile of yours, hon. It lit up the room for me and pretty soon it lit up my world. Without you, the world was a dark place...'

Peggy's hand had moved in his, her fingers entwining with his strong ones. 'You must have been wounded badly in the war...'

'I lost an arm up to the elbow and it was hell for a while, but I got through because I thought of you, Peggy. I hoped you would leave Laurie and come to me – but then, after some time of unhappiness for you, he died. We married and were happy together – and we went down to my cottage in Devon and then we opened a café. It was a success but very hard work and, in the end, you felt you would rather be in London... and it was easier for Fay's ice skating.'

'Fay is our daughter... Fay and Freddie, you said?' Peggy had nodded as he'd confirmed it. She'd looked at him then, her eyes clouding with emotion. 'Why can't I remember them? What happened to me to make me forget? They say I had an accident...'

'Not exactly. There was a march for equal rights; I think they called themselves the Freedom Riders. Some people objected to them and there was fighting, jostling in the crowd. A woman was attacked and hurt – you went to her aid and they turned on you, Peggy. I came to you as soon as I saw, but you were unconscious by then. I think one of them kicked you in the head, but I didn't see it all...'

'So it was my own fault...' Peggy's face had creased with regret. 'I'm sorry. I've ruined our lives...'

'Don't be foolish, my love. Those youths or men, whatever they were, are responsible for your illness – but never you. It was something you would always do, hon. You've always cared about others – and we all love you for it.' He'd held her hand tighter. 'We'll get through this, Peggy. I promise.'

* * *

Lying in her own bed, tears on her cheeks, Peggy knew that Able had brought her through it. Having Janet there had helped, because she still looked very much as she had when she had married her first husband, Mike, though older. Yet it was Able's kindness and patience, telling her about their lives, struggling to remember little details, like the time she took Fay ice skating and was told she could be a star if she practised enough, and the way Freddie had given up his chance with Manchester United's young players team so that another lad could have the place. Those were the things she treasured and Able had given them back to her.

It worried Peggy that she might never remember those twenty-odd years she had lost – so much love and laughter and sadness too. Able was telling her as much as he could, but there were things he wouldn't know... perhaps Maureen could help with some of that... and he'd mentioned another friend called Rose. Peggy couldn't remember Rose coming to the Lane and Able didn't know the details either.

'You were good to her then and she loves you. For some years, you all worked together in the little cake shop – Fay has her kitchen and office there now.'

So many things to remember, such a big chunk of her life missing. For a while, the despair had overwhelmed her in the hospital. Perhaps if she'd died then... but, no, she had a family who loved her, people who needed her. It was the thought of those who needed her that had made her fight. Janet had told her about Jon, the way he'd stolen stuff and then run away from home when Ryan had punished him.

'He needs you, Mum,' Janet had said. 'I try to make up to him for all he's suffered, but Ryan... feels guilty. It has been difficult since Jon was knocked down and hurt so badly. You were the one he clung to when he more or less rejected us. I've won him back some of the way, but he still feels happiest when he is with you.'

That had brought tears to Peggy's eyes. She wanted to be there for her young grandson. Jon was a mixed-up little boy by all accounts, but Able said all he needed was love and a firm hand to guide him.

Peggy smiled in the darkness as she recalled the look in her husband's eyes when he'd spoken of Jon. 'His anger and his defiance are just bravado,' Able had told her. 'When you show him how to cut out silhouettes or let him help you make gingerbread men, he is as happy as a sandboy.'

She had a big family and all of them were talented, busy and happy, except for Jon. Peggy wasn't sure why he was such a lost little boy, but from what both Janet and Able had told her, Jon seemed insecure and frightened. She'd wanted to reach out to him and it was one of the reasons she'd told Able she needed to get home.

'The doctors think you should continue the treatment they've started,' Able had told her, but Peggy had known what she wanted.

'I have to get home,' she'd insisted. 'I shan't remember anything here in this hospital, Able. Besides, I'm needed at home – aren't I?'

'Of course you are,' he'd told her. 'We all need and love you, hon.'

Most of her family were grown up, or nearly, but Jon was clearly in need of his granny's love and care. Peggy had felt drawn to the child, even though she couldn't recall his face. She knew that Pip and his family were fine. Her eldest son had telephoned a couple of times, telling her he loved her and would see her when she got home – but he didn't need her. His family were thriving. Jon was the one that needed her.

Peggy had hoped he would be waiting for her with the others when she got back, but perhaps Janet would bring him for a visit in the morning. On that thought, Peggy drifted into a peaceful sleep.

* * *

The next morning, Fay brought her tea and toasted muffins in bed and sat next to her, pinching bits of the muffin as Peggy drank her tea. Peggy thought it had happened before but still had no memory. Yet it felt right, as if this was what they did, and gave her a safe, warm feeling inside.

'Ryan telephoned a few minutes ago,' Fay told her. 'He wants to bring Jon to see you later this morning. He says Jon keeps on asking for his granny. Janet is staying in bed a bit longer; she says she is exhausted.'

'I expect she is,' Peggy agreed. 'She and Able shared the days and nights talking to me. No doubt she wanted to be home but felt she needed to be with me. I think she has her own troubles...'

'Oh, you know Janet,' Fay said, shrugging. 'Always up and down. Anyway, Ryan says that Jon insists he wants to see his granny, so you'll need to get up after breakfast. We thought you'd like a nice rest in bed, but Able said you'd hate that?'

'He's right,' Peggy replied and touched her hand. 'This is nice, Fay. It feels like we've done it before.'

'We have, mostly on Sundays,' Fay told her. 'It was the only morning you could have a little extra time in bed. You've always got up weekdays...'

'I had a busy pub to run and Laurie wasn't much help...' Peggy caught herself up. 'That was years ago. Surely, I don't have as much to do now that you and Maggie run things?'

'We still need you, Mum,' Fay told her. 'You do all kinds of things for us – you keep the books and the bills straight for one thing and you still help in the kitchen in the mornings. Sometimes you go to the boarding house and talk to your manageress, Pearl, make sure all is well there... it is just two doors away.'

'Yes, Able told me about it,' Peggy said. 'It is a good business, but I may sell the lease and the goodwill...'

'Sell the lease?' Fay stared at her. 'Why? You always say it makes money...'

'Yes, but I think I'd like to spend more time with Able,' Peggy said. 'Our holiday was ruined, but we might go down to the sea somewhere this summer. It might be a good way to really know each other again.'

'We thought you would want things to be as they were...' Fay looked at her uncertainly.

'Perhaps I will in time,' Peggy said. 'I'm still trying to find my way, love. It is early days yet.'

'Yes, I know – but it seems ages,' Fay burst out, her eyes filling with tears. 'We thought you might die for several days and then you were so ill – and I miss you...' She caught back a sob. 'I miss our little jokes and the things only we do...'

'I know you do, darling,' Peggy replied softly. 'I am sorry. I wish so much it hadn't happened. I shouldn't have done what I did...'

'It's like the time when you brought that girl here and she attacked you,' Fay said and smiled mistily. 'Gillian or whatever her name was – she stole from us and lied to us even about her name.'

'Did she?' Peggy frowned. 'Able didn't mention her. Why did I bring her here if she was a thief?'

'Because she was ill and you felt sorry for her,' Fay pouted. 'She upset everyone, even Dad. She put salt in our cake and Dad's apple pie...'

'She must have been a difficult girl then,' Peggy smiled ruefully. 'I shall have to learn to be more sensible, shan't I?'

'Mum! You are sensible. You keep us all right – and the poor girl did need help,' Fay admitted and ate a piece of muffin. 'Maureen is coming to see you at eleven. She wanted to see you yesterday, but Shirley needed her – that's her stepdaughter, and she is a doctor.'

'I know Shirley...' Peggy frowned. 'Little petulant Shirley all grown up and a doctor.' She shook her head. 'So much has happened...'

'Well, I'd better go,' Fay said, 'or you will never get up.' She kissed her mother's cheek. 'I love you, Mum, even if you don't get your memory back.'

'Thank you, darling. I love you, too.'

Fay went away and Peggy got out of bed. She wanted to have a quick bath before Jon and Ryan arrived.

* * *

Fay squeezed her eyes tightly together to stop the tears coming after she left her mother's room. It was true, she did adore her mother and would go on loving her whatever happened, but it just wasn't the same. All the shared memories and the little jokes they'd had were gone; all her mother knew of her was what Fay's father had told her and it wasn't enough. It was heartbreaking to see her mother struggling to find the right words. She wanted to love Fay, but there was something missing. Fay didn't blame her mother, but she railed at fate for stealing the comfort and assurance that had been the backbone of Peggy Ronoscki's life.

It wasn't fair and it wasn't right. Fay felt angry and frightened and upset, but she wouldn't give way to her tears again, because she'd promised Freddie and she always kept her word to him.

When she reached the bottom of the stairs, the telephone shrilled and she answered it, pleased when she heard Jace's voice on the other end.

'Fay, I'll be in London later today – could we meet or are you working?'

'I'd love to meet you – where?' Fay said.

'I'll pick you up in my car about five and we'll drive out somewhere nice – have a drink and something to eat.'

'Yes, thanks,' she said, 'and thank you for asking.'

'You know I think about you all the time,' he said and rang off.

Fay smiled. It was exactly what she needed. To get away for a while, forget everything that was hurting her so badly, forget that puzzled look in her mother's eyes when she looked at her.

20

'Ryan – Jon...' Peggy looked at the man and the young lad as they entered the big warm kitchen. Able had whispered to her that they were coming and she smiled and opened her arms to the child. He came to her slowly, uncertainly, looking up at her. 'How are you feeling, my love?' she asked.

'I'm all right, Granny,' Jon replied, his eyes wide and wistful. 'Dad says you've been very ill. He says you can't remember things...'

'I couldn't remember anything for a while,' she admitted. 'I am getting better and I remember that I love you very much, Jon.'

He rushed to her, hugging her about her waist and she held him close, bending to kiss the top of his head and meeting Ryan's hesitant gaze. He said, 'We've been worried about you. We would have flown out, but Janet thought it might be too much for you.'

'It might have been at the start,' Peggy agreed. 'I did feel very strange at first, but Able helped me.' Her husband came forward and smiled at Jon. 'We bought you a present, didn't we?'

'Yes, we did,' Able said. 'We got you a big aeroplane kit that you can make and also a racing car.' He handed Jon two brightly coloured boxes, one with a picture of a large plane on the side and the other a model car. 'Oh, and some American candy...' He produced a box of sweets from behind his back.

'Thanks, Grandad,' Jon said and hugged him. 'I like building models. Dad helps me. We got a Lego set the other day and we made a digger and a crane.'

'That's wonderful,' Able said. 'I shall look forward to seeing those when we visit.'

Jon turned to look at Peggy, who was inviting his father to sit down and have a cup of tea. 'Can I have my biscuits, Granny?' he asked.

'Of course you can,' Peggy replied and went into the pantry, coming back with a fancy tin. She placed it on the table. 'Are they right?

'Yes, thank you,' Jon said. 'They are my favourite... ginger snaps.'

'Yes, I know.' She smiled at him and poured tea into three cups. 'You'll want a glass of orange juice, Jon.'

Able was looking at her. Peggy saw the odd expression in his eyes. 'What did I say?'

'Ginger snaps are Jon's favourites,' Able murmured. 'I didn't know that, hon.'

'But...' Peggy turned away quickly, tears springing to her eyes. She'd known they were her grandson's favourite and if Able hadn't told her – what did that mean? Nothing else had suddenly come back to her and yet she'd known...

'I'm sorry Janet didn't feel up to coming,' Ryan said into the silence. 'She was just so tired, I told her to stay in bed. She may pop in later today, if she feels up to it – but we'll have you all over to lunch next weekend, if you'd like to come...?'

'Lovely. Janet must do as she feels able,' Peggy told him. 'She has spent the past few weeks at my bedside. I think she needs a little rest to get over it – it was hard for her when I was ill.'

'Are you better now, Granny?' Jon asked. 'Can I come and stay with you please?'

'Soon,' his father told him. 'Granny needs to rest a little longer and then you can come. Perhaps at the end of July or August, when there is no school... you've had some time off. You have to go back now.'

Jon nodded. He looked disappointed but accepting.

Peggy smiled. 'We'll do some nice things in the summer, Jon. Perhaps we'll go to the seaside if your father will let us take you?' She glanced at Ryan, who nodded his agreement.

'We'll take a cottage somewhere and everyone can spend some time with us,' Able suggested. 'You'd like that, wouldn't you, Jon? We can play cricket on the beach or football...'

'Yes, I should like that,' Jon agreed. He looked at Peggy uncertainly and she smiled but sensed the reserve in him. Jon understood that she wasn't the same and that nearly broke her heart. She wanted to enjoy his love and trust but knew that might never return if she could not share the memories they'd made together. Jon had clung to his granny, so Able had told her, but now he was a little wary despite the hug he'd given her. How she longed to be herself again. Would it ever happen or would she always have this feeling of being slightly removed, despite all the love that was being shown her?

* * *

'Peggy...' Maureen came straight to her when she arrived, just after Jon and Ryan had left, and hugged her. 'You look thinner, dearest. We've all been so worried about you. How are you?'

'I'm all right now I'm home,' Peggy told her, hesitating as if unsure how to go on. 'I thought you would look different. I know this is 1961, Maureen. My memory is stuck at the beginning of the war, but I remember you – as you were when you worked in your father's grocery shop. You've put on a little weight, but otherwise you haven't changed much – oh, I think your hair is different, but it suits you.'

'That is nice to know,' Maureen said and laughed. 'You always knew how to make me feel better, Peggy. I know I've changed, we all have, but Gordon says I am still beautiful to him, so that's all that matters. Now, how do you really feel? You can tell me.'

'Strange, a little disorientated – and scared,' Peggy confessed. 'I'm afraid I'll never remember the people I should properly – I didn't even know my grandson or the twins, Maureen. I know how much that must hurt them... it hurts me, too.'

'Yes, of course it does,' Maureen said. 'I wasn't sure how you would be, Peggy, but you're just the same, always thinking and worrying about others.' She smiled and moved closer. 'How about a hug?'

'Yes, please,' Peggy laughed a little shakily. 'No one seems to know how to behave with me. They are all acting as if they're treading on eggshells. Even Jon was on his best behaviour. He kept looking at me as if he didn't know me – and, of course, he knew that I couldn't remember him. Ryan didn't stay long. He said they needed to get home. Jon looked as if he wanted to stay and I wanted to keep him with me – but how can I when I don't remember anything about him, other than the things Able has told me?'

Maureen hugged her tight and Peggy responded. They were both tearful when they released each other. 'I don't know what to say other than it will probably come back. At least that is what Shirley thinks – you've been told about her?'

'She is Gordon Hart's daughter now and a doctor... you married him, Gordon, didn't you?' Peggy nodded. 'I'm sorry I've forgotten so much of our history, Maureen. I know we are best friends and I feel that... but...' She sighed. 'Able has filled in as many blanks as he could, but there are things that I sense but can't remember and he doesn't know.'

'It must be so frustrating,' Maureen said. 'To lose a large chunk of your life just like that... and why the best years? You were always so happy with Able.'

'Yes, I sense that,' Peggy agreed. 'At first, I was so disorientated and afraid, even of him. He was my husband and yet he was a stranger...' Peggy closed her eyes as if the memory of that first realisation was too hard to bear. Then she opened them again and smiled. 'He was so patient and loving and kind, Maureen. I think I fell in love with him all over again.' She sighed softly. 'That could only happen if we'd had a good marriage. If we'd been unhappy, we would never have reached out to each other the way we did.'

'I'm glad you feel you can trust him,' Maureen said. 'It must have been so hard for him when you didn't know him – some marriages would not have survived that.'

'I know. I am very lucky. My family are all doing their best to be kind and understanding...' Peggy allowed a note of frustration into her voice. 'I just want to be normal and useful. I feel as if I'm a helpless invalid at the moment...'

'Have you started to help with the cooking yet?' Peggy shook her head. 'Then you should, love. It has been your life and I think it is the way back for you. You might never recover all your memories, Peggy, but perhaps enough will return once you slip into your old life.'

'You *are* a good friend,' Peggy told her with a little laugh. 'Can you explain that to my family please? They keep telling me to rest and that there is no need for me to do anything.'

'You should do whatever you feel up to doing,' Maureen said. 'Treating you with cotton wool gloves will not help you be you – not the Peggy I know.'

'Thank you,' Peggy replied. 'I feel much better already. Shall we have coffee and cake or would you rather have a cup of tea?'

'I drink tea all the time at home,' Maureen confirmed. 'Your Able's coffee is the best, Peggy. I always enjoy a cup of coffee here – and I'd love a piece of cake. Shall we see what Fay has made for us?' She went into the large pantry and brought out the tin that was kept for home use. 'This is where she puts our cake, Peggy. I saw a wonderful concoction on the shelf, but I am sure that is for the restaurant, unless she has a private party to cater for?'

'I think it is something special. I saw it earlier when I gave Jon some of his favourite ginger snaps. He was always partial to those and Maggie makes them the same...' Peggy stopped and stared at Maureen in wonder. 'I remembered,' she said. 'I remembered he liked those biscuits. No one told me...' Her hand shook as she paused in the act of filling the kettle. 'Do you think my memory is coming back?'

'Yes, I do.' Maureen looked pleased. 'Shirley said some people get it all back in a whoosh and for others it just comes in little dribs and drabs...'

'Dribs and drabs...' Peggy burst into laughter just as Fay entered the kitchen. She looked at them in surprise. 'I remembered something,' she explained. 'We think my memory is coming back...'

'I hope so, Mum,' Fay said and ran to hug her. 'Why are you eating those biscuits? I made you a lovely fresh cream sponge specially...' She went into the pantry and brought out the sponge she had filled with whipped cream and laced with lemon drizzle icing. 'I know you love this – both of you do...'

'We thought it was for the restaurant,' Peggy said and smiled.

'Thank you, Fay. I do love lemon drizzle cake but filled with cream, well, that is a real treat. Isn't it, Maureen?'

'The best,' Maureen replied. 'Thank you, Fay, we shall enjoy that... but are we in your way?'

'No, we're using my kitchen to do the prep for this evening,' Fay told her. 'You have another hour before we need to start the lunches. We'll do a simple lunch – shepherd's pie, or quiche, or a ham salad today. That's all most people want in the middle of the day – and quite a few just want apple pie. Unless we do a hamburger with onions; we serve those some days, but it makes the kitchen smell so much...'

'Would you like me to make the apple pies?' Peggy asked as she cut the sponge cake and served Maureen and herself. 'Want some of this, Fay?'

'Not at the moment, and yes please,' Fay said. 'I mean, if you want, you can cook the apple pies, and I'll have a slice of cake later – if there is any left. Once Dad sees that he will be after it. You know what he is like for cream cakes!'

'Who is taking my name in vain?' Able asked, entering as if on cue. He was smiling at them. 'Is that for me?' He looked meaningfully at the cake.

'Not all of it,' Peggy replied. 'You'll get fat – except that you never do, do you?'

'No. I can eat all I want and I don't change by more than a couple of pounds either way.' He nodded at her. 'This looks good, Fay – almost as good as the apple pies your mum makes.'

'Nothing is as good as them in your eyes,' Fay said with a sniff, pretending to be put out, but then she laughed. 'It is so good to have you both home.'

'We're glad to be home,' Able told her. 'Aren't you going to have any cake, Fay – or do I have to eat all this?'

'I suppose I can take five minutes and leave Maggie slaving

over the brandy and chocolate mousse for tonight.' Fay giggled and sat down at the kitchen table. 'This is what we used to do all the time...' She smiled happily at them. 'It's lovely having you both here and Maureen too. Freddie will enjoy this cake; it's lovely, even though I say so myself...'

'Freddie's favourite is coffee cake, I think,' Peggy said and looked at Able. 'Did you tell me that?'

'I might have done, but I definitely didn't tell you about Jon's biscuits.' Able smiled at her. 'You look happy, hon. It's being home with friends. I'll leave you two to chat...'

He walked away, munching his cake and Fay followed, linking her arm into his.

Peggy smiled at Maureen. 'Those two...' she said and got up to pour more coffee. 'She has always been her father's girl...'

'Just the way Freddie is your boy,' Maureen replied. 'You know how it is, a father always makes more fuss of his daughter and mothers adore their sons.'

'Yes, Freddie is a lovely lad. I thought Pip might come up and see me...' Peggy said. 'He phoned me last night, but that isn't the same. I know he is busy but—'

'He'll come,' Maureen told her. 'Have you seen Tom and Rose yet?'

'No, not yet. I remember Tom as an enterprising young man – but I can't remember Rose yet...'

'It's going to take time,' Maureen told her. 'The best thing is not to try too hard or worry too much, Peggy. Let it just come back naturally and I'm sure you'll soon feel more comfortable.'

'Yes, I'm sure I shall. I already do and that's because I have such good friends and a lovely family,' Peggy said and a little shiver went through her. 'If Able hadn't been there for me I don't know what I'd have done...'

'Well, he was and he always will be,' Maureen reassured. 'So just relax and be happy.'

21

'You look beautiful,' Jace said when he called for Fay that evening. He was driving a Jaguar car, dark green and very sleek, and it smelled deliciously of new leather. Jace was wearing a dark polo-necked sweater under a black leather jacket and looked every inch the music star he was, his dark brown hair slicked back to keep down the natural waves. He kissed her cheek and handed her a box of special chocolates. 'Hope you like these; they are Belgian and delicious.'

'Thank you, they look lovely,' Fay said and smiled, but didn't return the kiss. She wasn't yet sure how she felt about him, because they never had time to be together. 'Have you had a good tour?'

'Yeah, it went well,' Jace said. 'I hope we don't need to do another for a while, though. I'm looking forward to being in one place for a while – recording and the theatre booking. I might actually get to see more of you.'

'That would be nice...' She felt a bit shy.

He nodded thoughtfully. 'How are things with your business – are you doing as well with your catering as you'd hoped?'

'No, not really,' Fay admitted. She'd tied her fair hair back in a ponytail and was wearing a pale blue shift dress, a white cotton jacket and white leather shoes with dangerously high stiletto heels. 'I've had some decent events to cater for but not enough. The restaurant is doing much better, though, so we're all right.'

'What do you want to do this evening?' Jace asked as he started the car and glided away from the kerb. 'Go for a meal or to the theatre?'

'I thought it might be nice to just go for a walk in the park or something,' Fay replied. 'You see enough of theatres, Jace. We might get something to eat later – or just have a drink.'

'It is a lovely evening; we could go by the river, find somewhere to eat there,' Jace agreed. 'I like the early summer best, when everything is still new and fresh. I like autumn too, but not winter. How about you...?'

'I agree, spring into early summer and autumn. I don't like it too hot unless I can lie on a beach or by the river...' She smiled at him. 'It was nice by the river that day in France.'

'Yes, it was. I've often regretted that I had to leave so soon after we met, Fay.'

She turned her head to smile at him. 'I agree; it would have been nice to spend more time together. I know we've kept in touch – well, more since you came over here for your tour – but you must be pleased at the way things have turned out, Jace? Your records are always in the top ten and you've done several tours this past year, haven't you?'

He was thoughtful for a moment. 'I've been lucky, made a lot of money, and I'd be lying if I said that didn't matter – but it isn't everything, Fay. When I'm on tour, I don't have time to make new friends – oh, the guys I work with are great, but...' He looked at her, suddenly intent. 'You know what I mean, Fay. It's you I miss... I want to get to know you better.'

'I'd like that too, but I don't see how...' Her eyes met his and she felt a little tingle at the back of her neck. 'You'll be returning to America in a few weeks, won't you?'

'I have a bit longer here. Remember, I told you, we have a show at the London Palladium. I've got those tickets I promised you,' Jace told her, 'but I've decided not to go straight back when the show ends. I wondered if we might spend some time together – go to the sea for a holiday?'

Fay was silent for a few moments, uncertain how to reply – unsure of what he meant. Was he asking just as a friend or something more?

He was slowing the car, drawing to a halt at the side of the road, though they hadn't yet reached the river. He switched off the engine and turned to look at her.

'You haven't answered my question?' he said, his eyes searching her face.

'I'm not sure...' She met his gaze doubtfully. 'Oh, I'd like to meet up, see you more often, but... if we went away together...' She drew a deep breath, because it was such a big step forward. 'I'm not sure it is a good idea, Jace. If I spend too much time with you, I might feel worse when we part... I might not want to part...' The last few words came out without her meaning them to and she blushed at what she'd said.

'That is what I'm hoping,' Jace told her and caught her hand, pulling her close to his side. 'I think I'm in love with you, Fay. It happened in France when we had that day together. I had to leave for the sake of my career, but I haven't been able to get you out of my head. I know that I told you I didn't care about settling down – and I need to tour for my work, but I shall buy a house soon and... I don't know. I suppose you could have a catering business in America as easily as here. You might find your cooking in more demand there.'

'I might,' she agreed. 'It's a big leap of faith, Jace – a lot to ask just like that...'

'But if we get to know each other – take that holiday – we could make it work. I know we could... and I'd help you to get started. Maybe we'd open a restaurant...'

'I'm not sure I'm good enough. I thought I might get work from some of your friends after your party,' Fay admitted. 'I didn't...'

'That's because I wouldn't share your details,' Jace told her. 'Several of my friends asked where they could contact you, but I didn't trust them to treat you fairly... Besides, I wanted to keep you to myself.'

'You refused to give them my details? Surely you must have known how important that was to me?' She stared at him in stunned disbelief. How could he have done that to her?

'Fay...' He saw the look of annoyance in her eyes and his reflected guilt. 'I know. I'm sorry... I suppose I thought if you were too successful, you would never give it up for me.'

'You're serious, aren't you?' Fay caught her breath. 'You withheld my details because you didn't want me to be successful – that's pretty rotten of you, Jace. I thought you were a good friend...'

Fay turned away, angry and disappointed. She'd counted on getting that work and felt disappointed, believing that she'd failed. How could he behave that way? He said he cared about her – but he'd done something that had stopped her getting more work and that upset and angered her.

'I am a good friend,' Jace told her and caught her arm as she moved to open the car door. 'Please don't be angry, Fay. I didn't want to spoil things for you. They were all raving about you, and not just your food, but you – the way you looked, your smile... I suddenly thought I might lose you. Even my drummer wanted to marry you and I know he was drunk, but all of them thought you were so wonderful. I just felt jealous and wanted to keep you for myself. I do love you. You know that...'

'Love! I don't call that love,' she said, suddenly furious. 'Making sure I failed when you knew how much it meant to me... that's not love.' She put her hand on the car door handle and opened it. 'I've heard enough!'

'Fay, please don't go. I do care about you and I do want you to do your fancy cooking – but in America, with me... I'm asking you to give me a chance... to marry me!' The last few words sounded desperate, as if forced out of him, but she wouldn't turn her head. She was just so angry with him. It was selfish of him to withhold her details like that and she was too disappointed in him to listen to his excuses. 'I'm sorry... forgive me!'

Fay was out of the car and walking away. She heard him get out and call to her again, but she just kept walking. She didn't know if Jace was following because she didn't look back. Tears wet her cheeks. Everything was so horrible. Her mother didn't know her and Jace – Jace had let her down. At that moment, Fay felt more miserable than she ever had before in her life. Her evening was spoiled and all she wanted was to be on her own. How could Jace say he loved her when he'd deliberately stopped her getting orders for her business? If he truly cared he would have helped her to become successful – and they could have got to know one another... they might have had something special, but Fay felt too disappointed in him to continue that thought.

She took off her shoes and started to run. Why had everything suddenly turned sour in her life? Fay knew she'd been lucky; she'd had almost everything she wanted, but now it all seemed to have gone wrong.

* * *

Fay didn't want to go home and have Maggie and her mother stare at her because she was early, so, after she'd stopped running, she replaced her shoes and walked around for a while and then found a café where she sat drinking coffee. At least, she bought one, but after one sip she left it because it didn't taste anything like the coffee she had at home. She watched food being brought to table and wondered why people came to eat there; it wasn't like the delicious meals she and Maggie served in the restaurant. Someone had ordered the apple pie, but instead of being crisp and delicious, it looked soggy and hardly browned.

She was a good cook! Fay sat up and looked about her. She was so much better than this – and she'd been thinking herself a failure because her orders for the catering business were so infrequent. Jace had contributed to that feeling but he wasn't the real reason she'd not succeeded. Fay knew in her heart that she'd expected too much too soon. She needed to advertise or get out and look for work somehow.

Her thoughts were wandering when she saw two women enter and sit down. They had clearly been shopping all day and were laden with bags with well-known brands printed on them.

'Are you coming to the food fair next week?' one of the women asked the other. 'I heard it would have all sorts of fancy things on offer. I think I shall go and see what it is like...'

'I'll come with you,' her friend said. 'I'm looking for a good caterer for my daughter's eighteenth birthday...'

Fay wished she had a printed card with her business details. If she had, she would have jumped up and presented it to them. She was aware that she didn't look like a professional chef in her high heels and ponytail, but she burned to let them know about her services.

Getting up, she paid for her coffee and left the café. Her lack of a business card had made her realise that she needed to do more if she wanted to be successful. There was no point in just moaning because the customers were not lining up for her services. She *was* good. She just had to let folk know – and, as she began to walk home, the germ of an idea came into her head. Fay had known about the food fair, which was being held at Olympia; she and Maggie had discussed visiting it but were too busy with the restaurant to take a stand there. However, if she had some cards made, she could leave a few in strategic places, and she would have some posters done too. Maureen would put one up in her shop and Fay would do some research, ask around and see where else she could get them put up. Perhaps more adverts in magazines would help, too. She'd placed one in *The Times* newspaper and another in the *Tatler*, but those women in the café would probably read *Woman* or *Woman's Own* magazines. Perhaps she could get an advert in one of them – or she might even get them to write an article for her.

* * *

Fay had started to smile as she caught a bus home. She'd been so angry with Jace, but her success was down to her. And now she was determined to make her dreams come true; she just had to trust in her own ability.

It was only as she got off the bus that she remembered what Jace had said about loving her and wanting to be with her. He'd begged her not to go, but she'd been so angry – and she still was annoyed that he'd deliberately withheld her details – but there was regret too. Fay remembered his last words as she walked away, uttered in desperation, '... I'm asking you... to marry me!' Had he really meant them? As proposals went, it wasn't exactly romantic – more half-hearted, as if it was being forced out of him.

'Oh, it doesn't matter,' Fay told herself fiercely. 'I know what I want and it isn't what Jace is offering...' Go all the way to America and hardly ever see her family! No, she couldn't think of such a thing. She pushed the thought from her mind. Jace was just like a comet that flamed brightly in the sky as it flashed by. Their lives could never coincide. Much better to forget him.

Maggie was in the kitchen as Fay entered. She was still cooking meals. Fay took off her coat, washed her hands at the sink and put on her white apron.

'I'm glad you're back,' Maggie remarked as she finished serving up a steak in brandy and mushroom sauce. 'I could do with a hand… Everything all right, Fay?' Her eyes met Fay's.

She sent her a warning look as her mother walked in, carrying a tray of dirty dishes. 'Are you waiting table tonight, Mum?' Fay asked to cover the silence.

'Carla had a headache and we sent her home,' Maggie said. 'Granny Peggy said she was perfectly capable of serving a few dinners so she did…' She smiled as Peggy nodded.

'Of course I am. How did your evening go, Fay?'

'Not as I'd hoped,' Fay replied with a wry twist of her mouth. 'Jace was asked several times for my details after the party we did for him – but he didn't pass them on. It wasn't because my cooking wasn't good enough that I didn't get any orders…'

Maggie stared at her. 'You couldn't have thought that, Fay?'

'Well, what was I to think?' Fay said. 'You've made such a success of the restaurant, Maggie – and yet the outside catering has almost come to a halt just lately. I've only had three orders this past month. I've decided I'll have some business cards printed and posters, too. I do have a small wedding next month. I'll leave some cards there – and I'll ask some shops to put up posters or have my cards on their counters. I thought I'd take some to the food fair, too. If I'd thought of it in time, I'd have taken a stand…'

'Good idea about the posters, Fay,' Peggy said. 'Maureen will put one in her shop and I'm sure some of the other traders will too.

I'll ask Paula to put one up in the boarding house and you can leave some cards there.'

'Thanks, Mum,' Fay smiled at her. 'You look better this evening. Are you feeling less tired?'

'I am always happiest when I'm busy, you should know that, Fay.'

'Yes, I do...' Fay heard the telephone ring. 'I'll answer that...'

Fay went into the hall. If it was Jace, she would let him speak, but she wasn't sure how she felt about his behaviour; she was no longer angry but she still hadn't forgiven him.

'Fay – this is Sheila. Can I speak to Able please – or I suppose you could take a message...?'

'Of course I can,' Fay told her. 'Is something the matter, Sheila?'

'Yes. Pip is in hospital. He hadn't been well for a while. That is why we didn't come straight up to London as soon as Mum came home – how is she today? Pip rang her yesterday and said she sounded a little better.'

'She feels easier, but her memory isn't back yet,' Fay replied. 'What is wrong with Pip? I know Mum was a bit disappointed because he hasn't come to see her – but if he was ill... Why didn't he say?'

'You know your brother, Fay. He never wants to worry anyone. He had an operation last night to remove a burst appendix after he was taken to hospital in a lot of pain, but they say he is making a good recovery.'

'Oh, Sheila, I am so sorry. You must be worried sick?'

'I am,' Sheila agreed. 'I had to let you know – but Pip was so adamant that we shouldn't tell his mother he was ill.'

'You want me to tell my father and let him decide what to tell her?'

'Yes, please,' Sheila agreed. 'I've been fretting, not knowing what to do for the best. Pip's family has a right to know if...' She caught her breath sharply. 'But he came through the operation and the doctor says he thinks he should make a full recovery...'

'I am so sorry, Sheila. I wish I could do something to help.'

'I can manage, but the children are upset, of course,' Sheila replied. 'Pip should have gone to the doctor ages ago, but he always leaves things...'

'He didn't tell you he was having pain?'

'No. I would have made him go to the doctor. I knew he wasn't well, but he isn't always – not since his accident. His lungs were slightly damaged in that car accident he had and he gets breathless at times.'

'Have you seen him since the operation?'

'Just for a few minutes. I am going in tomorrow for a longer visit.'

'Give him my love – and from all of us,' Fay said. 'We will be thinking of him.'

'I'm glad I've spoken to you, Fay. You must come down soon and see us...'

'Yes, I will,' Fay promised.

After she had replaced the receiver, she stood for a moment in thought and then went through to the bar, where she knew she would find her father. She could hear him laughing with a regular customer. He turned to look at her in surprise.

'Fay – is something wrong? Not your mother?' He immediately looked anxious and she hastily reassured him.

'No, Dad – that was Sheila on the phone just now.' She beckoned him to her and lowered her voice. 'Pip is in hospital...'

'It never rains, but it pours,' Able said. 'What is the matter with him, Fay?'

'Pip had an operation for a burst appendix... He is through the operation, but Sheila doesn't know yet if he'll be all right...' She saw the shock in his face. 'I know. Sheila wanted you to tell Mum but...'

'Yes, I shall do it,' Able told her firmly. 'Don't say anything now. Leave it to me. I shall be finished here soon and then I'll find the right moment.'

'Yes, all right...'

Fay smiled and nodded to some familiar faces and left the bar, returning to the kitchen.

Maggie looked at her. 'You were a long time. Was it Jace?'

'No, not Jace,' Fay said. 'I'll tell you later...' She picked up an order. 'Table five want apple pie, chocolate mousse and a raspberry ripple ice cream – that's your homemade one. Shall I do that?'

'Yes, please,' Maggie agreed. 'I've just finished the last of the mains. I've had a busy evening. Thank goodness Granny Peggy was here to help out...'

'It's nice to think I'm still of use,' Peggy said, returning with a laden tray of used plates. 'I think it is time we had a bit more permanent help, Maggie. I can help with the cooking but we do need another waitress...'

'I can help,' Rose Barton said and entered the kitchen. 'Able told me you were waiting tables, Peggy. Tom suggested I come round and give you a hand...'

'Oh, that is nice of you, Rose,' Peggy said. 'But what about Molly and Jack?'

'We have a babysitter this evening,' Rose replied. 'Tom took me to the pictures...' She stared at Peggy. 'Did Able tell you the names of our children?'

Peggy looked at her. 'I might have remembered... I've started to remember things. Maureen said it was dribs and drabs and that made me laugh...'

'Good. It is nice to see you smiling again, Peggy. Tom and I have been very worried about you.'

'Thank you for coming through, Rose. I was just saying we need another waitress permanently.' Peggy gave her a grateful look.

'I might know of someone – at least Tom might,' Rose said as she put an apron over her dress and picked up the tray for table five. 'One of his clients was saying his daughter, Amy, has just left school and wants to work in a restaurant as a waitress.'

'I'll telephone Tom in the morning,' Maggie said. 'We can interview the girl and see if she suits. Otherwise, we'll need to put an advert in the paper.'

Rose nodded as she went out with the tray and Peggy picked up the next one.

'Table seven's order is there,' Peggy said, placing the tab in front of Maggie. 'Table nine doesn't want dessert only coffee – very slim ladies – and table ten hasn't decided yet. Everyone else has been served, so we shan't be long before we're finished... apart from the washing-up. If you leave it, Paula's mum will do it in the morning.'

'Mrs Maggs did most of it before she left to catch her bus. I never leave dirty crocks and there are only a few,' Maggie said. 'We really should buy a machine to wash dishes, but they are expensive and for the moment Fay and I will do it together. We'll finish up – you go and help Able in the bar. You used to love that...'

'I still do,' Peggy said. 'Yes, I might pop in and see if any of my regulars are here this evening...'

Maggie looked at Fay as the door closed behind her. 'Right, now spill. I know something is on your mind. Tell me before they come back...'

'Pip is ill; he had an operation,' Fay said. 'I've told Dad and he will tell Mum himself.'

'It is serious then?' Maggie looked anxious.

'We don't know for sure yet, but it could be,' Fay confirmed. 'His appendix burst and they operated, but that can be nasty...'

'It's one thing after another,' Maggie said. 'Sheila must be so worried.'

'She is, but at least he is through the operation.' Fay served up the last order of apple pie. 'Good thing there are no more orders to come, there isn't much left.'

'That was Able's fault,' Maggie said. 'He said it was too long since he'd eaten one of your mum's apple pies and he devoured almost a whole one...'

'Trust Dad,' Fay said and laughed, then made a face. 'I don't think I'll be seeing Jace again.'

'You've finished with him then?'

'I was so angry, Maggie. He deliberately didn't pass on our details so I would go with him to America. He says I could work over there and he wants to marry me...'

'You turned him down?' Maggie stared at her.

'I didn't take him seriously. I was too angry to listen.' Fay shook her head. 'If he loved me, he would have wanted me to do well, Maggie. How could he do that to me?'

'I doubt he saw it that way,' Maggie told her. 'He wants you with him. He might help you to become a famous chef over there...'

'He said something about us having a restaurant together. I suppose he has the money to open a posh one...' Fay met her gaze. 'But isn't that selfish of him? What about my hopes and wishes?'

Maggie raised her fine eyebrows. 'Love can be selfish, Fay. He should have told you how he felt and let you decide – and it doesn't sound good that he didn't help you when he could, but perhaps he wasn't thinking straight. It says something that he was honest enough to tell you what he'd done. You should have heard him out and listened to his side...'

'Maybe,' Fay said. 'I doubt I'll see him again anyway...'

It was at that moment that the phone shrilled. Maggie grinned. 'I'll bet you a sherbet lemon that's him...'

'You're on,' Fay said and went to answer the phone. She tingled as she picked it up. Pray God it wasn't more bad news about Pip!

'Fay, I'm sorry...' Jace sounded dreadful. 'I know I acted badly, but I was confused, jealous. I do love you and I do want you to succeed in your career... I just want you to do it with me!'

'You've never said it before,' Fay said and felt a little breathless. 'What made you say it now?'

'I never said it because I was a fool,' Jace told her. 'When the record deal came through, I thought it meant everything – and it is important to me, of course it is – but without you... it doesn't mean much deep down.'

Fay was caught off guard because he sounded so sincere. 'I've forgiven you,' she said at last. 'I... might be a bit in love with you, Jace, but I need to get to know you.' She hesitated, then, 'I will take that holiday with you – but it doesn't mean I'll sleep with you. I want to know you better before I make any decisions about my future.'

'That's fair enough,' Jace said. 'I thought you might not want to see me again. I'm glad you're going to give me a chance. As soon as I can arrange things, I'll call you and we'll make plans.'

'Yes, do that – and we'll come to the show if you send us the tickets,' Fay said. 'Take care of yourself, Jace.'

'You too,' he said and replaced the receiver. Fay stared at it for several minutes before returning to the kitchen where Maggie had begun to wash the dishes.

'I owe you a lemon sherbet,' she said. 'I might be taking a little holiday in a few weeks, Maggie. You'd better look for your helper as well as someone to wait tables...'

'You're never going off with him just like that?' Maggie was disbelieving. 'What will Granny Peggy say?'

'I'll be twenty next spring,' Fay told her defiantly. 'Besides, it is only a holiday as friends!'

Maggie shook her head, but Fay ignored her. She was going to take that little holiday with Jace and see where it led – why shouldn't she?

22

'Pip is in hospital?' Peggy stared at her husband in dismay. 'I wondered why he hadn't come to see us.' She closed her eyes briefly. 'A burst appendix – you can die with that... Oh, Able, whatever will Sheila and the children do if...' She swallowed hard. 'No, it won't happen; it can't. Pip doesn't deserve this...'

'The operation was successful, though there is always a risk of infection with something like that; Sheila was upset and thought you should know.'

'Naturally, I want to know and of course she is upset,' Peggy replied. 'We have to go down and see him. Does Janet know – and the girls?'

'Fay took the message, so I'm sure she will have told Maggie,' Able said and reached for her hand. 'He may not be up to visitors, hon. Shall we wait and see what Sheila has to say?'

'No. I want to visit him in hospital. When he had the accident, I couldn't go. I had to stay here and look after things. Janet went, even though she was pregnant and you thought she might give birth on the journey...'

Able looked at her in his quiet patient way. 'I haven't told you about that... did you just remember it?'

Peggy met his steady gaze. 'I'm remembering more all the time now, Able. Working with the girls tonight made me feel needed again – made me feel normal. I think I might never remember everything, but if something jogs my memory it comes back, like Pip being in hospital; I remembered the first time... But it isn't me that matters for the moment. It's Pip. I'd like to go down tomorrow if we can?'

'We'll telephone Sheila in the morning and tell her we're coming,' Able promised. 'Just try to get some rest tonight, Peggy. It's a long journey and you've been very ill yourself.'

'I am well now,' she told him as she slid her arms about his waist. 'Thank you for all your care of me, Able, but don't worry. Maureen says I'm a tough old bird...'

Able gave a shout of laughter. 'That sounds like my Peggy. I thought I'd lost you for a while back there, but I haven't – have I?'

'You'll never lose me,' she said as she leaned into him, inhaling his masculine scent. 'I think we were meant to be, Able. From what you've told me and the things I remember, life hasn't been straight-forward, but we've always come through.' She looked up at him. 'I have to go to Pip because I didn't last time. I couldn't then, but I can now – do you understand?'

'Of course I do,' he said and bent his head to kiss her. 'Just don't fret, hon. We'll go down and we'll do all we can for them.'

* * *

'Oh, Mum, Able,' Sheila fell on them when they arrived late the next evening, hugging them both. 'I am so glad you came – I hope it wasn't too much for you?'

'I'm fine now, Sheila,' Peggy said and hugged her. She saw the anxiety in her daughter-in-law's eyes. 'How is Pip now?'

'Still a bit groggy,' Sheila said. 'They say he should be fine tomorrow, but he was hardly awake when I visited this afternoon. I think he was in a bit of pain, because he had an infection, which they are treating.'

'When can we visit?' Peggy asked. 'Is it just visiting hours?'

'Yes,' Sheila said regretfully. 'They wouldn't let you in at this hour. He isn't considered to be on the danger list now, so just two until four tomorrow – and again for two hours in the evening.'

'We'll have to wait until then,' Peggy sighed. 'I am feeling pretty tired after the journey, so perhaps it is as well...'

'I'll get you a nice cup of tea,' Sheila said. 'I wasn't sure what time you would get here so I just made some sandwiches and sausage rolls.'

'That would be lovely,' Able told her. 'We ate on the train, but a nice sausage roll with some pickle would suit me. I seem to remember you make a wonderful sweet piccalilli?'

Sheila beamed at him. 'Fancy you remembering that,' she said. 'I do and I have some all ready for you, Able. I know you like it...'

Peggy sank down into one of the comfortable old chairs and looked around her as Sheila went off to make tea. 'It hasn't changed much since we lived here, has it? I seem to feel it's the same.' The room had a familiar feel and she believed she recognised some bits of furniture.

'Not much change, apart from some of the decor,' Able agreed. 'It was comfortable then and it is now.'

'Yes, nice,' Peggy said. 'If we can manage it, I think we might buy a holiday home somewhere this way, Able. All the family can use it if they choose and we'll spend some time down this way, see more of Pip and Sheila and the kids...'

'I thought you enjoyed being a landlady again?'

'Yes, I do, but I also want to spend more time with you, just enjoying ourselves. I think I'm going to sell the boarding house. I have a long lease and the goodwill of the place should pay for a small cottage somewhere nice...'

'You don't need to do that, hon. I can find the money...'

'You had all the expense of the accommodation and the extra flight home.'

'I've sorted all that now. You don't have to sell your business, hon.'

'I think I shall,' Peggy said. 'I think it's time for us, Able. I might have died, but I was lucky and we should make the most if it. Besides, Maggie will need help until she is really on her feet and independent – and Fay. I'm not sure she is truly happy with her business...'

'Well, you know Fay,' Able said and Peggy nodded.

'Yes, I'm beginning to,' she said and then Sheila returned with a loaded tray and the talk became centred on Pip once more.

'Have you let Pip's work know he's in hospital?' Able asked as she poured their drinks and, when she nodded, 'What did they say? I think he's working on an important new project, isn't he?'

'Yes. He was supposed to fly out to America next week to talk to some people there...' Sheila hesitated. 'I think some important people over there want to recruit him on to a project they're working on. It might have something to do with space travel...'

'No!' Able stared at her. 'Pip is clever. We all knew that – but if he has been asked to join the space race... well, that's a feather in his cap.'

'Space race?' Sheila asked and Able grinned.

'Sorry. I heard it spoken of that way while we were in America. It's a race between America and the Soviet Union to see who can be the first to put a man on the moon. President Kennedy is determined it should be them...'

'Pip won't be well enough to go, surely?' Peggy said, frowning. She was silent for a moment, then, 'If he did take a job there, would you and the children go with him, Sheila?'

'I don't think it would be a permanent thing,' Sheila said, looking thoughtful. 'He might just work on something for a few months and then come home – but I suppose... if he really needed to live there...' Her eyes met Peggy's. 'Yes, I would in that case. After all, I could visit you sometimes...'

'Yes, you could,' Peggy agreed, but a little shiver went down her spine. 'I know I'm being silly but... No, you must do whatever suits you as a family.'

Able was eating a sausage roll. He looked at her, eyebrows raised.

She shook her head. 'I know what happened to me was my own fault, but it makes me worry for my family if they go to live there.'

'Pip will do what he thinks right,' Able said. 'You look tired, hon. Why don't you go up to bed? I'll bring the cases up in five minutes...'

'Yes, I will,' Peggy agreed.

'I'll come with you,' Sheila said and they went out together.

* * *

Able sat in his chair and finished his supper. It would do Peggy good to have a chat with Sheila, who was a sensible girl. He understood that Peggy's unfortunate experience had given her a dislike of the country he'd been born in, but that was natural enough. He'd tried to convince her that it was just an unpleasant incident, but he couldn't budge her idea that it was a terrible place. Able knew differently. They'd been having a wonderful time until the accident and Peggy had loved all the places, he'd shown her. Of course, she'd forgotten that too.

Damn! Why did it have to happen? His first anger at what had happened had faded now, leaving him saddened and a little anxious. Able was quite happy to spend his life in Britain with Peggy, but if Pip and his family went to live there, it would have been nice for her if they could visit now and then – but at the moment that was out of the question.

No use in worrying. Able had never been one to bay for the moon. They had to visit Pip in hospital and hope that he was fully recovered before anyone could think of the future. If he was well, he would want to follow this new and interesting lead in his career. Peggy would find that difficult. She'd only just told Able she was thinking of buying a place near her eldest son so that she could see him and his family more often. The news that he might be moving abroad was a shock for her...

Hauling himself up, Able shoved the small case under his left elbow and took the larger in his right hand. He'd taught himself to do most things one-handed and, in his experience, there was always a way to get round obstacles if you really tried...

* * *

'Mum...' Pip looked up at her and gave her a weary smile. 'It should have been me visiting you. How are you?'

'Much better,' she replied and bent to kiss his cheek. 'We brought you some cherries. Sheila says you like those better than grapes.'

'I always did, Mum,' Pip said. 'You shouldn't have come all this way after what you went through. I'm glad you did though...'

'I didn't come last time,' Peggy murmured. 'I had to come this time, because I could.'

'Are you beginning to remember?' Pip asked her. 'I couldn't remember some things for a while after my accident, but I didn't forget everything like you. It's rotten for you. I'm sorry I couldn't get up to London.'

Her eyes were anxious as she looked at him. 'You need to rest, Pip, take some time with your family, not go flying off to America.'

'Same old Mum,' Pip said. 'I suppose Sheila told you. I fly to America next week to see about working on a project there – and it might mean living out there for a while…'

'You won't go now? Surely you will postpone it?'

'If I have to – but it is important to me. I'll go as soon as I'm able.' He frowned. 'It is something I've worked hard for…'

'How long would you be away?' Peggy asked.

'Months, perhaps years. It depends on whether we're successful in getting a man on the moon…'

'Oh, Pip,' Peggy cried. 'It sounds marvellous – but are you sure it's what you want?'

He smiled. 'I find the idea exciting – don't you?'

'Yes, I suppose so. What is the point of it, though? Will it help us on Earth? Will it lead to a better life for people? It must cost an awful lot of money to run a programme like that?'

He sat up in his excitement and then groaned. 'I'm still sore – but the landing on the moon is only a part of the future. That's in satellites…' He lowered his voice. 'I'm working on it here now, but that's confidential. When we have those, it will lead to all sorts of benefits for mankind – things you couldn't even imagine…'

'I don't know – all these advances in science are fine, but what happens when they turn these things into weapons? We had a chance to fight the bombers in the war – but if the weapons are in space…'

Pip stared at her. 'You think deeper than many people, Mum. There is that side to it, of course, there is – but if we don't get there first...' He hesitated, then, 'America is the place to be right now. President Kennedy is behind us all the way. He wants America to be the first to land a man on the moon. I'm looking forward to meeting him.'

'You will be meeting him?'

'Yes, I expect so. I have to be briefed to make sure I'm not an enemy or an assassin but I do expect to be meeting him. He is very interested in the project.' He smiled. 'It's all very thrilling, Mum.'

'I can see that...' Peggy nodded. 'You are right. I know that, Pip. Perhaps I'm getting old. It all seems to be going too fast for me.'

Pip laughed and then grimaced. 'Don't make me laugh, Mum, it hurts. You getting old – never!'

'Oh, Pip,' she cried and bent to kiss his cheek. 'I had forgotten how much I love you – but I remember now. I remember you taking your bike to school, because you were so proud of it and how you longed to fly and you did in the war. Times have changed so much. You'll be wanting a spaceship of your own next....'

Pip smiled. 'I don't think that will be possible for a long time, but you never know. Perhaps one day...'

'I'd better go,' Peggy said. 'Able and Sheila are waiting to see you – so I mustn't be greedy, but I'll be here again this evening.'

'And then you should go back home,' Pip told her. 'I'm glad you came, Mum, but I don't want you hanging around here when you should be resting too. I'll be fine now. I promise.'

'I know,' she said, kissed him and left, though she wouldn't go home for a couple of days, just to be sure.

23

'Would you like to go to the pictures with me?' Freddie asked Greta when she served him at breakfast that morning. It was the end of July now and looked as though it would be a hot summer day. She'd brought him a grapefruit cocktail and egg on toast with a pot of coffee, all perfectly prepared. Her smile lit up her face when he asked if she wanted to go out and nodded. 'Good. I think you will like it – it's an epic called *Spartacus* ...unless you've seen it? It has been to London, but I missed it for some reason. We could see *Whistle Down the Wind* with Hayley Mills if you'd rather?'

'I haven't seen either; I've heard about them both, though, and I don't mind which,' Greta said. 'When were you thinking of going?'

'Well, we could go to a matinee on Saturday afternoon,' Freddie suggested. 'It is my day off this week. You could ask your aunt if you could have that off instead of Sunday. We'll see *Spartacus* this time and *Whistle Down the Wind* next time, if you like?'

Greta looked happy. 'Yes, that would be just right. She is visiting a friend of hers on Sunday and asked if I would look after things for her. So I think she will agree.'

Freddie nodded. 'How are you getting on with your night school classes?'

'I'm enjoying them,' Greta said. 'My tutor says I have an aptitude for typing and thinks I could get a good job as a typist, especially if I learn shorthand as well. I could be a secretary then.'

'Would you prefer that to what you do now?'

'Yes, I think so, though I wouldn't leave until my aunt found someone to help her, but she's always telling me anyone could do better than me so...' Greta giggled and glanced over her shoulder. 'I'd better go or she will be on the warpath.'

'Yes, you get on,' Freddie said and started to eat his breakfast. He was surprised when Muriel came and sat at his table as she normally sat with Steve or Guy. He looked at her and saw that she'd been crying. Her eyes were red and so was the end of her nose. 'What's wrong? Is there anything I can do to help?'

'Just be your normal cheerful self,' Muriel told him. 'I had a bit of bad news this morning, that's all...'

'I'm sorry,' Freddie sympathised. 'I know that doesn't help much. I can see you are very upset.'

'A friend of mine has told me that her little boy and her husband are both in hospital after a road accident. She has asked me to go and stay with her for a few weeks to help run her business and keep her company. I want to – but if I do, I have to give up this job. I can't expect Guy to keep it open indefinitely.'

'He will need to bring someone in from one of the other teams, but there are plenty of us to keep the beaches safe,' Freddie said. 'We've already lost Jill and... But you must go to your friend, of course you must, Muriel. She needs you or she wouldn't have asked.'

'I know...' She sniffed and took out her handkerchief, blowing her nose hard. 'I must, because she doesn't have anyone else to turn to – but I shall miss everyone here so much. I shall miss talking to you, Freddie...'

'We shall all miss you,' he replied. 'I know it's hard for you to give up this job, but it's what I would have done if my mum had needed me at home. She didn't because she has all the others – but, if your friend is relying on you, you can't let her down, Muriel.'

'No, and I shan't,' she said, gave a sniff and then smiled. 'I'm going to tell Guy after breakfast and then leave. I hope he will be as understanding as you are, Freddie.'

Greta returned with another breakfast and then asked Muriel what she would like. She was smiling and looked happy and Muriel remarked on it after she left the dining room.

'You've certainly made a difference to Greta,' she remarked. 'Before you came, she looked as if she was being put to the torture and would expire at any moment. Now, she is glowing.'

'Greta is happy because we are going to the cinema to see a film on Saturday.'

Muriel looked at him consideringly and then shook her head. 'No, she is happy because she thinks you are little short of God,' Muriel said. 'I know you're always thoughtful and kind, Freddie – you have been to me and if I was staying on through the summer, well, I wouldn't have minded a little dalliance with you – if you know what I mean. But, and please take this seriously, don't break Greta's heart. I'm not sure what she might do if you let her down.'

'I would never hurt Greta...'

'You're not in love with her, though, are you?'

'I can't answer that,' Freddie replied.

Muriel stared at him. 'You're still immature in some ways, Freddie, though very much a man in others. Have you ever made love to a woman?' She laughed as the hot colour swept up his neck. 'No, you don't need to answer. I know you haven't – but it means you haven't truly thought about the relationship between the sexes. In my opinion, it is almost impossible for a man and woman just to be friends, unless they are old and passionless. Greta is thinking about that side of things – and if you really don't want to hurt her, you should be careful.' She smiled. 'That's just a friendly warning. Had it been me, I would have gone to bed with you in an instant and waved goodbye with a smile – but she won't.'

'Thank you for the warning, but it wasn't necessary,' Freddie told her. 'I like Greta and I care about her. She was unhappy and I've tried to make her a little happier – as for the rest, well, we'll have to wait and see...'

Muriel stared at him in surprise. 'I stand corrected. You go deeper than I thought, Freddie Ronoscki. Lucky Greta if she gets you – don't forget to invite me to the wedding.'

Freddie shook his head. 'Don't make mischief, Muriel. I'm not ready for marriage yet and Greta is even less experienced than me. She has a lot of growing up to do first and so do I. In the autumn, I am off to college and, with any luck, Greta will have found a new life – something that will make her happy and give her confidence in herself. She is quite pretty when she smiles and could be very pretty if she had the right clothes and had her hair done...'

'Well, well,' Muriel said but shut up when Greta brought her breakfast tray.

Freddie stood up and looked down at her. 'Good luck,' he told her. 'I hope your friend's family recover.'

'Good luck to you too,' Muriel answered and Freddie walked away before she could resume her teasing.

He was well aware that Greta had attached herself to him and might well be thinking of love and marriage. Freddie didn't know how he thought about her if he was honest. He felt protective towards her and wanted to help her – was that love? Freddie wasn't sure. He only knew that he had to go ahead with his plans for the future, but whether Greta would one day be a part of that future he couldn't say. For the moment, he simply wanted friendship.

He thought over what Muriel had said to him. He'd been embarrassed when she'd asked him if he'd made love to a girl, not so much because he was still inexperienced but because of the way she'd looked at him. He was glad she wouldn't be around for the rest of the summer, because he would have been uncomfortable with her suggestions for a bit of dalliance, as she called it. No, he would settle for a girlfriend and then marriage one day, but he wasn't ready yet.

Somehow he would have to make Greta see that it was friendship he was offering her and hope that it didn't upset her too much…

* * *

Greta frowned as she started the chore of washing greasy plates and pans. It wasn't a job she relished, but her aunt did most of the cooking, because Greta wasn't very good at it. Perhaps if her aunt had spent more time showing her, she might have managed it, but she did tend to drift off into dreams.

Her dreams at the moment would have shocked her aunt. Greta smiled as she saw herself looking beautiful in a long white lace dress walking down the aisle towards a very handsome Freddie wearing a dark pin-striped suit and white shirt. What a wonderful day that would be – and how good life would be for them both. She would learn to cook to make him happy – she would do anything he asked.

A sigh escaped her lips and her smile dimmed. It was just a dream and Greta knew it. Freddie was her friend, but he wasn't in love with her.

Greta had seen photographs of Fay, Freddie's beautiful twin and one of Maggie, who was just two years older.

'You have such a lovely family.' Greta had looked at the pictures enviously. What she would give to be part of a family like that... but she knew it could never happen? Freddie could have any girl he wanted – that Muriel had been lusting after him for weeks! Greta knew a spurt of anger. She wasn't going to get her claws in her Freddie!

If only he was hers! Greta's smile returned as she slipped into another daydream. She could see the red-brick house they would live in, roses growing up the wall and over the door. White nylon curtains at the windows and they would have one of those new Formica kitchen tables with a blue and white top. They were nice because you could just wipe the top to keep them clean instead of scrubbing the pine table her aunt used in her kitchen.

'Daydreaming again!' Greta's aunt boomed at her. 'Get on with it, girl. There are all the beds to make – and we've lost another guest. That Muriel is leaving, so you'll need to clean her room right through and put clean bedding on. Unless they keep paying me for the empty rooms, I shall have to take on more lodgers...'

'Why do you keep doing this?' Greta asked her. 'If you dislike it so much, why don't you sell and go to live somewhere else?'

Her aunt stared at her for a moment in silence and Greta thought she was in trouble, but then she sighed. 'What would happen to you, miss, if I did? Tell me that? I could help my friend run her small hotel in Torquay – and that has a much better class of clientele, I can tell you. She's asked me several times and if I sold this place... But you would never get another job. I promised your father I would look after you and I shall...'

'I could find another job,' Greta replied. 'You don't need to worry about me, aunt. If you want to sell, do it...'

'Well, I might at the end of the season,' her aunt told her. 'In the meantime, get off and start on those bedrooms...'

'Yes, I will,' Greta poured the water down the sink and wiped her hands. 'Think about it, aunt. *I'm* not going to stay here forever...'

She went out then, leaving her aunt staring after her. Greta's heart was thumping as she went upstairs to start cleaning and bed making. She would have to work even harder at her typing because she had to make a success of her life somehow. She'd thought of herself as a prisoner here, but if her aunt sold the boarding house, she would have to look for work and if she wasn't ready to begin as a typist... But she would worry about that when the time came, she decided. For the moment, she wanted to think about her trip to the cinema with Freddie.

* * *

'Your aunt is considering selling up at the end of the summer season?' Freddie looked at Greta in surprise as they left the cinema early that Saturday evening after the epic story of slavery, courage and faith that had held them both glued to the screen. He paused at the edge of the pavement and halted at the zebra crossing. They waited until the way was clear. 'What will you do then – go with her?'

'No, not unless I have to,' Greta told him. 'I may have to find other work while I continue to learn new skills – but I suppose I can do that...'

'Some of the boarding houses close for the winter, don't they?'

'Well, yes,' Greta agreed. 'A lot of places here only open for the spring and summer, a few weeks into autumn. After October they shut for a few months and do other things – a lot of families have different jobs in summer and winter. The men go fishing and the women… I'm not sure what they do…'

'So it won't be so easy to find work here,' Freddie pointed out. 'You might have to go elsewhere.'

'Yes, I suppose so. I'll think about it when the time comes. We have bookings until the end of September and there might be one in October.'

'You've got a while to think then,' Freddie said, but he was thoughtful as they walked home from the cinema. He could smell fish and chips, toffee apples and candy floss. 'I'm hungry. Shall we get something to eat?'

'I have to get back,' Greta said, 'but we could eat some chips as we go if you like?'

'Right… come on, I'll treat you to a toffee apple for afters.'

Later, that evening, when Freddie was in his room alone, he sat on the edge of the bed thinking. Then he got out the leather notecase his parents had bought him and started to write a letter. He frowned as he took out his fountain pen and then began to write. Surely, with all the work going on in the Pig & Whistle and at his mother's boarding house, they could find somewhere for Greta – just until she was ready to start her new life as a typist and a writer of short stories.

He wrote explaining that his friend would be out of a job in a few weeks and asking if he could bring her home with him when he came. Freddie smiled as he sealed the letter, put a stamp on it and took it out to post it.

Guy was just returning to the house when Freddie got back. He smiled at him. 'Had a good day off?'

'Yes, thanks. Everything all right on the beach? Did you get Muriel's replacement?'

'Yes. Ted is one of the usual standby guards. He is normally on duty at the station but patrols when needed.' Freddie nodded. 'Fancy a game of cards before you retire this evening?' Guy asked. 'We'll play for pennies – just for fun really.'

'Why not?' Freddie replied. 'I was going to read a book, but I don't mind a game of cards.'

'We'll ask for a pot of coffee – unless you prefer hot chocolate?'

'Coffee will be fine,' Freddie said. 'I'd like a glass of beer – but we're not allowed it in this house, are we?'

'Mrs Phipps is against alcohol,' Guy confirmed. 'I have no idea why. A single glass of beer never hurt anyone – but she won't have it in the house.'

'Coffee it is then,' Freddie said and grinned. 'Save any lives today?'

'We had two girls fainting on the beach. Another one had sunburn – oh, and we had a jellyfish attack. One little boy got stung and we had to take him to the first-aid station, because he had a reaction.'

'Poor kid; that hurts,' Freddie sympathised. 'Just another day at work then.'

'Yes, afraid so,' Guy said. 'It's your turn tomorrow, Freddie. I'm visiting a friend, so you and Steve will be in charge of our beach. There is a sailing competition just down the coast at Eastbourne, so some of our senior lifeguards will be attending that, just in case.'

'Fine by me,' Freddie replied. 'That is what I'm here for.'

24

'There's a letter from Freddie,' Able said as he entered the kitchen that morning after they returned from visiting Pip. 'He wants to know if it is all right to bring a girl called Greta here at the end of the summer. He says, "Greta will be out of a job at the end of the season. She isn't much of a cook but can make beds and clean and she wants to learn typing and shorthand. She writes short stories and they might be good if I could read her handwriting! She is a friend, but I haven't told her she can definitely come until I ask – so is it all right, please?" What about that then? Do you think Freddie is in love?'

'Of course he can bring her here,' Peggy said instantly. 'He should know that... Write back and tell him so, Able.'

Able looked at Fay and Maggie, who had stopped their food preparation to look at him. 'What do you two, think about it?'

'Maybe she could wait tables,' Maggie suggested. 'Just until she qualifies as a typist. I could teach her to cook...'

'I don't think Freddie is ready for love and marriage yet,' Fay put in. 'I think she is just a friend, like he says. He mentioned her to me when he popped home for those few days. If he wants to bring her, it is all right by me.'

'Good, then I'll tell him to bring her,' Able said, a little smile on his face. He looked at Peggy. 'You haven't answered my question – do you think our Freddie is in love?'

Peggy looked at him. 'Do you want him to be? He's got a new job this autumn and plans for the future.'

'Doesn't stop him having fun,' Able said and then looked across the room at Fay. 'What about you? Who is this chap you're set on going on holiday with – if I let you go? Why haven't we met him?'

'He is busy,' Fay replied. 'I told you, Dad. Jace is a singer and a star; he is appearing at the London Palladium and we're going to the show next Monday evening. The restaurant isn't open in the evening on Mondays and Mum and Maureen said they would manage any orders from the bar for one night.' A little smile touched her lips. 'Jace's records are always in the top ten. He has asked me to go on holiday with him and I've told him it will be separate rooms. I'm not an idiot...'

'I know that, Fay,' Able said, 'but you are inclined to be impulsive. You do and say things without thinking them through. Your mother and I just want you to be happy and I want to meet him before you go gallivanting off.'

'I told you we met when I did that cookery course in France. He heard about a big record deal and had to fly out to America. He'd asked for my address and sent me a few cards from there but... then he came here for a tour and I did that party for him...'

'And ever since he has been ringing her and sending her cards,' Maggie put in. 'Tell them the rest, Fay – or I shall...'

Fay stuck her tongue out at her, but shrugged. 'Jace wants me to marry him and go and live in America...'

'No!' Peggy shuddered. 'Not you, too! I don't like it there – and you're too young to get married.'

'Do you love him?' Able asked in a more reasonable tone. 'Is that what you really want, Fay?'

'I'm not sure,' she replied honestly. 'I want to get to know him. I think about him a lot. I don't know if I want to marry him and live over there – what is it like, Dad?'

'It depends where you live,' Able replied. 'Like any other country, there are good and bad places...'

'He is thinking of Hollywood. Jace can afford a big house with a swimming pool and things like that...' Fay sighed. 'It sounds glamorous.'

'Glamour isn't everything,' Peggy objected. 'Besides, we would hardly ever see you. And what about your business? You were so sure what you wanted to do and now you decide to go off to the other side of the world!'

'It isn't that far these days. Jace is rich, Mum. We would travel by plane and that is much quicker than sea, as you know. You could visit and we would, too,' Fay said uncertainly. 'Don't say no, Mum. Please let me make up my own mind what I want...'

Peggy looked at her hard for a moment, then at Able. He nodded and she sighed. 'I suppose I have to – it's just that after what happened to me...'

'I wouldn't do what you did, Mum,' Fay stated. 'I'm not brave enough.'

Peggy hesitated and then smiled wryly. 'I doubt I've ever refused you anything, Fay – have I?'

'You did refuse to buy me a toy tortoise once. I wanted that thing so badly. It had a little wire attached and a handle you squeezed and it walked when you made it – and you said it was a waste of money...'

'Well, it was,' Peggy agreed, 'and I remember you sat on the pavement and screamed to get your own way, but I didn't give in. It was not long after the end of the war and we couldn't get toys for ages and then we could...' She looked at Able. 'You were busy in the café and we saw the damned thing in the department store...' She smiled and the tears were trickling down her cheeks. 'I do remember that, Fay. I remember all sorts of things about when you and Freddie were little...' Her voice cracked with emotion and a tear trickled down her cheek. She dashed it away impatiently.

Able reached out to take her hand. 'I knew your memory had been coming back more and more, recently,' he said. 'Has it all come back now, hon?'

'Not completely,' Peggy replied. 'There are still blanks. If someone mentions an incident like Fay just did, it brings more memories back; it's like a curtain that slides back and allows me to peep into a room and see things. I suppose I may never remember everything, but it doesn't matter. I know who I am and the people I love.'

'I'm sure it will all come back in time,' Able said and looked at Fay again. 'If Jace is going to live in Hollywood, you would probably be happy. It is your sort of place, Fay. I've always thought you need to spread your wings a bit before you settle – but, if you do decide you want to marry him, you will wait until we say – probably next spring...'

'Able!'

'Dad!'

Both Peggy and Fay looked at him.

'She is too young...' Peggy began.

'I want to get married now while Jace is here...' Fay said.

'Fay will be twenty next spring,' Able said in a forceful tone, as everyone, including Maggie, stared at him. He seldom spoke with authority but did so now. 'She may marry then with my permission, if she is sure of her own mind – and we shall visit her, Peggy. You had a bad experience, hon, but you can't let that stand in the way of Fay's happiness – can you? You'll want to see Pip and Sheila if they settle over there, too.'

Peggy looked at him hard and then inclined her head. 'As you say, Able. If it is really what she wants – but she does not marry anyone until she is quite sure.' She glanced at her daughter. 'If you marry it is for life – not just six months, Fay. You can't just walk out on it if you're bored or have an argument with your husband.'

'Fay, do you agree to wait?' Able asked sternly. 'If you do, I shall allow this holiday with Jace – but we want to meet him first. Do you understand?'

'Yes, Dad, thank you,' Fay said meekly. 'I'll tell Jace when he next rings me.'

'That will be tonight or in the early hours of the morning,' Maggie said and Fay threw a dishcloth at her.

'Beast!'

'Infant!'

'We shall leave you two to squabble,' Able said and took Peggy's hand. 'Let's go shopping, hon. It's time we had a little fun too – and I want to buy you a present.'

'It cost you such a lot for that holiday...' Peggy said hesitantly.

'All taken care of and no loan from the bank. Tom sold one of our houses this week and we both made a large profit, so everything is fine.'

* * *

Maggie looked at Fay after Able had persuaded Peggy to go out with him.

'You could have knocked me down with a feather,' she said. 'I don't think I've ever seen your father put his foot down like that before.'

'He doesn't,' Fay agreed. 'He always gives us anything we want, especially Mum – but I'm glad he did. It means I'll have time to be sure and I'll still be around for a few months to help you.'

'Thank goodness,' Maggie replied. 'Granny Peggy could have taken over the work you do when she is ready, but I need another cook if I'm going to expand the business.'

'Will you go ahead with getting another restaurant when you can – if I'm not here? Fay asked, looking a bit wistful.

'I expect so,' Maggie said. 'It may alter things a bit but—' She was interrupted by the shrill of the phone. 'It can't be Jace at this time?'

'I'll go,' Fay retorted and disappeared into the hall.

Maggie finished slicing potatoes for the Lancashire hotpot she was preparing as a pub lunch, frowning at her thoughts. She wouldn't tell Fay how much she would miss her if she left, because that might affect her decision. Maggie wanted her best friend to be happy.

Fay was glowing when she returned a few minutes later. 'I've got an order for a big celebrity wedding,' she chortled. 'Jace recommended me to a friend and they've asked for a meeting so we can plan the menus...'

'That is wonderful,' Maggie said and threw her arms around her, hugging her tight. 'I am so pleased. Let's hope someone answers that advert I put in the paper for a junior chef. We shall need it... Oh, that's the phone again...'

Fay went running into the hall. Maggie got on with making her pear upside down cake. When Fay returned, she could see the excitement in her eyes.

'Another order?'

'Yes.' Fay's eyes sparkled. 'I've been asked to do a tea this time – it's for a publisher of romantic fiction. They are giving it for their authors. I'll be able to do lots of fancy cakes and tarts...' She did a little dance around the room. 'It came from that advert in the magazine – and there may be a follow-up article. The business could pick up now, Maggie.'

'You deserve it,' Maggie laughed to see the joy in Fay's eyes. This was what she would miss if Fay went to live in America. Yes, she would carry on with her cooking, but it would never be quite the same...

* * *

Able looked at Peggy as he placed the beautiful diamond and ruby eternity ring on her finger. It fitted with her wedding ring and looked perfect.

'That is what I wanted to give you,' he told her. 'I intended to buy it on our holiday, but things went wrong – but I can give it to you now, hon. I hope you know how much I love and need you?'

Peggy smiled up into his eyes and then reached out to kiss him. 'I do love you so much,' she said. 'Even when I couldn't remember anything, that love came over strongly. I would never have made it through this without you, Able.'

'I just thank God you did,' he told her and his smile caressed her. His gaze held hers. 'You're not really upset about Fay's future plans – and we have to accept that they may happen, hon. If she loves this man and he can give her a good life...'

'Will he though?' Peggy asked. 'We don't know him. She doesn't know him well yet; she admitted it.'

'And that is why I think she truly loves him,' Able told her. 'If she'd said she was madly in love and couldn't bear to be away from him, I'd have thought it might be infatuation – but Fay can be sensible, it seems. She has changed her mind a lot in the past and by making her wait until next spring, it gives her a chance to change it again.'

'You are very wise, Able,' Peggy said. 'I shan't stand against her if she really wants it, but I can't help hoping she won't...'

'Ah, that's a different matter,' Able said. 'I would much rather she lived and worked in London, or Britain anyway – but I hope I have the strength to let her go...'

'We both have to one day,' Peggy said with a smile. 'Thank you for my beautiful ring, Able – and for everything you give me each and every day. I am very lucky.'

'We both are,' he said and then his eyes sparkled with mischief. 'I wonder what this girl Freddie wants to bring home is like? I didn't think he was ready for romance yet...'

'Oh, don't say he wants to get married as well,' Peggy exclaimed.

'I don't think so,' Able said. 'If he is in love – I doubt he even knows it himself. He is a slow and steady one. It will take him time to be sure and he won't hurry.'

'He's not like his father was, then,' Peggy said. 'I think I remember you being very urgent when you wanted me...'

'I knew what I wanted,' Able said. 'The moment I laid eyes on you...'

'Sure it wasn't when you tasted my apple pie...?'

'That might have made it more urgent,' he said, laughing with her. 'But no – it was you, Peggy Ronoscki – your body I loved and lusted after... and I still do.'

Peggy giggled like a young girl. 'Go on with you,' she said and gave him a poke in the ribs. 'We're far too old for...' She gave a shout of laughter as he pulled her to him right there in the busy street. 'Or maybe we're not... we'll see later.' Her eyes promised as she looked up at him and then she knew. It didn't matter if she never got all of her memories back; they could make new ones, because their love was just as strong and good as it aways had been.

25

'You were wonderful, Jace,' Fay said when she and Maggie were invited round to his dressing room after the show. 'I like the new songs – are they on the LP you've been working on?'

'Yes, both of them, but there's a lot of the older songs too. I think we have about six new ones – but I wrote one of those for you, Fay. You'll know when you get the album I'll send you.'

'When do you finish here?' Maggie asked him and he looked at her for the first time since they entered his dressing room. 'I have a friend who wants two tickets, so I said I'd try to get them for her... Shirley never has time to go and buy tickets,' she added as Fay looked at her. 'She wants them as a birthday present for her husband Ray. Apparently, he likes Jace's records.'

'I know the show is sold out,' Jace said, 'but I think someone in the band might still have their complimentary tickets. We all get a couple, but Mack usually doesn't bother to give his away. He's the one on saxophone.'

'He's brilliant,' Maggie said. 'But you all sound good, which is just as well, because Fay is always playing your records. I have to work to them...'

'Sorry about that,' Jace said and held out his hand in apology. 'I know we haven't met before – if I was rude, or ignored you, blame this one; she puts everything else out of my head.' He put his arm around Fay's waist.

'I should have introduced you properly,' Fay said, 'but you both knew who the other was. My father does want to meet you, Jace. You're invited to lunch any day this week – will you come?'

'What about tomorrow?' he replied with a pleased look. 'I'd like to meet the rest of your family – and we could have the afternoon to ourselves...'

'Don't you have to rehearse or something?' Maggie inquired.

'No, not tomorrow. It's just a repeat of today's show.' He pulled Fay closer. 'Shall we all go to a nightclub?'

'Not for me,' Maggie said. 'I'll get a taxi and let you two spend a little time together.'

'No. I'm not coming, Jace,' Fay told him. 'We have to be up early, busy day tomorrow. I'll be prepping while Maggie goes to market. I'll see you when you come to us for lunch and we'll spend the afternoon together.' She smiled at him and kissed his cheek. 'If I swan off to a nightclub and leave Maggie to go home on her own, Dad might refuse to let me go on holiday...'

'We wouldn't want that,' Jace laughed but seemed annoyed.

They talked for a little longer and then another member of his band entered the dressing room and they left them to discuss a slight technical problem.

After they left the theatre to emerge into the busy street and hail a taxi, Maggie looked at Fay sideways. 'I can see why you like him,' she said, 'but I'm not sure I do...'

'Why?' Fay demanded. 'What don't you like about him?'

'I don't know,' Maggie said truthfully. 'I'm just not sure he is good enough for you, Fay. Perhaps I wouldn't think anyone good enough... sorry. I wanted to like him...'

Fay pouted at her. 'I don't dislike your boyfriends.'

'I don't have any,' Maggie said and sighed. 'James is always too busy and...' She shook her head. 'Maybe I'm a jealous cat...'

'No, you're not,' Fay said and looked reflective. 'Jace can be selfish and he isn't always thoughtful. He ignored you until you spoke to him – and he wasn't pleased when I said no to a night-club... He isn't perfect, but neither am I.'

'Don't take any notice of me, Fay,' Maggie told her. 'I'm just tired I expect. Make up your own mind about him.' She stepped forward and hailed a taxi with its light on. It pulled over and stopped for them and they got into the back. 'All I know is that I want you to be happy – and your parents do too.'

Maggie felt uneasy as she undressed that night. She wasn't sure why she'd taken a sudden dislike to Jace – unless it was because when he pulled Fay to him, he'd looked so possessive. She had a sudden fear for her friend. Possessive men could be overwhelming, dominating the lives of those around them. Fay would never be happy with a man who tried to rule her – and yet perhaps Maggie was imagining things. She had no right to influence Fay. Perhaps she was a little jealous. There was no doubting that Jace wanted Fay. It was there in his eyes – but wanting and loving were not the same. Maggie hoped Fay wouldn't end up with a broken heart.

She slipped between cool sheets that smelled of soapflakes and thought about her own life. Maggie loved what she did; it was a full, interesting life – and yet, she also wanted someone of her own. Thus far, she hadn't been lucky enough to find the right man. She didn't want to give up her career, but the right man would understand that...

A picture of a man's scarred face came into her mind. His eyes –

the way he'd looked at her... but she didn't know him and it was foolish to think about someone she might never see again.

Sighing, Maggie turned over and went to sleep. Just before she dropped off, she heard the phone ring and knew that Fay had answered it. Jace must have rung her again, instead of going to the nightclub, and they would probably sit talking for an hour or more.

* * *

Fay was in the kitchen cooking breakfast for the family when Maggie came back from the market the next morning. The smell of bacon frying was enticing. Everyone was laughing and talking and she looked at them, feeling happy because her family was together again.

'Your mum is coming for lunch today,' Fay told her. 'When Mum said Jace was coming, she got all excited and asked if she could come too. What did you get for us?'

'Well, I got skate for the restaurant and cod and plaice as well – but skate is Mum's favourite, so we could have that ourselves. I've got loads of stuff in the fridge for this evening anyway...'

'Oh, good, I like that,' Able said. 'You can't always get it, so it makes a nice change. By the way, Maggie, someone rang for you early this morning. He is coming to the restaurant this evening and hopes to see you then...'

'James is coming to the restaurant?' Maggie was surprised.

'No, not James – some chap named Greg. I can't recall his second name...'

Maggie's breath caught in her throat. 'Greg Hayes. He is a racing driver but he had a terrible accident...'

'Yes, Freddie and I saw it happen on TV,' Able said. 'I didn't know you had such famous friends – both you and Fay. A famous singer to lunch and a racing driver this evening…' His eyes twinkled with mischief. 'Can I expect Her Majesty for tea?'

'Able! Stop teasing,' Peggy commanded and looked at her granddaughter. 'You never mentioned him, Maggie?'

Fay threw her a wicked look, very like her father's. 'She's got a soft spot for him, Mum – and I think he's mad about her…'

'Fay! Don't be daft. I've only met him a few times,' Maggie said, her cheeks flaming.

Fay arched her brows. 'You did it to me…'

'That was different. Jace had asked you to marry him. Greg – well, he helped me when I had a slight accident with the van.'

'Yes, I did notice the repairs,' Able said. 'They were well done – that wing had a tiny dent in it when we bought it and now it hasn't.' He frowned. 'Were you hurt?'

'Slightly. Greg took me home in his car and bathed a cut – and I cooked a meal for us. He brought me home afterwards…'

'In a very posh car,' Fay remarked. 'He has an apartment in London – and a lovely house in the country.'

'How did you know that?' Maggie demanded.

'Jace told me. He knew all about him and the accident… says he was one of the most popular drivers – and rich, apparently. Old money, Jace says.'

'He was just a stranger being kind, that's all.'

'He came to see you were all right the next day, and he brought friends here for a meal, but then he went off to America,' Fay said. 'He didn't say why or when he'd be back – but he wrote to you.' She laughed as Maggie glared at her. 'Freddie thought he was interested.'

'Then why just go off and not ask me out or say when he'll be back?' Maggie asked. 'Fay is right… I liked him and I would have liked to know him better, but that's all there is to it.'

'Then why is he coming here this evening?' Peggy asked and

they all looked at her. 'There are hundreds if not thousands of places to eat in London, Maggie. Why would someone like that come here if he didn't want to see you?'

Maggie felt her cheeks burn. 'I don't know,' she admitted. 'I do want to see him – but why hasn't he been in touch? Jace manages to send Fay cards all the time and ring her. If Greg wanted to be friends, why not say something before he left?'

'That is the question,' Able said and his eyes were filled with mischief. 'I have a feeling it may be answered this evening.'

Peggy looked at him suspiciously. 'What do you know that we don't, Able?'

'Ah, that would be telling,' Able replied, looking mysterious. 'I think we will leave that for Mr Hayes to reveal himself...'

'Now you'll have us all wondering and guessing all day,' Peggy said. 'Tell us, Able. What did he say to you on the phone?'

'Just that he wanted a reservation and was hoping to see Maggie...'

'So?' Peggy persisted.

Able met her gaze. 'I saw something about him on American TV just before we left – but it isn't for me to tell you. If Mr Hayes had wanted Maggie to know, I am certain he would have told her. He hasn't told me...'

'But you know,' Peggy said and looked at Maggie. 'I'll get it out of him, don't you worry.'

However, when Able finally told her privately, Peggy agreed that it wasn't for them to tell Maggie. Greg Hayes had a secret and it was his to share, not theirs.

* * *

Carla returned from serving at table ten later that evening. She looked excited and sort of secretive. 'Mr Hayes sends his compliments to the chef and asks if he can come to the kitchen to say thank you?'

'Yes, of course,' Maggie agreed, though she was feeling hot, tiny beads of perspiration on her brow. She dabbed at her forehead with the cloth she kept for it and then looked at Fay. 'Is my nose shiny?'

'Yes,' Fay told her truthfully. 'But he won't notice. You look beautiful, Maggie. You always do.'

Maggie finished plating up her latest order and stood back, allowing Fay to take the next order from the shelf. Her heart was racing and she felt strangely anxious. Able's teasing had put all kinds of things into her head and she'd imagined Greg married to a Hollywood star or winning a big race – or anything but the truth, which was apparent the moment he walked in and turned his face towards her. The scarring was still there, but much less of it and it seemed to have faded.

'Is it OK?' he asked and she nodded wordlessly.

'You had something done...' she said. 'Does it feel easier? I know you said it felt tight and irritated at times.'

'I hope it makes me look better,' Greg said, a question in his eyes. 'More attractive as a man?'

'You always looked just fine to me,' Maggie replied. 'Yes, it is much better, Greg. I'm sure she will like it... whoever she is...'

Greg smiled. 'I was wondering if she would come out with me tomorrow. I know you're busy most evenings. Perhaps we could take the morning if you could manage that...?'

'Of course she can,' Fay told him. 'Mum and me will do the pub lunches. Maggie can stay out all day if she wants. I'll ask Rose to help with the evening service.'

'Maggie...' Greg looked at her and she nodded.

'I'd like that,' she said a little shyly. 'Shall I pack us a picnic?'

'No, we'll find something to eat somewhere,' Greg replied. 'I'm going through to the pub now. Able invited me to have a drink and a chat. If you have time later, you might join us?'

'Yes, I will, when I've finished the mains,' Maggie agreed. 'Fay can see to the desserts; they are all prepared ahead.'

'That brandy and chocolate mousse was delicious,' he said. 'You are both talented cooks.'

With that he went out, leaving them alone in the kitchen. Fay served up the desserts for table nine and then looked at Maggie as Carla departed with a full tray.

'Well, what do you think of that then?'

'I don't know what you mean,' Maggie frowned. 'I'm glad he's had the treatment for his sake. I know he was very conscious of the scarring.'

'He went to America for treatment for you,' Fay told her. 'It is obvious, Maggie. He didn't tell you because he wasn't sure what they could do for him – but it is certainly a big improvement.'

'He didn't have to do it for me,' Maggie said. 'Surely he knew that?'

Fay looked at her. 'I think this is the last of the mains, Maggie. It's just the chicken casserole. I can do that. Why don't you pop upstairs and freshen up before you go through to the bar?'

'If, you're sure?' Maggie smiled. 'I would like to put something decent on...'

'Go on, I can manage here,' she urged and then her mother walked in, looking pleased. 'Mum will help if I suddenly get more orders.'

'You go and join your young man,' Peggy told her with a smile. 'And don't say he isn't – because he will be if you want him.'

Maggie gulped and ran. She had a quick wash and changed into a thin silk dress and slipped on some pretty white sandals, sprayed perfume behind her ears and went down to the bar. Standing in the doorway, she saw Able and Greg talking and laughing together. It was obvious that they got on well and it made her smile.

Greg turned his head to look at her and the look in his eyes made her draw a sharp breath. She felt tingling at the back of her neck as she went to join them.

'Greg was just telling me he is going into the mechanical side of racing,' Able told her. 'Going to join Lotus as an independent advisor on their cars.'

'You won't be racing again?' Maggie asked, her heart beating madly. 'Won't you miss it?'

'I'll still be involved,' he told her, his gaze firmly fixed on her. 'I'll be working in the factory, involved in design and helping to oversee the development of the new cars – and I may travel with the team for overseas races sometimes, but no, I shan't miss the driving.'

'Is that why you went to America – or part of the reason?'

'No. My future was discussed the evening we came here. I was offered the chance to drive for Ferrari – an Italian Formula One team – but I turned it down. I went to America because I was advised that I could get the right treatment for my scarring there – but I wasn't certain it would work, so I didn't tell anyone.'

Maggie nodded. 'It's wonderful that it helped you,' she said. 'Surprising what clever people can do these days...'

Greg nodded and sipped his beer. 'I'm relieved it is over,' he told her. 'Now, let's talk about you, Maggie. You look beautiful and Able told me that an artist you're friendly with painted some pictures of you. I think I saw them at a gallery in New York, but I wasn't sure it was you?'

'You might have done,' Maggie agreed. 'James painted them a couple of years ago. He says they are his best work...'

'I didn't think they were you, although I could see a likeness... but they were a bit ethereal, as if you were more fairy than human.

I don't see you like that, Maggie.' He didn't say how he saw her, but the expression in his eyes did strange things to the nape of her neck, sending little spirals down her spine.

'James says I've changed. He doesn't want to paint me now, because he thinks I've lost that innocent look.'

'Is James special to you?' Greg asked, his eyes still seeming glued to hers.

'He is a friend,' Maggie replied and she suddenly knew that was all James could ever have been to her. 'He likes my food and he forgets to eat when he's working, so I take him food sometimes… but not since he got back from America.'

Greg nodded. He turned, but Able had moved down the bar and was talking to some other customers. 'Shall we go somewhere we can talk?'

'We could just walk,' Maggie suggested. 'It was hot in the kitchen today. I like to walk at night when it is cooler.'

'I do too,' Greg agreed.

* * *

Maggie and Greg left the over-warm bar together and began to walk through the lanes towards Commercial Road, which was still busy even at this hour, the shop windows lit and the buses moving along the street, stopping to disgorge their passengers and take up new ones.

'Granny says that this was all dark during the war,' Maggie said, because they had been silent for a while. 'It must have been so difficult to find your way around London then…'

'Almost impossible, unless you knew every street,' Greg agreed. 'I like Able and your grandmother. I read about them being caught up in that riot. Able told me that she lost all her memories for the past twenty years or so. That must have been terrifying for her – alone in a strange country.'

'Yes, I suppose it was like being alone, because she didn't know Able,' Maggie said. 'She has come through it very well and remembers a lot of things now – but not everything, yet anyway.'

'Perhaps if she saw the right doctors?' he suggested.

'She'll fight it herself – the way she has all her life.'

'A very strong lady. I think you take after her in some ways, Maggie.'

'Yes, I might do,' she agreed. 'I hope I do.'

'Tell me about yourself,' Greg invited as they paused in front of a TV screen in a shop window that was showing news. 'Those poor devils trying to flee from East Germany to the West; so many of them are being killed, but they refuse to open up and let them go.'

'I don't think they will,' Maggie said and paused, then, 'What do you want to know about me?'

'I know you're a wonderful cook and beautiful, intelligent and generous,' he said, 'but I don't know what you like – what makes you happy?'

Maggie laughed. 'Do any of us know that? I'm happy in my work. It gives me pride to see a perfectly cooked and presented meal – but I do like other things. I enjoy music and I like horses. I don't often get the chance to ride, but I do when I'm on holiday. I was given a pony by a friend when I was a small girl and I loved it so much...'

'You should have your own horses,' Greg said. 'I suppose it is very expensive to keep them in town. Easier in the country, if you have a paddock or two.'

'Do you ride?' Maggie looked at him.

'Yes, I ride. I have a couple of horses... I'd like you to see my home when you have time for a little holiday? It's in Sussex and the countryside is beautiful – lots of places to ride or walk.'

'I'd love to come – for a couple of days. I'm too busy to take much time off at the moment.'

'You could come one weekend, when you get a chance, and ride the mare. She's about right for you – you're quite tall, taller than your cousin.'

'Yes, I'm taller than Fay,' Maggie agreed. 'She doesn't like horses – but we share most things, or we have done…' A shadow passed across her face. 'She is thinking she might go to America to live next year. I'll miss her. I've advertised for a new chef's assistant and I can manage the work – but she is a friend…'

'Yes, you miss friends,' Greg agreed, 'but you make new ones.'

'Fay is special to me,' Maggie replied thoughtfully. 'I want her to be happy, but I'm not sure she will be. She thinks she might be in love with someone and he wants to marry her – but I'm not sure he's right for her.'

'Isn't that her choice to make?'

'Yes, of course it is and I wouldn't interfere – but I think she might come home in a couple of years with a broken heart.'

'Although she might be happier than you can imagine?' he suggested in a reasonable tone.

Maggie laughed. 'Yes, that is true. Able won't let her marry until next spring when she will be twenty, so she has time to change her mind. If she still feels the same way then, I shall wish her happy.'

'Of course you will,' he said and smiled. 'Where shall we go tomorrow?'

'I'd like to go where it's cool; it's going to be hot again – why not on the Serpentine?'

'In a boat?' Greg looked at her. 'Did you know I like boats?' Maggie shook her head. 'Well, I do. I've got a boat moored up at Henley. If I fetched you early, we could go there?'

'That would be lovely,' Maggie said. 'I work in London, but I love being in the country whenever I can. One day I'll own a couple of restaurants and live in a nice little cottage not too far from the sea...'

'Will you, Maggie?' Greg laughed softly. 'Yes, I am sure you will, if it is what you want.'

26

'Well?' Peggy demanded that evening when they were alone in their bedroom. 'You've met them both – so do you approve of the girls' choices?'

Able's gaze narrowed in thought. 'I liked Greg Hayes. Decent chap, seems to think a lot of Maggie. He has old money behind him, Peggy. If she wanted him, he could give her all she ever dreamed of – the restaurants, big house and all the rest, and I think he would look after her...'

'I liked him,' Peggy agreed. 'The money doesn't matter if he loves her and she loves him. Maggie wouldn't marry him if she didn't...' She looked at her husband. 'What about this singer then? What did you think to him?'

'I'm not sure,' Able said and frowned. 'On the face of it, he seems to care about Fay. He probably has even more money than Greg – but... I don't know if he is right for our Fay.'

'I didn't like him,' Peggy said decisively. 'I know that's unfair, because I don't know him – but he wasn't at ease with us the way Greg was this evening. He seemed moody. He made jokes and held

Fay's hand a lot but... I think he loves himself more than he loves her. Something wasn't right with him...'

'Yes, I fear that your instinct may be true; he seemed a bit selfish to me,' Able agreed. 'We can't forbid her to see him, hon. Fay would just resent us and I wouldn't put it past her to run off with him. You know how impetuous she can be...'

'Yes, that's what I'm afraid of.' Peggy looked anxiously at him. 'I think he will hurt her if she goes off with him. He doesn't seem the type to settle down to me.'

Able's deep tone gave away his feelings as he growled, 'I wish she'd never met the chap – but we still can't forbid her to see him, hon.'

'I know – but I think one of us should have a little chat with her, before she goes on this holiday. Try to make her see that she could ruin her life by marrying the wrong man. I made a mistake the first time. Laurie was often thoughtless and selfish. I don't want Fay to make the same mistake when I know how much better life is with the right man...'

Able yawned and eased his shoulders. 'Let's get some sleep. We'll see what happens in the morning. Fay isn't an idiot and perhaps she will see what's wrong with Jace for herself...'

Fay was tired after the busy service was finished. It had been hot and airless in the kitchen and she'd felt restless. She went straight up to her room and stripped off her work things, then had a wash and got in bed. However, sleep eluded her as she tossed and turned.

Her parents didn't like Jace. They'd been polite and welcoming as they always were, but they didn't like him. Jace hadn't seemed easy with them either. She had thought he would fit into her family, but he hadn't. First Maggie had warned her to think carefully and she was pretty sure her parents would do the same when they got round to it. What was wrong with Jace that he'd acted the way he had, making stupid jokes and touching her all the time? He'd been ill at ease, even angry, an odd, almost resentful, expression in his eyes that made her wonder at the change.

She'd walked a little way down the street with him after lunch and he'd seemed more like himself. 'Is something wrong?' she'd asked. 'Only – you didn't enjoy yourself with my family, did you?'

'Not much; I had my reasons,' Jace had admitted. 'I felt I was on trial, Fay – and your mother didn't like me. It made me uncomfortable and I reacted badly, sorry.' He'd muttered a curse. 'I'm upset about something, that's all...'

'It doesn't matter,' she'd told him, but it did. Fay had hoped it would all be wonderful and her parents would relent and let her marry this year – if she wanted to.

Tears stung her eyes as she turned them to the pillow and then thumped it hard. How could she marry a man her parents didn't like and go halfway across the world, knowing that she might never see them? Jace would never want to come on holiday to see her family, which meant she would either not see them or she would have to come back alone.

Oh, damn it! Fay buried into her soft pillow and let the tears fall. Why couldn't Jace be nice, the way Greg was with Maggie? She'd felt a little jealous when she'd seen the way he looked at Maggie that evening. Fay knew instinctively that Greg had gone through treatment which must have been uncomfortable, even painful, and he'd done it for Maggie, because he wanted to look better for her.

Fay couldn't imagine Jace doing that for her. Not the man she'd seen that lunchtime. The thoughts kept running through her head and she didn't know what she wanted; she was in turmoil. A part of her wanted to throw caution to the wind and go with Jace, but another part of her was warning her she would be sorry if she did.

He'd told her their holiday was booked to start the day after his show ended and he would be picking her up at eight in the morning. Fay groaned as she fought her whirling emotions. Did she love him enough – or was she only infatuated with his fame and his wonderful voice? He was good-looking and his job was glamorous – but life was more than that; it was about family and friends... and most definitely love.

Fay was restless a long time, tossing and turning. Maggie was having time off in the morning and Fay had offered to stand in for her. She would be dead tired at this rate. Finally, sleep overtook her and she gave a gentle snore.

She was sleeping soundly when Maggie peeped in at her early the next morning and she didn't wake until her mother came to rouse her.

The lecture she'd been half expecting didn't materialise. Instead, Peggy asked if she had enough money for her holiday and any new clothes she wanted to buy before they left.

'I've got plenty of clothes,' Fay said, 'and I have some money saved. Besides, Jace is paying for it. It was his idea...'

'Yes, but you'll need money,' Peggy said. 'I'll give you some if you need it?'

'I have enough thanks, Mum,' Fay replied and then looked at her. 'You didn't like Jace much, did you?'

'I don't know him,' Peggy said. 'You like him as a friend and that's what matters but... No, I shan't interfere. You're old enough to know your own mind, Fay.'

'Thanks, Mum,' Fay said and kissed her, but perversely she wished that her mother had warned her to be careful. 'I wish I was more like you – I'm not like Dad either. Where did you get me from?'

'I think you might be a bit like my mother,' Peggy told her. 'She could never make up her mind and Able says his mother was a bit that way as well – so maybe it is an inherited thing from way back. Or maybe we've just spoiled you?'

Fay laughed. 'I've been spoiled. I know that...' She caught her mother's hand. 'I like him a lot, Mum, but I'm not sure I want to give up everything for Jace. I don't think he would do it for me...'

'You are a sensible girl despite the spoiling,' Peggy said and kissed her. 'I just want you to be happy and so does your father.'

* * *

'I didn't say much to her,' Peggy told Able later. 'I think she knows in her heart he isn't right for her, but she has to make her own mind up.'

'Perhaps we should just let her grow up,' Able suggested. 'She needs to test her wings, hon. We have to let her – even if she flies too near the sun.'

Peggy inclined her head. They both wanted to tell Fay it was a bad idea to go away for a holiday with Jace and an even worse one to marry him, but it would probably only make her set her mind on him even more. It was only right that she had freedom to choose and all they could do was watch and hope she would not get hurt too much.

27

Greg had found them a quiet spot to sit and talk, behind them a smart restaurant situated on the riverbank at Henley. It was a busy place with the buzz of chatter and laughter, but here, on the wide expanse of grass that led down to the water's edge, there was a tranquil peace, broken only by the humming of bees in a flower bed and birdsong. The river looked beautiful, clear and sparkling in the sunshine as it flowed through a serene scene of sloping, well-kept grassy banks, wild flowers, an ancient wooden jetty and graceful willows at the water's edge. Out on the water, a rowing boat was streaking past, the oarsmen pulling hard as they trained for one of the regattas that were held here regularly. Greg's house-boat was moored a little further down and they'd walked to look at it: a small wooden boat with a polished oak deck and wheelhouse, all beautifully kept. Now as they sat, just talking and sipping their drinks, water rippled lazily, a family of swans seeming to float by on the dark surface. In the hazy summer sunshine, it was a glorious haven.

'The swans look as if they're gliding, but there's a lot of work going on underneath,' Maggie remarked and sipped her long cool drink of orange juice over ice.

'I suspect a lot of life is like that,' Greg said and smiled at her. 'This is a lovely spot – but anywhere would seem perfect to me if you were there.'

She looked at him, cheeks slightly warm. 'You don't know me yet. I can get cross if things go wrong at work and my nose shines when I'm busy.'

'Your nose looks fine to me,' he replied with a smile. 'I knew you from the minute we met – the way you looked at me. Didn't you feel it, too?'

'Yes, I did,' she said. 'Why did you go through all that pain to have the scar treated? You didn't need to do it for me. I think I fell in love with you when you came to my aid, or when you stopped being cross – my knight in shining armour...' Her eyes sparked with mischief. 'Mind you, the fancy car and apartment might have had something to do with it.'

'Only borrowed, I'm afraid,' Greg teased and she laughed.

'Good job I don't care about them then.' Maggie met his eyes. 'I didn't believe in love at first sight until I met you and then I told myself I was dreaming.' She reached out to touch his hand. 'When you just went off to America that way, I thought it was just me being silly...'

'Oh no, Maggie. I was the foolish one. I fell hard for the brave young woman who had just driven into a lamp post but was more worried about her cases of wine than herself. I should have told you how I felt before I left for America, but I got the offer of immediate treatment and I knew it was much too soon to speak of love.' He touched his face. 'It feels so much easier, not as tight as it did. I wasn't certain it would work, but I can smile properly now.'

'Your real smile is in your eyes,' Maggie said and her fingers entwined with his lovingly. She'd fallen for him that first night but hadn't believed it and they'd had so little time together. Now she knew instinctively he was the one for her.

'Your face lights up when you smile,' he replied, one finger caressing the back of her hand. 'The moment I saw you, I felt I'd been hit by a whirlwind that would change my life. It was the reason I decided not to race again but to take the job Lotus offered me.'

'Oh, Greg... won't you miss the racing?'

'No. I meant what I just said, Maggie. I am in love with you – and for me that means a life together.'

'I love you too...' She gave a little sigh.

'What is wrong, my darling? You can tell me.'

'What are we going to do, Greg?' Maggie asked, her hand holding tightly to his. 'My grandmother and step-grandfather have spent a lot of money renovating and expanding at the Pig & Whistle. Able had to buy the property from the brewery to do what we wanted. Your work will be miles away. I can't just walk out and come with you. Besides, I want to run the restaurant.'

Greg's soft chuckle made her look at him and smile.

Maggie gazed into his eyes. 'I know you haven't asked me to marry you – but you are going to, aren't you?'

'Yes, but I'm not going to demand you give up everything just like that,' he said. 'You could hire a chef to take your place in time, but I have a new job too and I'll have to concentrate on that for a while, which means I'll travel back and forth. We can live in London and use the country place for holidays or I might sell. You mean more to me than any house, Maggie. I can rearrange my life to be with you. Besides, if you take more staff on you don't need to be there the whole time. You can still do your share and oversee things.'

'Yes, I could,' she agreed. 'It's what I planned to do when we could afford another restaurant – but that is for the future.'

'It doesn't have to be,' Greg told her. 'I could finance a restaurant wherever you chose...'

'I would rather you didn't,' Maggie replied, the love in her eyes softening the words. 'I have to earn it. I want to succeed, not use your money to finance something that might fail – and it might. It isn't that easy to get a regular trade. At the Pig & Whistle I had a head start. I'm content with that for the moment. One day, if and when I'm ready, you can be my partner in a new venture.'

Greg looked into her eyes. 'Are we going to have a long, slow, courtship or get married and accept that our jobs will keep us apart sometimes?'

Maggie took a deep breath and then made her decision. 'I'd like it if we got married sooner rather than later and just let things work themselves out.'

He leaned forward and kissed her. 'I can't believe I'm so lucky...'

'We're both lucky,' Maggie breathed and put a hand to his face, caressing it with her fingertips. 'I think it was fate that we met that night.'

'I'm glad it happened the way it did, but please be more careful in future. You are a brave wonderful girl, Maggie, and I don't want to lose you.'

'You won't,' she said and kissed him softly on the lips. 'You haven't met my mother yet or my stepfather. 'I'll get them to ask you to dinner next Sunday and you can meet them then.'

'I'm afraid I don't have a family – my parents died a few years back and I was an only child.'

'I'm sorry – that must have been hard for you.'

'It was – but I have a lot of friends.'

'I'd like to meet them.'

'You will.' He reached for her hand again. 'I like your grandparents. I hope your mother and stepfather will be as easy to get on with.' He looked at her thoughtfully. 'Who do I ask for your hand in marriage – Able or your stepdad, or your mum?'

'We just tell them. I'm old enough to marry without consent. Ryan won't say much and Mum will like you.'

'I hope so, because I want to be with you for the rest of my life.'

'Me too,' Maggie said and then laughed. 'And I tell Fay she is the impulsive one...'

'Why – what has she done?' His eyebrows rose in amused enquiry.

Maggie's smile shaded. 'Oh, she wants to go on holiday with a singer named Jace and then, if she decides she's in love with him, marry him and go to live in Hollywood... but I'm not sure I like him...'

'Jace is an unusual name...' Greg's gaze narrowed and the laughter left his eyes. 'If it's the man I think... she would be making a big mistake.'

'Why, what do you know about him?' Maggie stared at him. 'You have to tell me, Greg. Fay is my cousin and I don't want her to get hurt.'

'It isn't my place to tell tales.' He frowned. 'I can't tell you something that was related to me in confidence – but if I were you, I'd advise her to be very careful...'

Maggie bit her lip. Suddenly, the peaceful atmosphere was spoiled. 'Please, don't leave it like that,' she begged. 'If you know something that we ought to know, you should tell me. Please, Greg. It's important to me.'

He hesitated, then, 'Perhaps you have the right to know in the circumstances. Have you heard of a girl called Mitsy?' Greg asked and Maggie was transfixed as she nodded.

'She is Jace's roadie, carts the kit about for the band, very strong girl.'

'Yes, that's the one. Mitsy's mother works for me sometimes –

comes in to clean the house when I'm away. She is a very sad lady at the moment—' Greg paused uncertainly, then, '—Mitsy killed herself in the bath two days ago. Cut her own wrists with a razor blade and bled to death. Her mother believes it is because of this Jace... she was pregnant.'

Maggie felt the colour drain from her face. 'You think it was Jace's baby, don't you?'

He didn't answer, but the suspicion was in his eyes. 'She didn't tell her mother who the father was, but she was mad about Jace and it seems likely, though we can't know for certain...'

'You think he threw her over when she discovered she was pregnant and that's why she killed herself?'

Again, Greg didn't answer. He'd told her what he knew; the rest was speculation.

Maggie felt sick. 'I want to go home,' she said.

'I'm sorry. I shouldn't have said anything – but it was in my mind because I spoke to Mitsy's mother on the phone yesterday and she told me she hadn't been in to clean, because she'd been so upset. It is an unpleasant thing to tell you, Maggie. I'm sorry I've upset you... spoiled things.'

'Upset me? I'm angry rather than upset,' Maggie told him, eyes flashing. 'Not with you – but with Jace. How dare he make out he loves Fay and has been thinking of her all this time when he's been... It's disgusting. And to cast off the girl because she was pregnant...'

'I don't know the whole story, Maggie, just her mother's thoughts – but I'd advise your cousin to make sure she knows what she is doing...'

'I certainly intend to...' Maggie sniffed hard. 'I think it will break her heart, but if she marries him, he'll break it anyway...' She glanced at her watch. 'It's time we left. I need to be back for the dinner service this evening.'

'Yes...' Greg looked at her regretfully. 'I'll be away for a few days now, working, but I'll be back to meet your parents next Sunday... if you still want me to?'

'Yes, of course, I do.' She reached out and touched his hand. 'I'm not blaming you in any way, Greg. You didn't want to tell me, but it was right that you did. If I can save Fay from making a mistake, I must.'

'Yes, of course you must,' he agreed. 'It won't be easy for you – and she may not believe you...'

'At least I can warn her. It is up to her what she does...' Maggie looked regretful. 'I shan't tell anyone about us, Greg. I can't if Fay is miserable. We'll have to wait for a while.'

'We can see each other, get to know one another,' Greg said. 'We both know what we want, but there is no rush. I just want to be with you as much as possible.'

'Me too,' Maggie replied. 'We'll meet as often as we can – but it will be difficult if Fay is upset...'

He nodded. 'I don't think your Fay will like me very much when you tell her what I've told you.'

'I shan't say who told me, just that I've heard something...' Maggie sighed. 'She was looking forward to this holiday, I think...' It was going to be so hard to shatter Fay's illusions, but it had to be done.

* * *

'No! It is a lie. I don't believe it. I won't,' Fay cried when Maggie told her what she'd heard later that evening. 'How do you know? Who told you such a wicked lie?'

'It came via Mitsy's mother,' Maggie replied sadly. 'It is horrible. I don't want it to be true, Fay – but you have to ask him!'

'Why are you being so nasty about Jace – all of you? Mum and

Dad don't like him. I know he was acting oddly when he came to lunch yesterday...' The colour drained from Fay's face. 'He said he wasn't himself... that he was upset over something.' Her eyes met Maggie's. 'Do you think he'd heard about Mitsy – that she'd killed herself? Is that why Jace acted that way? I couldn't understand it. He never has before. He said it was because my parents didn't like him, but if...' Fay's eyes filled with tears. 'It can't be true, Maggie. Jace wouldn't do that... he couldn't have... not if he loves me.'

'I'm sorry, Fay,' Maggie told her sincerely. 'I hate hurting you like this, but you had to know. I couldn't let you go off on holiday with him – and perhaps marry him, if he isn't to be trusted.'

For a moment, Fay looked at her rebelliously and then her body sagged. 'I know you didn't want to hurt me,' she said, 'but you have. Please, Maggie, don't tell Mum and Dad about this. I will ask Jace for the truth, I promise you – and I'll know if he lies.'

'Are you in love with him? You weren't sure...'

'I wasn't sure, but after he behaved badly and I considered whether I should go on that holiday... I realised that I cared about him and I was willing to overlook the way he'd been, so I must love him a bit, mustn't I?'

'It sounds as if you do,' Maggie agreed. She wanted to put her arms around Fay and hug her, but knew that at the moment she wouldn't want a show of affection. 'I promise not to tell anyone else. I know that the story about Misty killing herself and being pregnant is true – but not if Jace was the father. Only he can tell you that now.'

Fay nodded and lifted her head proudly. 'I thought I could forgive him anything but – not this...' She closed her eyes briefly. 'If Mitsy was having his baby, he should have helped her, married her – or at least promised to give her all she needed for the child's future.'

'Will you forgive me for telling you?' Maggie asked anxiously.

'You did the right thing,' Fay replied, 'but I can't help wishing you hadn't...'

* * *

Fay cried herself to sleep again that night. She felt miserable, unsure and angry all at once. If she couldn't trust her own instincts, how would she ever find love? She'd really believed that Jace loved her, but if he was cheating on her all the time with Mitsy... he didn't truly love her. Not in the way Fay wanted to be loved – the way Maggie was loved.

Fay had wanted to ask Maggie about her day out and whether Greg had asked her to marry him. She was certain he was going to and had thought Maggie might come back wearing an engagement ring. It had been so obvious that they were in love.

'I wish Freddie was here,' Fay sighed before she fell into a restless sleep, in which she was drowning in a raging sea. Then Freddie swam out and rescued her and suddenly everything was all right again.

28

Freddie was woken early by the frantic knocking at his bedroom door. He struggled to open his eyes, being deeply asleep, but the urgent sound of Greta's voice had him jumping out of bed. It had been a sultry August night and too hot for pyjamas, so he was just wearing underpants, and he didn't have time to find his dressing robe because she was clearly desperate.

'Is there a fire?' he asked, because the smell of burning was quite strong.

'Only in the kitchen. I burned the kippers and the toast... and the toaster is ruined, as well as her best frying pan.' Greta gulped. 'I was writing a story down and... and Aunt Edith is furious. She said she's had enough of me and told me to leave now...'

'She can't do that.' Freddie took her hand, urging her into his room. 'Turn your back while I get dressed... though I suppose it is too late for that now.' He laughed ruefully as he hastily pulled on the shorts and cotton shirt he wore on the beach. 'Is she just angry or does she really mean it?'

'She means it,' Greta said calming down. 'She's had an offer from someone to buy the boarding house, but they want an answer now – so she's going to sell...'

'But why throw you out for burning the toast?' Freddie stared at her.

'And her kippers and I ruined the toaster – and I broke her best teapot earlier. I burned her best silk blouse yesterday when I was ironing it. She says I'm stupid and can't do anything properly because my head is filled with nonsense... but I was trying to do the ironing, take her cake out of the oven – and then someone rang about a booking. I only left the iron for a moment to take the cake out, but the sleeve was up against it and it singed a little bit...'

'If she thinks you're stupid, she shouldn't ask you to iron her best blouse,' Freddie said. It seemed to him that Mrs Phipps expected her niece to do far too much. He thought for a moment then, 'Would you like to live with my family in London and help out there until you get the job you want? They've said it is all right to take you – and I'm going up this weekend. Guy says I can have two days off, because I've done extra duties this week. I can take you and then come back and finish my job here...'

Greta hesitated and then nodded. 'If you think they won't mind... I wanted to be with you for the summer, but I can't stay here now. I said some terrible things to her. I know I shouldn't but I did...'

'Pack your clothes,' Freddie said. 'We'll go up on the train later this evening, after I finish for the day. You can sleep in the carriage, because I'll be there to take care of you.'

'Oh, Freddie, you are wonderful,' Greta said and launched herself at him, hugging him and kissing his cheek.

'No need to strangle me,' he told her but laughed. 'I dare say your aunt won't be best pleased with me, but if I have to, I'll move to another boarding house.'

'Oh, she won't take it out on you, your room is being paid for,'

Greta said with a sniff. 'I'll pack my things and bring them to your room and then I'll spend the day on the beach...' She lifted her head defiantly. 'She can cook the breakfasts herself and make the beds and see how she gets on.'

'She will probably apologise when she sees you,' Freddie suggested, but Greta shook her head.

'She said I had to apologise and she would let me stay until she's sold the place, but I'm not going to. Ever since I came here to live, I've been nothing but a skivvy for little more than my food and lodging. I'm not going to apologise for telling her the truth.'

'No, don't,' Freddie agreed. 'Come to the beach and when I take my break, we'll have some chips and a cold drink together.'

The look Greta gave him was little short of adoration and Freddie was reminded of Muriel's warning. Yet there was nothing else he could do but offer his help. Greta had no one but her absent father, very little money and, at the moment, not much chance of finding another job. His parents would agree he was doing the right thing, and he was fond of her – but as a sort of sister. Perhaps when she knew him better, she would get over her crush and find someone else. Or perhaps they would drift together as people sometimes did. Freddie could only hope that his actions now didn't end up breaking her heart in the future...

* * *

Greta's possessions fitted into one shabby suitcase and a couple of carrier bags. Freddie ordered a taxi to take them to the station, but he only had his rucksack so managed to carry most of her stuff himself as they got on and off the train. Once in London, he found another taxi and spent the next few minutes watching the wonder and astonishment on Greta's face as they passed large department stores and impressive buildings.

'It's so busy – and big,' she said, looking at him in excitement. 'I thought Newquay was busy when I first went there – but... However do you find your way around?'

'You learn the number for the bus you want,' Freddie told her. 'It's the easiest if you haven't got luggage. In time, you know where you're going – and if you get lost, you ask a policeman. That's what I did when I was a kid... there aren't as many about as there were then. I think most of them are in patrol cars now, but someone will know if you ask.'

Greta nodded, but looked a bit apprehensive. 'I'll get used to it,' she said but seemed overwhelmed.

'Remember, you will be living with my family,' Freddie reminded her. 'They will look after you, Greta. You only have to ask them what you need to know. Mum has lived here most of her life. She knows it all.'

Greta smiled. 'I can't wait to meet her – and your twin and your cousin, Maggie.'

'I hope you will be happy...' Freddie felt a twinge of doubt. He'd acted for the best, but London was a big place and it would take her a while to become used to living there. 'It can't be worse than living with your aunt anyway.'

A little shudder went through her. 'Did you hear what she called me when we left? She said I was a slut to run off with you and even when you said I would be living with your mother, she still kept saying it...'

'Yes, I heard it,' Freddie said ruefully. 'I'm not sure she will have me back in her house, but Guy says he'll move me to one of the others they use if she continues to be unpleasant. She was rude to him, too...'

'I'm not going to think about her any more,' Greta replied with a determined lift of her chin. 'She knows that she will have to employ someone in my place and that will be expensive.'

'Well, she ought to have treated you better,' Freddie looked at her and realised that he felt very protective of her. She hadn't been treated well and his doubts fled.

'Your family will like me, won't they?' she asked him as the taxi began to slow down and she looked out of the window.

'Yes, of course, they will,' Freddie reassured. He liked Greta and knew that his family would too. 'They are expecting us. I rang before we left and told them what time we'd arrive.'

* * *

Freddie took Greta into the Pig & Whistle the back way, under the arch and past the new extension, which was set out with tables laid with bright yellow clothes and little vases of flowers. The smell of cooking was in the air as they went in through the kitchen door and found everyone sitting drinking coffee before the day's work started. All eyes turned to them, curiosity in their faces.

His mother was the first to speak. She stood up and came towards them, a smile on her face. 'Hello, Greta. I'm Freddie's mum, Peggy, and I'm glad he brought you to us. I hope you will be happy.'

'Thank you, Mrs Ronoscki,' Greta said nervously.

'Call me Peggy – and this is my husband, Able – my granddaughter Maggie – and Freddie's twin, Fay.'

'I've seen photographs of all of you,' Greta told her. 'Freddie keeps them in his room and I dust them every day.' She looked at Maggie and then Fay. 'You are both so beautiful...'

'Don't tell Fay that, she is already impossible to live with,' Able said and laughed. He had stood up when Peggy did and now offered his hand. 'Join us at the table and have some coffee. Would you like some breakfast?'

'I told Greta about the pancakes you sometimes make for us,'

Freddie said. 'She loves them but hasn't had any for years and none the way you do them.'

'Well, why don't I make some this morning – if Maggie will let me use her kitchen?' He looked at her teasingly and she nodded.

'That's a wonderful idea, Able. I think we might make some as a dessert for lunch – with an orange, sugar and brandy sauce. We could do cooked strawberries with them too.'

'That sounds wonderful,' Greta said. 'I've never heard of anything like that before...'

'They have a fancy name Crêpe Suzette.' Maggie said, 'but we just call them pancakes. People know what they're getting then...' She smiled at Greta. 'Shall I show you your room while Able makes your pancakes? You will be sharing with me for the time being... but there will be a room free at the boarding house after next week so you can have your own room then if you like.'

'Oh – yes, thank you,' Greta said and glanced at Freddie, who nodded at her.

They left the room together as Freddie said, 'I'll bring your bags up in a few minutes, Greta.'

'I'll come up too,' Fay called. 'I just want a word with Freddie.'

She went to him and hugged him as the door closed and whispered in his ear. He looked at her raising his eyebrows. Fay wanted to talk in private.

'Now?' he asked and she nodded. He followed her out into the hall and then through to the restaurant. 'What is so important you have to talk now?'

'I don't know what to do, Freddie...' Tears welled in her eyes and then it all poured out, about the way Jace had behaved when she invited him to lunch with the family and the secret Maggie had revealed. 'I'm supposed to go on holiday with him this Sunday, but how can I?'

'Have you told Mum or Dad about this?' Freddie asked and she shook her head. 'You know what they would say, don't you?' Fay nodded. 'You are in love with him then. If you weren't, you wouldn't think twice... it isn't an easy decision?'

'I just feel so mixed up in my head,' Fay admitted. 'If he treated Mitsy so badly then he... well, I couldn't marry him, Freddie. Yet I do care – more than I thought I would. What do I say to him?'

'You'll just have to ask him for the truth,' Freddie said. 'You know it's the only way, and you will know if he is lying, Fay. Look in his eyes. He can't hide his guilt; it will show even if he lies.' She gulped and he saw that she agreed but was dreading the truth. 'Look, love, we all care for you, but we can't make this decision for you. Jace might be innocent. Even if Mitsy's mother thinks he was the one that hurt her, she could be wrong. You have to face that it also may be true – and you've told me you don't want to marry him if it is.' He reached out and took her hand. 'It will hurt either way. If you give him up now, you'll be torn with regret and disappointment – but if you marry him knowing what he's done, you will never trust him and that will lead to heartbreak in the end – but much worse and for longer.'

Fay inclined her head and the tears trickled down her cheeks. 'I know. I just wanted you to say it...'

Freddie reached for her and hugged her, letting her cry into his shoulder.

She gave a sniff and looked at him. 'Take Greta's things up. I'll go up and see her in a minute.'

Freddie nodded and left her. He knew she was hurting but despite her tendency to be impulsive, she was sensible underneath and he was confident she would make the right decision.

* * *

Maggie's room had twin beds in it. Greta was sitting on the first one when Freddie knocked and entered. She was looking a little lost, but her face lit up when she saw him.

'Should I unpack?' she asked. 'I'll be moving into the guest house next week...'

'You could probably stay here longer if you don't mind sharing with Maggie?'

'I wouldn't mind, but this is her room.' Greta looked around. 'It's really nice – much nicer than the room I had at my aunt's house. Maggie is lovely. She told me I could stay here if I want, but if I prefer a room to myself, I can have it next week.'

'Why not stay here for a bit longer,' Freddie asked. 'Give yourself a little time to get used to the change, Greta.' He hesitated, then, 'I'll be away for a while, back in Hastings and then to college. You can use my room if you like?'

'Then you won't have anywhere of your own when you get back. I'll stay here for a while and then move into the boarding house when I'm ready. Maggie says she will teach me to cook. I told her I'm hopeless, but she says everyone needs to be shown and I can start by doing preparation. I can't burn things then, can I?' She gave a little giggle. 'Maggie said she burned her first cake.'

A little knock at the door heralded Fay's arrival. She entered and smiled as if she hadn't a care in the world. 'Able says the pancakes are nearly ready. He's done them with maple syrup and we can have strawberries with them. You are in for a treat, Greta.' She went to kiss Greta on the cheek. 'Welcome to Mulberry Lane. Come on, before the pancakes spoil.' She linked her arm through Greta's. 'You can talk to Freddie later – and when he has gone back to Sussex, I'll show you where the buses and the underground is. We'll go shopping together and you can help us in the kitchen until you find the job you want. You'll have plenty of time to write your stories and you can use Maggie's typewriter to practise on until you get your own.'

Freddie smiled as he watched them walk down the stairs. Fay had made her decision. He could tell without her saying a word, and now she was turning her attention to Greta. Smiling, he followed them downstairs. Fay was drawing Greta out, asking what clothes she liked and talking about hairdressers and a visit to the cinema. She would do as he'd ask and look after Greta for him – and that meant she wouldn't be going away with Jace anytime soon...

29

Jace had pulled up outside in his car that Sunday morning. Fay went out to him. She opened the passenger door and got in, turning to look at him, but didn't shut the door.

'Where are your cases?' he asked, looking at her in surprise. 'You haven't forgotten we're going away today?'

'I have to talk to you,' Fay said. She took a deep breath. 'I've been told something – and I need you to tell me if it is true...'

She saw his gaze narrow. 'Who has been telling tales?' he demanded.

'That isn't important,' Fay countered. 'I've been told Mitsy killed herself because she was pregnant – is that true?'

'God help me, yes,' Jace's voice grated harshly. 'It hit me for six when I heard. I was still reeling from it when I came to your home for lunch. I hardly knew what I did or said that day...'

'Mitsy was in love with you. Did you... did you let her down, Jace?'

'Did I...?' Jace's eyes blazed with sudden anger. 'You can't think... Is that what this is all about, Fay, why you haven't brought a suitcase? You believe I was the father of her child?'

'Were you?' Fay asked, but even as she spoke, she knew it wasn't true. Jace wasn't guilty; he was angry – with her. 'I thought....'

'Her mother thought so too,' Jace said bitterly. 'She accused me of being the cause of Mitsy's misery and her stupid actions...' He took a deep breath. 'Get out, Fay. Go back to your family. They don't like me because of what I do, because they think I'd be bad for you – but I thought you would have faith in me. For God's sake! If I'd been the father – if I hadn't wanted to marry her – I would have stood by her. I gave her money to help her when she told me she was leaving, but it wasn't my child. She had a fling with Keith – my drummer...' He nodded as Fay's eyes widened. 'Keith told me himself. He said she got drunk one night and they sort of fell into bed together...'

'I'm sorry...' Fay attempted, but she could see it was no good. 'She was in love with you. Why did she...?' She shook her head. 'It seemed... I'm sorry, Jace. I do love you...'

'You thought I'd been with her and thrown her off and would do the same to you?' Jace said bitterly. 'So that's what you really think of me? I can do without that kind of love.' He gave her a hard look. 'Just go, Fay. I'll be in touch when I'm not angry – maybe...'

Fay hesitated and then got out of the car. She shut the door and he drove off without looking at her. A little sob of despair left her and she stood there staring after him, tears on her cheeks. Why hadn't she trusted him? Why had she believed Maggie?

Turning, she went back into the kitchen, feeling stunned and reeling with the pain. Maggie was standing with her back to her. 'It wasn't him,' she cried. 'You told me it was Jace... but it was that drummer. The one on drugs... and now he's gone and we're over...'

Maggie turned and the shock was in her eyes. 'Oh, Fay... are you sure?'

'He was so angry that I thought it was him...' Fay burst into tears. 'He told me to get out of the car and he's gone. I shall never see him again.'

'I'm so sorry.' Maggie stared at her helplessly. 'I thought you had to know, because... but I was wrong. I should have asked him myself...'

'How could you?' Fay said. 'Even I didn't have a telephone number for him, because he was always moving around. You should have kept it to yourself, let me discover my feelings and decide what I wanted to do for myself – but no, you had to tell me, and I believed you.' Fay's voice rose shrilly. 'You didn't like him and you wanted me to stay here, so you spoiled it all for me... I hate you!'

Fay whirled around and ran from the kitchen, pounding up the stairs to her room, where she threw herself on the bed and started to sob. She cried and cried until she had no more tears and then lay curled up in a ball. Jace had looked so hurt and angry – and she loved him, she really did. It was true that she'd been dithering, not certain she was ready to give up the life she loved to go with him to a new one in America, but now she felt empty inside. Jace had gone and nothing else seemed to matter.

* * *

'What is wrong, Maggie?' Peggy asked as she entered the kitchen and found Maggie there with tears on her cheeks. 'You look as if the world just tumbled around you. Did you burn something?'

'No, I've made a terrible mistake... and I've broken Fay's heart,' Maggie said and then sat down and told her grandmother about what Greg had reluctantly told her. 'I thought Fay had to know. She confronted him with it – and it wasn't true... The baby's father was his drummer...'

'Oh, Maggie,' Peggy said and reached for her hand. 'You mustn't blame yourself.'

'Fay blames me. She hates me...'

'Fay will come to her senses,' Peggy soothed. 'You were only acting as her friend. I might have done the same.' Maggie looked at her. 'It might have been better to just tell Fay that Mitsy had taken her own life and let her ask Jace about it... But that is hindsight and that is what we all need but don't have.' Peggy smiled at Maggie. 'I'll go up and talk to her.'

'Tell her I didn't mean to hurt her...'

'Fay knows that, Maggie. If she said she hated you it was just a wild moment.'

'She must be so unhappy. I know I would be if—'

'—if it was Greg?' Peggy nodded. 'I know you love him. We'll talk about you and Greg later, Maggie.'

* * *

Peggy got up and left Maggie to resume her work, walking up to Fay's room. She knocked. There was no answer, but the door was not locked so she went in and found Fay curled up in a ball, her fist pressed against her mouth. Her eyes were dark with misery as she looked at her mother.

'He's gone. You will be glad...'

'No, I'm not, Fay,' Peggy said. 'I love you and I want you to be happy. If Jace is the one you want, then I would rather you went off to America with him than stayed here to break your heart. I just wasn't sure... he seemed a bit offhand when he came to lunch...'

'He'd just heard the news about Mitsy. He told me when I accused him... it upset him and he wasn't himself. He isn't usually that way, Mum. I wouldn't love him if he was...'

'No, I don't suppose you would,' Peggy said. 'I should have known that, Fay. Forgive me for misjudging him – and can't you tell him you're sorry?'

'I did and I told him I loved him, but he said he could do without that sort of love and told me to get out of the car....'

'He was angry and he had a right,' Peggy replied. 'It was an unfortunate mistake. Maggie was told part of the story and she was trying to protect you – someone she loves. She didn't mean to hurt you, Fay.'

'I know. I shouldn't have blamed her,' Fay said and gulped. 'Even Freddie said I had to ask for the truth – but he did warn me it could be a mistake. I should have been more... diplomatic...' She sniffed and wiped her nose with the hanky Peggy gave her.

'Diplomacy has never been your strong point, my love,' Peggy told her. 'Learn a lesson from this, Fay. If anything like this happens again, ask the right questions in the right way but don't accuse.'

'I didn't... but it was in my mind and he knew that,' Fay admitted. 'What am I going to do, Mum? Jace will never forgive me. I know he won't...'

'Oh, he might,' Peggy said and leaned close to kiss her cheek. 'I've forgiven worse and I still love you. If Jace loves you, he will come back – but is he the one?'

'Yes, he is,' Fay said. 'I know I said I wasn't sure but...' She broke off and hugged her. 'I love you and Dad and Freddie, of course – and Maggie and the others... but Jace is a piece of me. I want to be here with you, but I can't bear it that I've lost him.'

'Write and tell him,' Peggy suggested.

'I don't have an address or anything... He is always moving around and may go back to America sooner than he'd planned,' she said on a little sob.

'I don't know what to suggest, but I'll ask your father. He has contacts in America. Perhaps he can help you get in touch with him if he does go back...' She saw the look in Fay's eyes. 'I know you want to do it now this instant, but it isn't possible. I'm afraid that this time you have to wait – first for Jace to contact you and if he doesn't and you still want to try to heal the breach, through his record label or something of the sort...'

Fay looked at her, rebellion flaring in her eyes, but then in a moment it had gone and she inclined her head. 'I know, Mum. I've always been impatient. I find it hard to wait for anything I want – but you know that... don't you?'

'Yes, I do, Fay,' Peggy said. 'I've remembered so much of yours and Freddie's childhood. There will probably be gaps but not many. I feel much more like myself now I'm back where I belong.'

'I do love you...' Fay flung her arms around her and hugged her. 'I don't know why you love me, because I've been such a selfish silly daughter, but I know I have the best mum in the world.'

'I love you too and Freddie, more than I can say—' Peggy broke off as Maggie came to the bedroom door. She peeped round the corner.

'May I come in please?' She looked at Fay and then Peggy. 'There is a telephone call for you, Mum. It is Pip. He says he feels much better now and wants to talk to you...'

'I'll take it in my bedroom,' Peggy said and glanced at Fay as she left the room. 'All right now, love?'

'Yes, thank you,' Fay said. 'Come on, Maggie. You don't have to leave. I'm sorry for what I said to you.'

'I wish I hadn't told you...'

'No, you did the right thing. I should have just mentioned Mitsy and let Jace tell me. He was so angry...'

'Yes, well, he had the right,' Maggie said. 'I am sorry, Fay. If I could change things, I would...'

'You were worried for me because you care,' Fay croaked, her voice hoarse from emotion and crying. 'I would have done the same – except anyone can see that Greg is potty about you. When are you getting married? Come on, don't pretend you aren't just as potty about him, because I know you are.'

Maggie hesitated, then, 'We would like to get married soon. Greg is going to be working for Lotus on racing car design and advising. He has a big house in Devon, but we shall live in his apartment in London for a year or two.'

'You've got it all worked out,' Fay accused. 'When were you going to tell us?'

'That she is getting married?' Peggy's voice came from the doorway. 'I guessed after she had that day out with Greg.'

'Granny Peggy!' Maggie cried. 'You couldn't have...'

'Well, I did,' Peggy told her. 'I knew why you didn't say, of course – Fay wasn't settled and you were worried about the business. You thought we'd spent a lot of money and we might feel you were letting us down.'

'I shan't leave you in the lurch...'

Peggy smiled. 'You must do whatever you wish, my love. Able invested in the property and we'll keep it running for a few years – and then, when you both want to move on, we'll sell. It will be split two ways. Able and I will take half and the other half will be yours, Fay and Maggie. You'll be free to use your share as you wish. Neither of you is tied to the business, because I can employ cooks to keep it running and I'll be here until we retire, which won't be for a few years yet, I hope.'

'Mum – that's so generous...'

'Granny... you can't... When I asked if I could take over, I never meant the whole thing, just the restaurant...'

'Able is very happy with his investment. He reckons that we

could run it ourselves if you two get married and move away. We'd need more staff, of course, but we'd manage...'

'I feel so guilty,' Maggie told her and then gave her a hug. 'Just when we've done all that expansion, I go and fall in love. I wasn't going to get married for years...'

'Love just comes,' Peggy said. 'Look at Able and me. I fell in love with him twice. Besides, you are much too beautiful and talented, as well as warm and loving – so what are your plans?'

'We'd like to get married. We shall live in London, for now, and he will go back and forth to his work. I suppose we might spend some long weekends and holidays at his house in the country.'

'What a delightful prospect,' Peggy said, smiling. 'And what about you, Fay? What are you going to do?'

'Carry on with my business,' Fay confirmed. 'I would have gone with Jace if...' She caught her breath. 'I might one day if he will forgive me...'

'He'll come back,' Maggie offered. 'I know he will – he did before when you quarrelled.'

'That was different...' Fay looked at her. 'What had Pip got to say, Mum? Is he feeling better?'

Peggy beamed at her. 'Pip is out of hospital and feeling much better. He will be flying to America very shortly. He wants as many of us as can manage it to go down there for a holiday when he comes back.'

'We haven't done that for ages,' Maggie said. 'I've got a new young chef coming for a trial period on Tuesday. If she is good enough, I'll take her on and she can look after things while we all go...'

'That would be lovely,' Peggy agreed. 'All of us together. Maureen and Rose would pop in to keep an eye on things – and of course there is Greta... What do we do with her? Should she come with us or stay here and help?'

'Come with us of course, if she wants,' Fay replied into the momentary silence. 'We can't possibly leave her here when Freddie asked us to look after her.'

'Is he in love with her?' Maggie asked, looking doubtful. 'I suppose she could be pretty if she had her hair done properly...'

'Maybe...' Fay's eyes sparkled and she sat up in bed. 'I've got an idea...'

30

'I don't know...' Greta looked at Fay as they sat in the hairdressing salon waiting for their turn some days later. It was one of the more exclusive salons in London and they'd been lucky to get appointments so quickly. 'Do you think I should? I've never had highlights in my hair before.'

'It will make it look lighter,' Fay told her. 'I've had them done several times. It's fun to change your look, Greta. Come on, live a little – have a different style and then we'll go and buy some new clothes.'

'I'm not sure I can afford—'

'I'm paying,' Fay said firmly. 'You are going to be my assistant at a special wedding, so you need to look smart.'

'Oh well,' Greta sighed and accepted her fate. 'I'll do whatever you think best, Fay. I do want to look nice when Freddie comes home...' Her words faded away and she blushed.

Fay saw the look in her eyes. 'You're in love with Freddie, aren't you?'

'Does it show so easily?' Greta asked anxiously. 'I've been

trying to hide it. I know he has lots of plans for the future and he is so lovely that he could have any girl he wanted.'

'Yes,' Fay agreed instantly. 'Freddie probably could choose almost any girl he liked. However, he likes you and Freddie is usually too wrapped up in his sport to notice girls. Besides, I want him to have a wife who will adore him and do everything for him – so that means she will have to be able to cook...' She laughed as she saw Greta's fallen look. 'No, don't worry. There are three good cooks at the Pig & Whistle and if we can't teach you, no one can – if you count my father's pancakes, that makes four of us.'

'I'll try hard to learn,' Greta said and smiled at her. 'I'd do anything to deserve Freddie...'

'Hmmm,' Fay murmured. 'By the time I've finished with you, he will have to work to deserve you.'

'Why are you being so kind to me?' Greta asked. 'I am grateful, but I don't know why you should want to help me like this...'

'One, because Freddie asked me to look after you, two because I like you, and three because I need something to take my mind off Jace...'

'You miss him, don't you?' Greta said. 'Why did you quarrel with him?'

'Because I was afraid,' Fay admitted. 'It was all too sudden when he told me he wanted to marry me and take me to live in America. I couldn't decide what to do and then, when I heard a tale about a girl who worked with him... well, I got it wrong. He was angry with me for thinking the worst and went off in a mood. I'm not sure I'll ever see him again.'

'If he loves you, he will come back,' Greta said. 'You are so pretty, Fay, and an exciting person to be with – I'm sure he will get over his anger and come back.'

'Mum says he'll come back if I'm patient, but that isn't my

middle name...' She broke off as the hairdressing assistant beckoned them. 'It's our turn now. So are you going to leave it to me?'

'Yes,' Greta agreed. 'You decide what I should have done, Fay.'

* * *

Two hours later, the girls emerged from the salon, both with shining hairstyles that turned heads as they walked along the street. Greta's hair had been cut in an avant-garde style that framed her face, with a soft fringe and a bounce in the curled-under ends. Her mousey-brown hair now looked shades lighter because of the carefully blended streaks and the change to her appearance was already striking.

'Is that really me?' she asked Fay as she caught sight of herself in a mirror in a shop window. 'I look so different...'

'In a good way,' Fay told her. 'You wait until we finish our shopping, Greta. I know just the kind of clothes that will suit you – I've seen them in Selfridges, and that is just here...'

Fay led the way into the large store and into the women's clothing department. Sensing Greta's hesitation, she steered her towards a rail of summer dresses and began sliding the hangers along, picking out various garments and handing them to Greta. Clutching a handful herself, she approached the assistant watching them from a distance.

'We'd like to try these on please.'

'Yes, miss. Please come this way.'

They followed her to the dressing room and Fay hung her bundle on the hangers provided. Greta did the same and then looked at her.

'Start trying them on then,' Fay told her. 'I think the navy and white spot, the pale pink shift dress and the white tiered dress will all suit you, but let's see if I'm right. You might prefer that stripy shirt dress and it is nice too...'

Greta took off her plain grey skirt and grey blouse and tried on the three dresses Fay had suggested. They all fitted and looked wonderful. Greta had never seen herself in clothes like these and just stared at her reflection in the mirror.

'They are too good for me,' she whispered, but Fay shook her head.

'Those three will be for going out in,' she told her firmly. 'Now, that plain navy shift dress is right for when you help me at the wedding – and the black skirt and white blouse for working in the kitchen. We want a nice pair of pedal-pushers; they are jeans cut off just below the knee, if you didn't know – and a couple of cotton tops for relaxing in on holiday, and we're done for now... Oh, and you'll need some shoes, too. A pair of heels and some white sandals.'

Greta glanced at the ticket on the navy and white dress and gasped. 'It's five pounds, Fay... You can't spend all this money on me; it's too much.'

'Oh, I'll make it up when you're scurrying around helping me set up the tables at weddings and parties,' Fay said airily and then the mischief peeped through. 'But it will be worth every penny to see Freddie's face when he sees you. He is sure to come to Pip's for a day or two when we go down there, if not before – and I can't wait to see him realise that his little mouse has turned into a beautiful young woman.'

'Oh no...' Greta began but then looked at herself in the mirror. 'I do look very different...'

'You look marvellous,' Fay told her, smiling in a way that was very like her twin. 'Freddie won't stand a chance...'

'Fay! You're wicked,' Greta retorted and had a fit of the giggles.

When the salesgirl came to inquire if they were getting on all right, she found them laughing at their secret joke, but her expression of puzzlement turned to a pleased smiled when they told her what they wanted to buy.

'Oh, that's nice,' she said. 'And you're in luck, because you will reach the discount level. We are giving two pounds off every sale above ten pounds...'

'In that case, we'll have the stripy shirt dress too,' Fay said. Greta gave a half-hearted squeal of protest, but Fay insisted and they finally left the shop half an hour later loaded down with parcels.

* * *

'How did you manage to get two discounts?' Greta asked when they were standing in a queue for the bus home.

'I told the girl that half the purchases were yours and half mine – so we both qualified.'

'But they were all for me...'

'We know that and she knew that, but she went along with it,' Fay said. 'I think they are having a competition with Harpers – that's the big store at the other end of Oxford Street. They've got discounts on, too. If we hadn't found what we wanted in Selfridges, I would have taken you there. We'll try there, next time.'

'I've got enough clothes to last ages...'

'Oh, they will do for a start,' Fay said airily. 'Once you get used to decent wages, you will be able to buy nice things for yourself, Greta. Besides, those stories are sure to sell and they will bring in a few pounds extra. I loved the one about the lifeguards. When that happens, you'll be busy, happy and rich.'

Greta giggled. 'I'll settle for the first two. I like to be busy and

I'm happier since I came to live with you than I've been in a long time...'

'Good. Freddie will be pleased with me.' Fay gave a satisfied nod as they clambered on board their bus. 'This evening you can help me serve up the desserts. I'll show you how to make them look so delicious that people want to eat more than one...'

'I could eat more than one of your mum's apple pies,' Greta said. 'I've never tasted such delicious things as you eat at home – let alone the food you serve in the restaurant.'

'Now all you have to do is learn to make it...'

'I'll try,' Greta sighed. 'I really will...'

* * *

'Gosh, you have been busy... Greta, you look wonderful,' Maggie exclaimed as they walked into the kitchen loaded down with bags. 'What a transformation... Oh, that sounds rude, but you look so different.'

'I know I do and it isn't rude when you say it,' Greta said. 'I wasn't sure, but Fay persuaded me to have the highlights and I'm so glad I did.'

'Well, she was right,' Maggie said and then smiled at Fay. 'There was a phone call for you while you were out, Fay. I spoke to Jace and explained what I told you and he is coming round this evening.'

'Jace is coming this evening?' Fay stared at her and then gave a squeal of delight. 'What did he say?'

'He didn't get much chance,' Maggie said. 'I informed him you were at the hairdresser after crying your eyes out for days and then read him a lecture... he ended up apologising to me for his behaviour at lunch the other week and then said to ask you if you would see him this evening. I told him to come at six, before we get really busy.'

'Oh, Maggie, I love you!' Fay grabbed her and danced her around the kitchen while Greta stood and laughed to watch them. 'I thought he would never forgive me...'

'I think he now understands that he owes you an apology. He should have told you about Mitsy himself – and he should have taken time to be with you instead of rushing here, there and everywhere. I told him I wouldn't allow him to hurt you a second time and if he loves you, he has to make sacrifices too.'

Fay stared at her. 'You said all that and he is still coming this evening? I am impressed, Maggie.'

'I want you to be as happy as I am,' Maggie told her. 'So if he was a selfish brute, he would have cleared off into the blue – now, at least, you'll know he loves you.'

'Yes...' Fay looked at her mistily. 'Thank you...'

* * *

Jace arrived at five in the evening, bearing three large bouquets and a huge box of perfume with a fancy bottle and a large red bow.

'I bought flowers for Maggie and your mum, too,' he said and placed them on the table in the hall. 'The perfume is Chanel and is for you.' He hesitated, then, 'You look lovely, Fay. I'm sorry I went off like that. I was angry that you thought... But, as Maggie pointed out, it looked as if I was the father of Mitsy's baby... I know what she said to you and it was easy to think the way you did.'

'I should have been more trusting...'

Jace shook his head and leaned forward to kiss her as she tried to apologise. 'No, I'm the one who hasn't behaved as I ought,' he insisted. 'I knew I loved you in France, but I didn't tell you – I just went off for over a year and then breezed back into your life. Mitsy did have a crush on me. I thought that was all it was, because I'd made it clear I wasn't interested but...' He shook his head. 'Can we go somewhere we'll be alone?'

'Come into the extension.' Fay took him through the restaurant. The tables were all set, but it would be a couple of hours before the first customers arrived for the evening service. 'Mitsy warned me off so...'

'Yes, Maggie told me. It did look as if I'd been playing the field – but I wasn't interested in her...' Jace took a deep breath. 'I had a row with Keith, told him what I thought to the way he'd behaved and asked why he didn't offer to marry her... He said he had, but she wasn't interested. He blamed me for breaking her heart and told me I deserved it if you broke mine.'

'I'm sorry—' Fay began but Jace silenced her with a kiss.

'Keith said he'd had enough and was leaving the band. I asked him to stay and he said he wasn't going to live in America. He wants to stay here in England and make records and just tour occasionally...' Jace sighed and looked at her. 'I have a contract to fulfil for another year. I have to go back – which means I'll need another drummer. I want you to marry me and come with me, Fay – will you?'

Fay took a deep breath and then reached up and kissed him. 'Yes, I'll come, if my parents will allow it – but I want to come home sometimes to see my family.'

'We'll visit – and when my contract ends, we'll come back to live,' Jace promised. 'I would stay now, but when I signed for the American company, I was almost an unknown. They took a chance on me and I've been more successful than I ever dreamed, but it kept me away from you...'

'I couldn't have got married then,' Fay told him. 'I was too young and my parents wouldn't have agreed – they won't let me marry until next spring... but perhaps they might if you explained...'

'I'll do that,' Jace said. 'Do you think they have time to talk to me now?'

'Yes, I think they might,' Fay smiled and took his hand. 'Everyone is in the kitchen, Jace. Come with me now...'

31

'Well, so much for making her wait until next spring,' Peggy said much later that evening, when they had closed for the night and she and Able were alone in their bedroom. 'Do you think she will be happy?'

'I hope so,' Able replied. 'Jace isn't such a bad bloke after all now he's explained why he was a bit off the day he came to lunch. He'd had a nasty shock and been blamed for something that wasn't his fault by Mitsy's mother. It is enough to throw anyone off balance.'

'It is a tragedy that the girl took her own life,' Peggy said. 'She must have been very mixed up in her thoughts to do that, Able.' She shook her head. 'So we're having a small family wedding and our little girl is off to America in a month... I can't quite believe it...'

'Jace has a two-week tour booked next week in France and then he'll be back to take her on honeymoon before returning to America. He was able to change a few dates. He should have been off to America next week, but his record company came up with this tour in exchange for him returning a month later than planned.'

'He must have pulled a few strings,' Peggy said thoughtfully. 'I took some convincing, but I do believe he loves her and I know she loves him.'

'We have to let her go, hon,' Able told her with a gentle look. 'I believe Fay needs to spread her wings. Let her see a bit of the world and marry this man. He's promised to come back to England when his contract ends. We don't know they will be happy – but you can never have guarantees. Some marriages that look bright don't work and others you wouldn't give a straw for their chances last forever.'

'I know...' Peggy rested her cheek against his chest as he bent his head to kiss the top of her head. 'I'm lucky and I want a good marriage for Fay – but I know I can't wrap her in cotton wool all her life.'

'She will be through her contracts for the catering by the wedding,' Able said. 'Maggie has a new cook coming to help in the restaurant – but I'm not sure what to do about Fay's business. Do we just let it go or do we find a good cook to take over?'

Peggy looked up at him. 'We have a good cook standing right next to you.'

'Too much work for you...'

'No, it isn't,' Peggy said and smiled. 'I've got Maureen and Rose to help out – and I will take on an extra chef myself. We'll keep it going for a year or so, and, if Fay wants it back when they relocate to England, she can have it.'

'Peggy, you've been ill yourself...' Able looked at her anxiously.

'And I'm better now,' she reminded him with a determined lift of her chin. 'I still have a few holes in my memory, but most things are there. Keeping busy is good for me, and Maggie only needs me now and then – even though she pretends she can't manage without me. It is the logical thing to do, Able, and silly to throw away a business that is just beginning to pick up.'

Able sighed and gave in. 'As long as you don't do too much...'

'Sitting around makes you old,' Peggy retorted and smiled up at him. 'You're not ready to retire yet, are you?'

'No.' He laughed and drew her close. 'You always manage to get your own way, don't you? I always wondered where Fay got it from...'

'Cheek! I am not as changeable as your daughter.'

'Let's hope she doesn't change her mind this time.'

'Oh, I don't think she will,' Peggy said. 'I haven't seen that glow in her eyes before.'

'No mystery to me, my darling. Fay is her mother's daughter all the way. She just needed to grow up and falling in love will make a woman of her. A beautiful woman just like you...'

'Daft,' Peggy said and gave him a soft punch in the chest, but her eyes were glowing just the way Fay's had when she'd looked at Jace when her father said they could get married when Jace returned to London.

* * *

'Fay is getting married in just over two weeks' time?' Maureen looked at Peggy in astonishment. 'Well, I thought I was the one with big news but... I'm not sure that doesn't top it...'

'What kind of news?' Peggy looked at her anxiously. 'Is Gordon all right?'

'A few twinges, but otherwise the same,' Maureen told her. 'No – Shirley rang me last night. She and Ray are having a baby...'

'That is wonderful news, Maureen,' Peggy said and hugged her. 'I know how excited you must be. It is lovely being a grandmother and this is your first...'

'Shirley had all those years training to be a doctor and she was reluctant to take time off, but I told her she can go back when she's ready, because I'm willing to babysit as much as she needs.'

'Well, that is lovely; the best news you've had in ages. We both have something to celebrate...' Peggy hesitated. 'Maggie is engaged, but she isn't getting married just yet. She wants Fay to have her special day first...'

'Goodness me!' Maureen exclaimed. 'Both of them. What about the restaurant?'

'Maggie will continue to run it; they'll be living in London for now – and I'm going to take over Fay's business, keep it running until they come back. I was going to ask you to help – but it looks as if you'll be busy.'

'I'll help when I can,' Maureen said. 'We always worked well together, Peggy, but I shan't be regular every day.'

'I shan't be working every day that's what I like about it,' Peggy told her. 'Fay does one wedding every month or so and a few dinners and parties. I think I can manage that. I'll be taking on a chef to help anyway...'

'As I said, I'll give you a hand when I can. Gordon wouldn't mind if I was out a few hours and he played nursemaid. He is over the moon about it – a grandfather. He can't wait – in fact, he cried when I told him the news.'

'It looks as if we'll both be busy,' Peggy said. 'Did you hear any more about visiting kiddies in hospital? You were waiting to be put on a list, I think...'

'Yes, I've just been told I can visit one or two afternoons a week, so I shall do that – it made me want to cry when Shirley told me about some of the children who get no or very few visitors. I'll take them books and puzzles and a few sweets.'

'Come round with Shirley when you get the chance,' Peggy said. 'I'd love to see her. Tell her I am thrilled at her news.'

'I shall,' Maureen promised. 'So, tell me, when is the wedding and where?'

'We shall have the reception at the restaurant of course,' Peggy told her. 'Fay said they were having a church wedding at the beginning of September, but it hasn't been finalised yet. I'll send an invitation – for Shirley and Ray as well, of course.'

'And what does Freddie say to all this?' Maureen asked.

'He says he'll be home then, getting ready to go to his new position. His summer job in Hastings finishes about then.'

'You will just get him back and he'll be off again.'

'Yes.' Peggy sighed. 'You look after them for their formative years and then they fly the nest – just the way Shirley went off for her training. I wish Freddie was coming back to London, but the place he was offered at University was in Cambridge, though he will apply for a job in London at the end of his course. He will be fully qualified by then. It isn't that far. He will be able to visit now and then...'

'And what about that girl he brought home?'

'She is working in the kitchen. Fay is determined to teach her how to make breakfast before she leaves – and I've promised to show her how my son likes his apple pie and other things.'

'I thought she kept burning things at her aunt's place.'

Peggy grimaced. 'She has been known to let things burn but nothing drastic. We're about and we keep an eye on her. She cooked the sausages for our lunch yesterday and there was nothing wrong with them...'

'You will be the one who ends up teaching her,' Maureen said and Peggy laughed.

'Yes, I probably shall, but it will be worth it if...' She shook her head. 'It is only for a while. Greta is learning to type and Maggie says she is good. She does the menu cards beautifully.'

'Well, if she can do something. Not every girl can cook...'

'No – and Freddie isn't a bad cook himself,' Peggy said. 'If he wanted to, he is perfectly capable of cooking a meal.'

'Are you thinking...?'

'No.' Peggy shook her head. 'One little bird flying the nest is enough for now. Maggie will be next, but she'll stay around for a few years anyway – and Freddie has to complete his training if he wants to be a teacher. Besides, I think he isn't ready yet.'

'But you wouldn't mind if – one day…?'

'One day, if that's what they want. Fay says that Greta is head over heels for Freddie – but I'm not sure he thinks of her that way. Not yet anyway…'

'Freddie is very unassuming,' Maureen said. 'And he might not realise he was in love either. He just cares about all his friends. He sent Gordy a parcel the other day. Football magazines, seaside rock and a baseball cap. Gordy has hardly taken it off since. He thinks the world of him…'

'Freddie is good with youngsters,' Peggy said. 'He is going to make a wonderful teacher. I'm selfish enough to hope he isn't in love with Greta and will have the freedom to have fun for a few years yet. He should be able to go out with whoever he pleases – don't you think?'

'Yes, but then I'm the mother of a boy too,' Maureen said and laughed. 'We can't run their lives for them – but your Freddie is sensible. I doubt he will jump in with two feet.'

'I do hope not – and I know that is unfair to Greta, but Freddie is too young to take on the responsibility of being a husband just yet.'

'What does Able say?'

'He thinks Freddie will get a shock when he sees Greta all made over by Fay, but doesn't think he will rush to get married.'

Maureen nodded. 'They grow up and want their own lives. I sometimes look at Gordy and think he's still a child, but he isn't really – sixteen this year. Where did all the time go, Peggy?'

'We enjoyed it,' Peggy said and laughed. 'Has Gordy decided what to do when he leaves school?'

'He is staying on to take his higher exams, but I think he might get an apprenticeship as a plumber. He talked about professional football for a while and toyed with the medical profession, but then his father introduced him to a friend he used to work with and Gordy went with him for a day to earn some pocket money. He enjoyed it and has been helping out for most of the school holiday. He likes soldering the pipes and they let him have a go at it.' Maureen shrugged. 'It is a good job, I suppose. He has a bit longer at school and then he'll decide.'

'It is always handy to know a plumber,' Peggy said with a smile. 'Now, shall we have coffee and some of the lovely coffee cake Fay has made for us?'

32

'I'm sorry to see you go,' Guy said when he went on to the station with Freddie on his last morning in Hastings.

'You're leaving too at the end of the season, aren't you?'

'I've made a few applications,' Guy said, 'but I don't have a place at college yet. I've been offered a job with the coastguards, on the lifeboats, so I might take that if nothing else comes along.'

'You are coming up for Fay's wedding, though? I told her about you and she said to bring you as my friend.'

'Yes, why not? I'm due a few days' leave and the team here is pretty strong. We shall get less children on the beaches now they're ready to return to school. The older visitors don't usually get into so much trouble; they are content to sit in their deckchairs and paddle at the water's edge.'

Freddie nodded. 'It has been a busy season and we've been lucky there were no fatalities – at least, none since Jill, and hers wasn't really a beach accident.' Freddie's eyes were shadowed with sadness. He would never forget Jill or what had happened to her.

'Yes, that was a terrible thing to happen, especially as it was your first rescue. You've made one or two this season, Freddie, but you always remember your first.'

'Well, I'd better get on my train, thanks for bringing me,' Freddie said as he saw the guard beginning to check the doors. 'Make sure to come up for the wedding...'

Freddie sprinted to the train and got onboard just before the guard slammed the last door and blew his whistle. He leaned out of the open window and waved at Guy, who was standing there, watching the train leave. Freddie gave a last wave and then took his seat. He suspected Gut was a bit lonely, even though he was in charge of the team and seemed to have friends – but no family.

The summer had been fun, busy and filled with little incidents and laughter when the team got together in the evenings. They'd had food on the beach at night sometimes, playing team games and drinking cold beer or iced orange juice. One or two had got a little drunk, but Freddie had stuck to one beer and then water. He'd missed seeing Greta at breakfast time, but he hadn't had to move. Mrs Phipps had simply avoided him and the new girl had been very chatty with all the others, while only speaking to Freddie if necessary.

Guy had laughed over it. 'She thinks you seduced Greta and ran off with her and has been warned to be wary of you.'

He'd seemed to think it very funny, but Freddie hadn't much cared for the idea, but he'd kept quiet and got on with his job, refusing to let the dark looks he encountered from Mrs Phipps affect him. Yes, it had been a good summer, but he was glad to be going home to see his family – and Greta. Yes, he wanted to see if she had settled all right...

* * *

Fay flew at him when he walked into the kitchen that evening. She hugged him and then looked up at him, her eyes glowing. He could see she was happy and smiled at her.

'No need to ask how you are,' he said. 'I'm glad it all turned out well in the en—' His words ran out as he suddenly saw Greta. She was wearing black slacks and a loose white blouse with an apron over them, but she'd changed. It wasn't just the smarter clothes, but he couldn't work out what it was. 'What on earth have you done to yourself, Greta?' he asked without thinking.

Greta's smile vanished and her hand went to hair and then he saw it had been cut in a fashionable style and surely it was lighter? 'You don't like it,' she said and looked as if she would burst into tears.

'I do like it,' he assured her quickly. 'It's just... you don't look like you...' He was putting his foot in deeper. 'You look fine,' he added hastily, but the damage had been done and he saw that he'd hurt her without meaning to. 'No, I mean it, Greta. You're really pretty but...' He floundered uncertainly. 'I thought you were pretty anyway...'

'You couldn't have,' Greta said. 'I look much better now...'

'You look gorgeous,' Fay came to her brother's rescue. 'If you're expecting lots of compliments from Freddie, don't. He usually tells me I look "OK".'

Greta nodded and turned away, getting on with her job of chopping vegetables. She concentrated hard and wouldn't look his way and Freddie cursed himself for being so clumsy. He wasn't sure whether he liked the new style or not. Greta's hair had a soft natural wave to it when she didn't scrape it back off her face. She'd worn it loose and wind-blown on the beach, and he preferred that to the sleek cut she wore now, but the lighter shade was nice and so were her new clothes.

'Come on, I'll help you unpack,' Fay said and took his arm. 'I want to show you my wedding dress.'

'Isn't that unlucky?' Freddie said but went with her with a feeling of relief.

'Only if you're the bridegroom,' Fay told him, 'And, if I'm wearing it before we meet at church – but it's only a superstition…'

'Did you do that – Greta's hair and clothes?'

'Yes, I thought you'd be pleased. You told me to look after her, so I did – don't you like it?'

'The colour is nice, but I'd rather see it more natural…'

'It makes her look modern and interesting,' Fay said. 'Don't be such a grouch, Freddie. She wanted to look pretty for you.'

'I thought she was pretty before – when she smiled. It was just her unhappiness – but I didn't mean to hurt her. Her hair is very smart and nice… just different.'

'You old stick-in-the-mud!' Fay exclaimed. 'It serves you right if she stops bothering what you like and pleases herself.'

'I want her to do that anyway,' Freddie said and sighed. 'I do care about Greta, but I'm not sure yet whether… and I need to finish training and find a job and get settled before I could think of getting married. I'm not like you… going off to the unknown at the drop of a hat…' He was teasing her now and Fay poked him in the ribs.

'You will come out and visit us in your long summer holiday next year, Freddie? Please say yes. Jace will pay for the flight, or if I am earning lots of money out there, I will…'

'I might,' Freddie agreed. 'I could probably find a beach job there for the summer or a pool attendant or something…'

'You'd be our guest, no need to work – but Jace intends to have a pool, so you could help keep that right.'

'I might be able to combine the two,' Freddie agreed. 'They

have a lot of pools out there, so I'd be able to get a job cleaning them or something of the sort.'

'As long as you come and stay.'

'I'll do that,' Freddie confirmed. 'But you'll come back sometimes, Fay – and it's only for a year or so, until Jace is out of contract...'

'That is what he promised, but I know a lot of the work is out there and he's since told me there may be a film offer coming... nothing definite yet, but if it happens, he'll want to do it and...' She shook her head. 'I love my family and I want to see them – but if Jace needs to be in Hollywood...'

'You'll stay with him?' Freddie nodded. 'It's only right you should, Fay. We'll always have a connection and you know I'll be around if you need me?'

'Of course I do,' she said and hugged his arm. 'Dad says he'll persuade Mum to come out, though she is reluctant after what happened last time.'

'You should be all right where you're going,' Freddie assured. 'President Kennedy banned segregation and although there is still going to be some who don't like it, it should stop those riots. We hope anyway.' He smiled at her. 'Don't forget you're half American, Fay. I imagine Dad is secretly pleased you're going to explore his homeland. Just keep out of trouble.'

'I'd never be brave enough to do what Mum did,' Fay said with a little shiver. 'She just does things a lot of people would fear to do – and perhaps that's one of the reasons we all love her.'

'Where is she?' Freddie asked. 'Not in the kitchen...'

'No, she went to babysit for Rose and Tom. They are going to a dinner dance and the girl who was supposed to do it let them down...'

'Oh, typical,' Freddie said and laughed. 'I suppose they would do the same for her.'

'They have many times,' Fay agreed. 'You should unpack and then go into the bar. Dad is in there with just Carla this evening. You can give him a hand with serving the drinks.'

'Yes, I will,' Freddie said. 'I'll see you later – and I'll apologise to Greta, too.'

'No, just leave it. She must accept you as you are, Freddie – kind, generous and thoughtful, but not one for fancy words.'

With that, Fay gave him a quick hug and left him to unpack. Freddie was thoughtful as he did so. Perhaps Fay was right. There was no point in making a thing out of his blunder. Until Freddie had done all the things he needed to do, there was no sense in Greta waiting for him. She should go out with other friends and enjoy her life. They were friends and that was all there was to it...

33

Fay had helped with the planning and preparation for her wedding. Instead of the usual fruit cake, which needed to be kept and fed with alcohol for a few weeks prior to the feast, she'd made a huge fresh cream torte. It had layer upon layer of sponge, whipped cream and fruit. She'd used tinned fruit as it was sweeter and she could be sure of the quality, adding the layers of cream and fruit the night before her wedding. It sat in the big fridge along with many other tasty little treats and Maggie was preparing the actual meal with Carla, Greta and the new chef's help. Peggy had also employed a young woman to help with the catering business and she would be giving them a hand, too.

Peggy had baked some of the cakes and quiches, but, as the bride's mother, she would be too busy on the day making sure everything ran smoothly. Maggie was going to slip out at the last minute and come to the church, leaving her staff in charge of the finishing touches. It would be a bit hectic for her, but she'd insisted she was going to do the wedding breakfast and wouldn't be swayed.

However, it was a buffet rather than a three-course lunch and that made it easier. It was what Fay wanted and she'd handed Maggie a list of the various dishes, she preferred. Most of it was fiddly little bits and Fay had spent ages doing them herself and freezing them in the new chest freezer they'd bought for the restaurant, but the exotic salads, sliced meats, spiced chicken wings and fresh salmon mousse were all down to Maggie.

Now, on the morning of her wedding, Fay was in her bedroom with her mother, Maureen and Rose. She'd done her hair herself and put it up in a French pleat at the back with a few wisps across the forehead. Her headdress was a tiny single coronet of pearls and crystals with a short veil and her dress was shorter than the traditional wedding dress. It was full-skirted, lace over silk, and ended just below her knees, swaying like so much gossamer as she walked. The sleeves were barely there, showing her arms through the fine lace and her shoes were white brocade with kitten heels. Around her throat, she wore a single pear-shaped diamond on a white gold chain; it was a gift from Jace and suited her perfectly. It also went well with the diamond drop earrings her parents had given her, and her huge pear-shaped diamond engagement ring.

'There will be some money for you in your bank,' Able had told her. 'The catering business will still be here when you come back and it will be yours if you want it – and I've given Jace a gold cigarette case. He told me to spend my money on you and not a joint present, but I wanted him to have something.'

Fay had hugged him and thanked him. 'You've always given me too much,' she'd said. 'Thank you – and Mum too. I don't know why you're so good to me...'

'Because we love you,' he'd said. 'That won't change, Fay, and you'll always have a home here if you want it... but I don't think you will. I think it will suit you out there and you'll love it.'

'I'm excited,' Fay had murmured as she hugged him again. 'But I'll always want to come back...'

'Have your adventures first,' he'd advised. 'It's what you need, Fay. You always did...'

Reflecting on her father's wise words, Fay kissed her mother, Maureen and Rose as they exclaimed over how lovely she looked. Then she went downstairs to where her father and Freddie were waiting. The look on their faces said it all.

'You are beautiful,' Able said and kissed her cheek, taking care not to crush her dress.

'You look fine,' Freddie, a man of few words, agreed. 'Jace is a lucky man...'

'Pop to the kitchen doorway so they can see you,' Peggy suggested and Fay did as her mother suggested.

Greta, Carla and the others all exclaimed over how lovely she looked and then Maggie came rushing down the stairs, having done the quickest wash and change of her life. She was wearing a simple pink shift dress and a white hat and shoes.

'Gorgeous,' she said. 'Come on; if you don't get a move on, Jace will think you've changed your mind...'

* * *

Jace was standing at the altar waiting for her. He was wearing a white suit with a pale blue shirt and dark blue snakeskin shoes, his tie matching his shoes and a blue orchid pinned to his lapel. Seeing him, Fay could hardly suppress her giggle. He looked every inch the rock star and she thought a few of her mother's regulars would raise their eyebrows when they saw him at the reception. A few of his band were in the church and their outfits were little short of outrageous, varying from bright pink and purple to deepest black.

Jace had only a few friends on his side and it had filled up with people from the lanes, because the church was packed. It seemed that everyone wanted to see the famous singer Fay was marrying and a lot of them had been invited to the reception, some to a simpler evening affair in the pub after Fay and Jace had left on their honeymoon.

Fay walked demurely at her father's side to stand beside Jace. He turned his head to look at her and grinned. Fay couldn't hold back her little giggle of pleasure. She'd broken with tradition with her short dress, but it wouldn't be the bride everyone would be talking about in the next few days.

The ceremony was lovely, as was the church, which had been decked out with lots and lots of white flowers. Jace had arranged it with a local florist and it smelled heavenly. Fay sort of floated through the next twenty minutes or so and then they were out in the sunshine, being showered with confetti and rice.

Her niece, Sheila and Pip's daughter, had been her only bridesmaid, because Maggie said she would rather just do the wedding reception and hadn't got time to dress up and pose for the camera. She'd shot off in their van as soon as the first pictures were taken and Fay knew she'd be in the kitchens making sure everything was perfect.

* * *

And it was, of course. The tables were set with white flowers, fancy napkins – Greta had turned out to be good at shaping them like fans – and pristine white linen cloths. The wine glasses were red and there were pink ribbon bows on the tails of the balloons, which were also red. Here and there were trails of sparkling silver stars that glittered in the lights of the restaurant and beside each plate was a small silver box containing rum truffles that Fay had made herself. Everyone complimented the bride and groom on entry, exclaiming over the pretty scene. However, the long tables set out with the buffet soon had the guests lining up to fill their plates.

Greta, Carla, Alice and Felicity, Peggy's new cook, were standing behind the bar. Maggie appeared soon after the bride and groom arrived and checked that everything was in place. Nicky, her new chef, was in the kitchen and made a brief appearance with some strawberry sorbets and then disappeared again.

'She made these,' Maggie whispered to Fay when she snatched a moment from greeting guests to sample the sorbet. 'Nicky is turning out to be better than I thought when we took her on.'

'Good. You will need her, Maggie – you'll need a lot more staff when you marry.' Fay glanced around the room. 'Is Greg here?'

'He will be,' Maggie said. 'I hope in time for when we cut the cake...'

'You don't get to see him much?'

'It's just while he's settling into his new job. I think we might have a Christmas wedding, but we don't mind, we're happy just to have whatever time we can manage together...' She smiled at Fay. 'I'll let everyone get over yours first...' Her eyes were drawn across the room. 'Greg has just arrived. If we don't have another chance to talk privately before you leave – be happy, Fay. I shall miss you. We all will, but it is only right that you go where your heart is.'

Fay caught her hand. 'Everything is beautiful, Maggie. Thank you...'

'You're welcome.' Maggie squeezed her hand and went off to greet Greg.

Jace put his arm about her waist. 'You'll see her again,' he whispered in her ear. 'You can invite her to stay whenever you like, Fay.'

'I know.' She smiled up at him. 'I'm looking forward to our new life together, Jace. It will be an adventure...'

He laughed and bent his head to kiss her. 'Do you think people are ready for a slice of that magnificent cake? I know I am...'

She laughed up at him. 'Come on, then. Let's cut it and see if it tastes as good as it looks...'

* * *

Freddie watched as his twin and Jace cut their cake. It wasn't the normal wedding cake but looked wonderful and was meant to be eaten on the day. Maggie had taken over now and was handing out slices to everyone. Some preferred a slice of the smaller but traditional fruit cake, but Freddie wanted a slice of the fresh cream torte.

'Good grief, is that Greta?' Guy's question broke Freddie's thoughts. She was handing out slices of the fruit cake and Guy was staring. 'My God, she is gorgeous...'

'Yes, I suppose she is...'

Greta was wearing a red striped shirt dress and white sandals. She had a little frilly apron, because she was serving the cake before she enjoyed herself.

'I'll see you later,' Guy told him and made a beeline for Greta. Freddie stood and watched as he chatted to her and noticed the pink tinge in her cheeks and then she laughed. Freddie felt something he never had before – a sharp twinge of jealousy. She looked so relaxed and happy. Surely, she wouldn't take Guy's compliments seriously? She wouldn't fall for his charm offensive? Clearly, he was now interested in a girl he'd hardly noticed before.

Freddie turned away and went to be served his slice of the magnificent torte. He sat at a table on his own and ate it with a spoon and fork; it was too squishy and soft to bite or hold in the fingers. It tasted delicious and he considered claiming another slice before it had all gone, but, as Guy moved away to speak to Fay and Jace, Freddie found himself approaching Greta.

'Just a small slice,' he said. 'You should get yourself a piece of the torte, Greta. It is delicious.'

'I think I'd prefer something less creamy,' she replied. 'Guy said it was too rich for him and I might agree.'

'He doesn't know what it tastes like,' Freddie retorted. 'The fruit and the light sponge cake melt in the mouth. Fay made it herself.'

'I know. I helped whip some of the layers of cream.'

Freddie nodded. 'How are you enjoying life here?'

'Very much, thank you.' Greta's smile was shaded. 'I had a letter from my father – redirected by my aunt. He didn't get my letter and says he is stuck in East Germany and not sure when he can get out...'

'It's not a good time to be there – they've clamped down on things and it looks as if they are starting to build a wall to keep everyone in...'

'He told me not to worry, said he will get out soon...'

'Perhaps he will. I hope so for your sake – but if he shouldn't, you will stay with us until you're ready to make a home of your own?'

Greta nodded. 'I'm applying for a typist's job soon. I'll move into the boarding house now that Fay is married. I can still work for Maggie sometimes, unless...'

'Unless what?' Freddie asked, but she shook her head and turned away to cut more cake for another guest.

He took his slice and sat down. Guy joined him after a minute or two, bearing wine glasses.

'Your sister said to bring you wine. They are having the toasts soon.'

Freddie nodded. 'When do you start your job with the coastguards?'

'Oh, I didn't get a chance to tell you. I've got a place at teaching college at Oxford. I've decided to take that instead; it's time to settle down...'

'Is that what you want then?'

Guy was looking across the room at Greta, hardly listening. 'I never realised how pretty she was – all that time she served breakfast and I didn't notice. She's done her hair differently. I really like it. She looks a bright modern girl now, instead of a little mouse.'

'Her aunt kept her under,' Freddie replied. 'It's being free to do as she wants now...'

'Well, I like it,' Guy said and then looked at him. 'Is she your girlfriend, Freddie? I don't want to tread on your toes – but I'm interested...'

'We're just friends,' Freddie told him, but his hands clenched under the table.

'Good, because I'm going to ask her out...' Guy got up and walked over to Greta. She was just about to take off her apron and she laughed as he said something to her and picked up a glass of wine as Able announced the toasts. Greta went to sit with Guy at an empty table.

Freddie watched her laughing and talking with Guy and cursed himself for being a fool. He'd thought only of setting Greta free from her old life and not about his feelings when that happened. Now it had and he was jealous.

Maggie's voice brought him back to the moment. 'She does look lovely, doesn't she?'

'I thought she was pretty before – but her hair is nice. She has let it go back to its natural curl today. It looks even better than when it was styled.'

'She just needed a bit of help to get started and Fay did that,' Maggie said. 'Does Greta know how you feel, Freddie?'

'I doubt it. I didn't know myself until just now – but it doesn't change anything, Maggie. I still have to go away and work hard if I want to achieve my aims...'

'Greta knows that – she just isn't sure that you want more than friendship.'

'I've always told her we're just friends...'

'And now that your handsome friend has arrived on the scene, you want more.' Maggie laughed. 'You'll have to win her back...'

'Win who back?' Greg said and glanced across at Greta and Guy. 'Yes, I see.'

'And it is Greta's choice. If she wants him...' Freddie shrugged but couldn't help feeling hurt.

'You can't just let him snatch her from under your nose, Freddie,' Maggie urged. 'Fight for what you want...'

'I'm going to say goodbye to Fay before she goes up to change.' Freddie got up and went to his sister, kissing her cheek and shaking hands with Jace. He didn't even see Greta's gaze following him or the way she got up and left the reception as soon as the toasts were over.

* * *

Maggie found Greta in the kitchen wrapped in a big apron and helping with the washing-up.

'Didn't you want to enjoy the reception?'

'It was lovely, but I liked to help set it up more than circulating. I don't know many of the guests...'

'You know Freddie and Guy...'

'Yes, and you and your family...'

'Why didn't you stay with Guy for a while?'

'He asked me if I would go out with him later this evening...' Greta lifted her head and looked at her. 'I said no. He never so much as looked at me before. I'm still me, Maggie, even if I look different.'

'Why don't you tell Freddie what you just told me?'

'Why? He wouldn't be interested...'

'You might be surprised,' Maggie said. 'Freddie isn't one for effusive compliments and he likes your hair the way it is now... natural, though he does like the colour. He has always thought you pretty.'

Greta's eyes widened. 'Did he tell you that?'

'Just go and see what he's doing,' Maggie suggested. 'Why don't you take a couple of those delicious sorbets from the fridge? There are a few left for us...'

Greta nodded wordlessly and did as she was bid.

Freddie was sitting alone. He looked up and smiled as she approached his table and offered the sorbet.

'These are lovely,' she said. 'So cool and simple after all that rich food...'

'Thanks,' he said and looked at her. 'Have you been crying?'

'Doesn't everyone cry at weddings?'

'Mum did in church and so did Dad...' Freddie reached for her hand. 'I'm sorry if I didn't say how lovely you looked before, Greta. You do – but you always did when you smiled.'

Greta smiled at him and he nodded.

'No wonder Guy was bowled over – are you going out with him?'

'No. He's all right, but I don't like him as much as I like you, Freddie...'

Freddie touched the back of her hand with one finger. 'You know I've got a year of teacher training ahead before I get a proper job?'

'I have a lot to learn, too,' she said shyly. 'It doesn't stop us being good friends, does it?'

'No, because we are friends and I think we always shall be – even when we're old. We might grow old together, Greta, but we have to wait and do some more growing up first. Do you agree?'

Greta looked at him and then giggled. 'You're not very romantic, are you, Freddie?'

'No, but I'm trying,' he said. 'I'm used to people just knowing I care about them...' He laughed as their eyes met and he saw mischief in hers. 'All right, I do love you, Greta. It took me a long time to know it but...'

Greta leaned across the table and kissed him. Just a soft, brief kiss that left him wanting more. 'I love you just the way you are,' she said. 'Don't ever change, will you, Freddie?'

'I doubt it,' he said. 'I'm not romantic but I'm good at remembering birthdays and I think you have one very soon. Shall we go somewhere nice? I thought about a posh meal out and then dancing...'

'Yes, please. Oh, Freddie...' She broke off. 'Your mother is signalling. Fay and Jace are about to leave. Shall we go and throw rose petals over them?'

'Yes, let's,' he said and took her hand and they ran to join the others sending Fay and Jace off to a wonderful new life.

34

'Well, that all went off well,' Able said when they were at last alone in their room. 'She looked beautiful and so happy; didn't you think so?'

'Fay is beautiful and I don't think I've seen her happier,' Peggy agreed. She sighed. 'They will be on the plane first thing in the morning, heading off to America...'

'And you are already missing her,' Able said and drew Peggy to him. 'She had to leave home one day, hon.'

'I know – it was just a bit too soon for me,' Peggy said, 'but I believe she is happy and that is all that matters.'

'Fay will have to stand on her own two feet now,' Able said and nodded to himself. 'I think you'll find it will be the making of her. We spoiled her as a child and as long as she had us, she would always run to us. Now she has to look to her husband and herself.'

'I know,' Peggy said and laughed. 'I am a fusspot...'

'Well, I doubt you'll have time to miss her that much,' Able pointed out. 'You've taken on her business and the orders for that are beginning to flow in. I wonder how you will manage it all sometimes.'

'I'll take on more staff if I have to, which is what Fay always intended. Besides, Janet will be living here and Jon – so there will be an extra pair of hands when I need them.'

Able stared at her. 'When did that happen?' He frowned, then, 'I noticed that Ryan wasn't in church or at the reception…'

'They've agreed to a trial separation,' Peggy said. 'I wasn't going to spoil the wedding, but I've known for a couple of weeks.'

'That is a pity,' Able replied. 'I knew things were a bit fraught, but then I thought they had made it up…'

'Ryan wants to follow his dream and live in Wales on a small farm. He wanted Janet and Jon to go with him, but she refused. She says she's had enough. She went off to Scotland with him but doesn't feel she wants to live in another remote location and nor does Jon. She feels Jon will be happier here. Besides, she wants to do her own thing… I think she means renovating property.'

'Well, she can help us in the business if she likes,' Able offered. 'Tom wouldn't object and she had some good ideas when she gutted that cottage near Pip's…' He looked at her. 'Did Sheila say if Pip had definitely taken that job in America?'

'She didn't say much, but we'll know more when we go down for our holiday. We had to put it back because of the wedding, but I think we're all looking forward to it…'

'Yes, I think most of us will get there for at least a few days. Freddie told me he'll come for a weekend, because they've given him some days off for study.'

'Janet will come down with us,' Peggy said. 'She wanted to stay at the boarding house, but I told her I was selling the lease. Pearl is taking it over and I think that is only fair, so I said they could come here until she knows what she wants. You don't mind?'

'When have I ever minded anything you do?' Able asked and kissed her. 'This has been an eventful time, our big trip ending the way it did with you so ill and me wondering if I'd lost you. Now Fay is married and off to her own big adventure. I could do with a bit of peace and tranquillity.' He yawned. 'I'm tired...'

'You're getting old,' she teased.

'No, just needing to feel comfortable again.'

'Yes, it has been a bit like a whirlwind.' Peggy reached out to him. 'What with Pip's illness and then me worrying about him living in America – and it will be Maggie getting married next, although she says not until after Christmas, as they are both too busy... but she won't be leaving us, not just yet anyway.'

'Good or I'd have you taking on her job as well.' Able shook his head at her. 'Oh no, Peggy. I'm putting my foot down there. Maggie will continue to run it or she will put staff in – or we'll sell. You've got more than enough lined up for the next year or two.'

'Yes, Able,' Peggy said and snuggled up to his chest. 'Of course you're perfectly right. Shall we go to bed?'

MORE FROM ROSIE CLARKE

We hope you enjoyed reading ***Life and Love at Mulberry Lane***. If you did, please leave a review.

If you'd like to gift a copy, this book is also available as an ebook, large print, hardback, digital audio download and audiobook CD.

Sign up to Rosie Clarke's mailing list for news, competitions and updates on future books.

https://bit.ly/RosieClarkeNews

Why not explore the bestselling ***Blackberry Farm*** series from Rosie Clarke...

ABOUT THE AUTHOR

Rosie Clarke is a #1 bestselling saga writer whose most recent books include *The Mulberry Lane* and *Blackberry Farm* series. She has written over 100 novels under different pseudonyms and is a RNA Award winner. She lives in Cambridgeshire.

Visit Rosie Clarke's website: http://www.lindasole.co.uk

Follow Rosie on social media:

twitter.com/AnneHerries

bookbub.com/authors/rosie-clarke

facebook.com/Rosie-clarke-119457351778432

Sixpence Stories

Introducing Sixpence Stories!

Discover page-turning historical novels from your favourite authors, meet new friends and be transported back in time.

Join our book club Facebook group

https://bit.ly/SixpenceGroup

Sign up to our newsletter

https://bit.ly/SixpenceNews